DAN

D0328860

O what can ail thee, Knight-at-arms
Alone and palely loitering;
The sedge is wither'd from the lake,
And no birds sing.
'La Belle Dame sans Merci'
John Keats, 1795–1821

No Birds Sing

Jo Bannister

No Birds Sing

St. Martin's Press ✹ New York

Library of Congress Cataloging-in-Publication Data

Bannister, Jo
No birds sing / by Jo Bannister.
p. cm.
ISBN 0-312-14382-6
1. Shapiro, Frank (Fictitious character)—Fiction. 2. Donovan,
Cal (Fictitious character)—Fiction. 3. Graham, Liz (Fictitious
character)—Fiction. 4. Policewomen—England—Fiction.
5. Police—England—Fiction. I. Title.
PR6052.A497N6 1996
823'.914—dc20   96-7296   CIP

First published in Great Britain by Macmillan

First U.S. Edition: August 1996

10 9 8 7 6 5 4 3 2 1

Part One

Chapter One

Strolling through Castlemere with Thomas Stirling on a Sunday morning made Mrs Cunningham feel like a young woman again.

Coming to town with Mr Cunningham was like taking part in military manoeuvres. So long for the drive in: mark. So long to find a parking space: mark. (They had a Ford Fiesta but Mr Cunningham drove as if it were a Chieftain tank.) So long to shop: 'Quickly, quickly, you 'orrible little woman, a Peruvian grand-mother with gout could get round Tesco's faster than this,' or 'Look, we're three minutes behind schedule already! Better do Safeway's at the double.'

How different, then, walking these same streets with Thomas. He never hurried her, considered his time well spent if he had no more to show for it than the memory of her smile. They wandered, they chatted – mostly Marion Cunningham chatted, Thomas paying solemn attention to all her opinions. They paused to admire the sights – the castle crumbling on its hill above the diamond, the Georgian frontages below, the sparkle of canal water glimpsed through the Brick Lane entries, the boats in Mere Basin bright as bath-time toys.

Sometimes she reached out and touched him,

almost as if to prove that he was real. For reply his cornflower gaze adored her. When she was with Thomas she never gave Mr Cunningham a thought.

It didn't matter that the shops, except for the newsagent on the corner, were closed. They windowshopped. Mr Cunningham never window-shopped; but Thomas allowed himself to be steered from one display to the next and never cared what he was being invited to admire as long as it was pretty.

Today they stopped at the jeweller's. When Marion was a girl old Mr Reubenstein sold costume jewellery and alarm-clocks from a shop the size of a goat-house in one of the entries. His son Mr Reubenstein expanded into a proper shop in Castle Place selling better jewellery, silverware and a nice class of crystal, and *his* son Mr Reubenstein expanded into the shops on either side to create Rubens, a glittering array of jewellery, presentation-ware and *objets d'art*. It was all here: the precious, the semi-precious and the merely pleasing. Mr Reubenstein the latest was no snob when it came to selling. He agreed with Thomas: he'd put anything in his window if it was pretty and turned a profit.

Mrs Cunningham was looking at the rings. Some were new, others antique; several were a shade ostentatious for good taste but Mrs Cunningham didn't mind. She loved their fire, their sheer *joie de vivre*. 'Oh look, Thomas,' she said, pointing to a cluster of amethysts around a single diamond, 'that's a hundred years old. It was first worn by a lady when my grandma was in her pram.'

Thomas Stirling said, 'Ruggle,' and set about chew-

ing the ear off his teddy; which Mrs Cunningham took
to mean much the same as *tempus fugit*.

Thus preoccupied – Mrs Cunningham with the
ring, her grandson with his bear – they did not for a
moment notice that they had been joined at the glittering window by a third party; and indeed, to take the
non-speciesist view, a fourth.

'Lovely, aren't they?'

Mrs Cunningham looked up, enthusiastic agree-
ment on her lips; but she was so taken aback that all
she could manage was a sort of non-committal moo.

Politely, the man showed no signs of having
noticed. 'Every inch a gentleman,' thought Mrs Cunningham in mounting hysteria. But what did he
expect? – standing there in his green felt fedora, his
tartan muffler and his calf-length burgundy corduroy
coat, like a man thrown out of a *Doctor Who* audition
for being too peculiar.

It may have been the smear of lipstick that finally
did for her, it may have been the puff of blusher; it
may have been the brassy curls permed within an inch
of their life peeping out from under the hat. Or it may
have been the dog – if it was a dog and not a skinned
rabbit – squatting on its naked rump at his feet. It wore
a blue collar studded with rhinestones, and that was
all. Its freckled fawn body was devoid of hair. There
were tufts on its feet, a plume on its tail, an explosion
of hair like a punk's Mohawk on its head, but its cat-
sized torso was nude. It gave Mrs Cunningham a bored
yawn revealing an absence of teeth.

She backed so hurriedly she almost fell off the kerb.
'Whoops,' said the strange man mildly. Flustered and
embarrassed, Mrs Cunningham flashed him her most

brilliant smile, wheeled the pram and set off across Castle Place like a galleon in full sail, her raincoat flapping round her. Her cheeks flamed.

She realized her behaviour was provincial but she'd been startled. Her willingness to live and let live was as well developed, she hoped, as in any middle-class woman of her generation – beside Mr Cunningham she seemed a dangerous libertarian – but her subconscious was honed by small-town mores fifty years before when an apparition in lipstick and a green fedora would have had insults, and worse, hurled at him in the street.

By the time she reached Dorinda Day's on the far side of the diamond she had regained enough self-possession to slow down and, under the guise of studying the latest thing in cruise wear, steal a backward glance at what the strange man was doing now. But in the time it took her to cross Castle Place he had disappeared, possibly into one of the shops, possibly up the steps to the castle. She gave a sigh that was mostly relief but just a little disappointed.

But she had little time to ponder who he'd been, where he'd come from and where he'd gone. In an instant the open space that all week was packed with parked cars and traffic and now held only a handful of strollers like herself, enjoying the April sunshine or fetching the Sunday papers, was filled with sound: an anarchic roar that drummed the ears and made Thomas Stirling drop his bear and howl in protest.

It came from the direction of Cambridge Road and filled Castle Place like water filling a bucket. Mrs Cunningham just had time to recognize the bellow of a high-powered car before it shot into sight, a big black

4×4 with bull-bars; and not enough time to complete the indignant thought, 'They'll cause an accident going at that speed!' before the behemoth slewed across the square where thirty seconds earlier she'd been pushing the pram. Then it mounted the pavement where, a few seconds before that, she and Thomas had been window-shopping. Mrs Cunningham gripped the handle of the pram until her knuckles turned white. In the instant that she realized what the vehicle was going to do, it did it.

There was toughened glass in the window of Rubens, and a grille designed to stop an opportunist brick without denying potential buyers a view of the goods. It might have been cellophane for all the resistance it offered. Safe in its cage the big dark bonnet smashed through glass and grille, spraying them and the wares they guarded in a rainbow arc of spinning, glittering, prism-scattered light.

By the time the air had cleared of stars Mrs Cunningham could see the monster entirely inside the shop, all five doors open, small dark figures – four of them, and perhaps they only seemed small beside the over-sized car – tossing in everything they could reach in a minute and a half. There was no time for discrimination, they took it all: gemstones and rhinestones and Christening mugs and charm-bracelets and watches.

At the end of ninety seconds they piled back in the car, the engine gunned – the sound drowning out the wail of the alarm – and the 4×4 lurched back through the wreckage of the window, spun on a rear tyre and shot off down Bedford Road at the foot of the diamond. First it disappeared from sight, Mrs Cunningham and half a dozen other stunned observers staring after it, then the fighter-plane roar of the engine faded into the distance.

For perhaps another minute only the shrill of the alarm, the broken glass tinselling the pavement and the gaping hole in Rubens' window display testified to what had happened. No one ran for the police. No one chased after the big dark car. The sheer speed of the episode, from a normal sleepy Sunday morning in Castle Place back to the same thing with burglar alarms, had paralysed them. Mrs Cunningham had one hand to her mouth: she couldn't have said why, but nor could she have moved it.

Then a new siren joined the first and a police car shot out of Market Lane, slewing to a halt in front of the ravished jeweller's. Two officers leapt out. The man dashed through the breach into the shop, the WPC – seeing Mrs Cunningham clinging to the pram – hurried over to check that she was all right. 'Did you see what happened?'

Mrs Cunningham nodded.

'You were standing here?'

Mrs Cunningham shook her head. 'Only a moment.' Her voice shook, too. 'Just before it happened we were over there. Right there. Right – there.'

WPC Wilson looked across the square and back to Mrs Cunningham, and frowned. It was a long way for a middle-aged woman to push a pram in a few seconds. 'Thank God you moved. Why did you – was there some kind of warning?'

'My guardian angel,' said Mrs Cunningham. She began to laugh. 'My guardian angel, constable, wears a green felt hat and make-up, and has a boiled rabbit on a lead.' Then the laughter turned to tears, and she lifted Thomas Stirling out of his pram and hugged him as if she meant never to let him go.

'Coincidence?' Detective Inspector Liz Graham pitched it precisely midway between a statement and a question. It didn't mean she had no opinion, rather that she wanted to hear Shapiro's first.

Detective Superintendent Frank Shapiro gave a morose shrug. 'What's the alternative? A ram-raider with a social conscience?' He glared at the papers littering his desk. It was the same desk he had had as Detective Chief Inspector. Most of the papers were the same too. It was Sunday afternoon.

'Could be. It's not in their interests to turn this into a murder inquiry.' She stood at the window gazing down at the canal, a tall woman who wore the CID uniform of tweed jacket, trousers and brogues with rather more style than most of her male colleagues. Long fair hair with an exuberent natural curl was tamed into a pleat for work, and her green eyes sparkled with intelligent good humour.

A persistent girlishness had somehow survived the bludgeoning effort of turning a job she had a talent for into a career until now, at forty, she had the rank she'd earned with a senior officer she liked and respected. People who'd known her through the struggle for acceptance reckoned she'd finally cracked the secret of dropping a year with each birthday. At last summer's Castlemere Horse Show she won a red rosette in the Pairs Jumping (Any Age) partnered by a seriously competitive seven-year-old on an Exmoor pony.

'So they sent a sweeper up ahead to clear the path?' Shapiro was unconvinced. 'Why not put out cones, or ask for a police escort?'

Liz grinned. She knew him well enough to recognize that gentle irony as the smoke-screen behind which he did his thinking. He was always open to rational argument, possibly because rational argument mostly proved him right. Yet coincidence tended to be the last thing they considered, when nothing else made sense. 'He was the look-out. It was his job to take a last look at the shop before they hit it, to make sure the area car hadn't just stopped for ice-creams at Cully's.'

Shapiro pictured the incident in his mind's eye. He was of an older generation than Liz, a thirty-year-man who wasn't the height of fashion when he started. He scraped through recruitment with question-marks against his height (modest), his bulk (immodest, even as a young man) and his manner (diffident going on vague). Only a note pointing out the wisdom of encouraging minorities got him a probationary posting. But the rest of the way to Detective Superintendent he made on merit, and the sheer ability that lay behind the broad amiable face and slightly disorganized manner had been a matter of public knowledge for so long now there was almost no one left who remembered what unpromising material he was once considered.

He nodded slowly. 'All right. They're not committed, they can change their minds right up to the moment they hit the window. There's a look-out on the street in case anything goes wrong at the last moment. If the area car *had* been doing the ice-cream run they'd have just kept driving.'

It was Liz's turn to look doubtful. 'Most look-outs

try to blend into the background. They don't dress up like something from an end-of-the-pier show.'

'Agreed,' said Shapiro. 'But that car was doing sixty when it hit Castle Place: the driver had just a few seconds to decide whether the raid was on or off. He hadn't time to hunt for the one chap who knew if it was safe to proceed. The look-out needs to be obvious from a speeding car a hundred yards away.'

They weren't arguing. They were trying to work it out, and that made sense. Liz thought it possible to push the hypothesis a little further. 'The woman with the pram said he vanished before the car arrived. So the plan is, if he's still there when they reach the target they keep going; if he isn't they do the job. That works. If the coast's clear and they do the raid the look-out's already offside so there's nothing to connect him to it. If he's still there, there's no raid.'

Shapiro was leafing through his papers. 'There's no mention of a Quentin Crisp look-alike at any of the earlier incidents.'

'I'm not convinced this is the Tynesiders at all.'

The Detective Superintendent elevated a shaggy eyebrow. 'Really?' He could invest a single word with enough polite disbelief to send most junior officers back-pedalling for their lives. But Liz mostly considered her opinions before expressing them, which made her harder to shift. Shapiro was forced to run to a second word. 'Why?'

She thought for a moment. 'Every police force in the country is watching out for a gang of ram-raiders who first struck in Middlesbrough five months ago and have reappeared at three- or four-week intervals in Harrogate, Barnsley, Mansfield, Nottingham and Leamington Spa. We're calling them the Tynesiders, though they could be from the Isle of Wight for all we know, because that's where they made their debut.' A strong forefinger tracked their progress down the map on the wall.

Usually Shapiro had a map of Cambridgeshire and Northamptonshire pinned up but today it was a larger map of England. It was not a new map. Either it was a very old map, that had had a lot of pins stuck in it tracing the course of a lot of criminal enterprises over the years, or it was the one that hung beside the dartboard in the canteen. To avoid perforating it further, Shapiro had tacked on stickers to represent the ramraiders' activities. They described a wobbly but essentially vertical line down the centre of England.

'Logically,' said Liz, 'their next port of call is somewhere round Oxford and it shouldn't be for another week or more. They're fifty miles off course, and though I don't know why they follow that particular routine I can't see them changing it when it works so well.'

Shapiro shrugged. 'Perhaps they think it's time to throw in a wild card. Make it harder for us to second-guess them.'

Liz stared. 'Has anybody come close to second-guessing them?'

'Not that you'd notice,' admitted Shapiro.

Liz nodded. 'Then there's the look-out. Nobody's reported that before.'

'Nobody'd have reported it this time if Mrs Cunningham hadn't got talking to the Queen of the May. Anyway, it's obviously a disguise – even Quentin Crisp doesn't look *that* much like Quentin Crisp! As long as he's easily identifiable he doesn't have to stand out like a lighthouse. Maybe last time he was the one pushing the pram; or he was a jogger in a fluorescent shell-suit, or a blind man selling flags on the corner. Anything that the driver would spot in the couple of seconds he has to make his decision.' He picked up a couple of faxes, discarded them again. 'There's not enough detail in these. Get Scobie to phone round, see if that rings a bell with anyone.'

'We'll give it a shot by all means,' she agreed readily. 'But I still think it'll turn out to be another crew. Ram-raiding isn't that devastatingly original any more. And the Tynesiders have attracted enough attention in the last five months to inspire copy-cats.'

'Their timing's not that rigid – they've hit two towns in a fortnight before,' said Shapiro. He had an almost sentimental attachment to the idea. 'Yes, we're a bit off-line for them, but what's fifty miles on the motorway? Maybe one of them's got a granny in the area that it's time he visited. Ram-raiding may be old hat in the cities but it's a new departure for Castlemere. And—' He stopped.

'And?'

He scowled. '*And* I have a gut feeling about it. Fine, feel free to laugh – poor old Frank, used to be a decent detective until he started getting indigestion and thinking it was ESP. All I know is, some people can sense where there are underground streams and I get feelings about crooks. And my guts don't think these crooks are home-grown.'

'Well, we'll know when we catch them,' Liz said diplomatically.

'We'll know before that. If it's the Tynesiders, and

if they stick with their usual MO, they'll hit us again soon – maybe tomorrow, maybe Tuesday. I want to be ready. I'm staking our overtime budget that if we watch all the likely targets till then we'll catch them in the act.'

'You can't do a full surveillance of a dozen shops for two days! It'd cost a fortune.'

'It doesn't have to be all day.' Shapiro was working it out as he went along. 'They rely on surprise, on getting in and out again before we know what's happening. They don't want to get caught up in traffic, and they don't want to be roaring through town in the middle of the night when everyone within earshot will guess what they're up to. Sunday morning's good, they've used Sunday mornings before. Weekdays they come in before the morning rush – between six-thirty and seven-thirty – or twelve hours later, after the commuters are safely home and before they set out for a night on the tiles. If we do ninety minutes morning and evening for two days we'll get them.'

'Unless they're home-grown, in which case they'll go on a blinder and won't do it again until they've spent whatever they made this time.'

Shapiro glowered at her. He trusted his instincts, but not to the point of ignoring hers. If she was right his next request for overtime would be about as successful as Donovan's next promotion board. 'The lookout in the green fedora: isn't that a bit sophisticated for the home team?'

She smiled. 'Ask them when you catch them. If they recognize both the words "fedora" *and* "sophisticated", they're imports.'

In a way she hoped he was right. If it was the

Tynesiders it should be possible to predict their next move. Of course, police in Harrogate, Barnsley, Mansfield, Nottingham and Leamington had probably thought the same. But even knowing a crime was imminent you couldn't seal off a medium-sized town for days on end. It made sense to do two or three quick raids in an area before moving on. The homework – learning the road network, the emergency exists, the ways they could go if those ways were blocked – only needed doing once. If Castlemere had been on that same vertical line she'd have had no doubts. But why would whatever was drawing them south suddenly pull them fifty miles east? Why would the Tynesiders change anything about their MO when it had served them so well?

'All right,' Shapiro said as if he had the clincher, 'then think about this. The chap in the green hat could be a local in fancy-dress, but what about that dog? That's not a Jack Russell in drag. Have Donovan check the vets, see if any of them treats a Chinese Crested Dog.' He'd had the public library opened specially to lend him the *Observer Book of Dogs.* 'I'll bet you lunch at The Ginger Pig that they don't.'

'You're on,' said Liz. 'But it'll have to be Morgan – Donovan's in London, remember? We'll check the hotels too. If our friend isn't local, whether or not he's with the raiders, he's staying somewhere. He can disguise himself, but how do you set about disguising a naked dog? With a toupee?'

Shapiro grinned. Her sense of humour was one of the best things about Liz Graham. And her creativity, that had kick-started more stalled investigations than he could remember; and her willingness to do the

15

groundwork while waiting for the lightning-stab of inspiration. A chauvinist, which Shapiro was not, would have gone on to note the aesthetic differences between the average DI and this tall handsome woman who shopped in London and Cambridge and not on the bargain rail at Suits Is Us in Viaduct Lane. She was a good detective, a good friend, good to have around.

The grin faded on Shapiro's face with the awareness that she probably wouldn't be around much longer. She was too good a detective to end her career as DI at a station the size of Queen's Street. She'd done work that would have won her promotion before now but for the glass ceiling. She'd broken through it to get here, and she'd break through it again; and Shapiro was too good a friend to hope they'd keep her waiting much longer.

But his heart sank wondering who they'd send him then. A dead-beat with no ambition to go any further, or a whizz-kid who couldn't wait to: Shapiro couldn't decide which he wanted least. There was no one of his own they'd promote into the job. Donovan would make a good DI in his own way; but he'd gone his own way too often in the past to expect another promotion. There was no one else.

'Frank?'

He blinked. 'Sorry. Just thinking.'

She smiled. 'Perhaps I should stop calling you Frank now you're a Superintendent.'

'And perhaps you shouldn't,' Shapiro glowered. 'Superintendent – what do you do with it? Chief Inspector you can shorten, but if people start calling me Super we'll have the place sounding like a finishing school.'

Not as long as Donovan works here, thought Liz. 'We were talking in the car,' she said. 'Donovan thought I should call you sir with a small S, he should call you sir with a capital S, and the constables should just grovel.'

Shapiro scowled. 'The next time Sergeant Donovan calls me sir with any sort of an S and it doesn't sound like a deliberate insult will be the first. Remind me: where is Castlemere's answer to Terry Wogan?'

Liz chuckled. Donovan had many good points, if you looked hard, but geniality wasn't one. 'Scotland Yard – the counter-terrorism course. That you and I both got out of going to? He'll be on the late train tomorrow night.'

'The train? Why didn't he take his bike?'

'I wondered that. He said he went to Scotland Yard in motorcycle gear once, and three different people tried to arrest him.'

Chapter Two

The train rattled through the dark. It was the last service of the evening, dubbed the Luvvies Train because of its popularity with patrons of the London theatres. But it took a particularly dedicated luvvy to travel beyond St Neots, especially on a Monday. Mostly those left in the emptying carriages were tired men and women who'd been in London on business that was a bit too much for one day and not quite enough for two.

Such a one was John Holloway, managing director of Holloway's (Boots & Shoes) of Castlemere. He'd been visiting the London retailers, listening to their views on why some lines sold like hot cakes and others like soggy sandwiches. But the conversational possibilities of soles, welts and toe-caps were exhausted by mid evening so he caught the last train home.

After it left the InterCity line and struck off across country there were only six people remaining in the first carriage: Holloway, a teenage girl in jeans and a woolly jacket, a woman of about fifty with a briefcase, a couple in their early twenties and a man in a black leather jacket slumped in the corner. He appeared to be asleep, except that once when Holloway glanced his way he caught the glint of a hawkish watchful eye under the heavy lid.

With nothing more to go on than that – the jacket might have made some people wary but Holloway had the greatest respect for black leather – he felt himself growing uneasy. He was a pragmatic man of fifty-nine: travelling late had never worried him before. That it was bothering him now made him wonder if perhaps subliminal danger signals were being broadcast, and though he wasn't sure what they meant he thought he knew where they were coming from.

For now he did nothing. But he decided to observe the order in which these people left the carriage. If the couple and one of the women left at Castlemere, and the man in the corner didn't, Holloway thought he'd travel further rather than leave the other woman alone with a man with those eyes.

But the dark miles poured steadily past the window, marked only by the lights of the occasional farmhouse, and nothing happened. The girl got up and walked through to the next carriage. The man in black watched her but made no attempt to follow. Holloway looked at his watch. A few more minutes and they'd be in Castlemere. He began to feel rather foolish. He thought he'd been wrong, that what had seemed like danger signs were only the disagreeable vibrations given off by a tired man at the end of a long day. He thought he was probably giving off some of his own.

Then, down the train, just close enough and loud enough to leave no doubt as to what it was, a girl screamed.

Holloway felt a sudden certainty, though he hadn't heard her speak, that it was the girl from his carriage.

But whatever had happened the man in black wasn't responsible; the cry had brought him from his seat and he was half way to the connecting door, a tall angular man who moved like an assassin.

The second carriage was as sparsely peopled as the first: a couple who might well have been to the theatre, two middle-aged women, two teenage boys. One of them went to get up but the man gestured him back like reprimanding a puppy. 'Stay here. I'll deal with it.' His voice was thick with purpose and an Irish accent.

There were more people in the third carriage: so many it seemed some were having to stand. One was the girl from the first carriage, and she'd have been screaming still but for a gloved hand clamped on her neck and the lancet point of a knife pricking the skin under her ear. Her face was creased up in terror, her mouth a ragged 'o', and she was shaking.

The man holding her had a ski-mask over his face. Beside the girl he seemed big, but not big enough to stand out of a line-up of ordinarily well-built men. Two other men wore the same uniform of dark ski-masks, gloves and jeans. Each had a rucksack that the passengers were filling with valuables.

The man holding the girl was in charge, yelling orders and menaces. 'You want to get home tonight? In one piece? Then do as you're told. Hold on to your rings and we'll cut your fingers off. Hold on to your earrings and we'll cut your ears. Give 'em up and we'll be on our way, but if anyone tries to stop us I'll kill her.' His hand jerked and the terrified girl, her face framed by a floss of fair hair, danced like a marionette. 'So nobody rushes us, nobody pulls the communication cord, nobody plays the hero. 'Cos if this turns nasty people are going to die, and one of them's going to be her.'

The sight of the knife stopped Detective Sergeant Donovan in his tracks. His instincts told him to go for it, that he could reach the man before he made the giant mental leap between threatening to kill someone and doing it. But it was too big a gamble for the sake of some jewellery. If he did nothing and no one got hurt, that would be enough. If he started a war that ended with a teenage girl getting her throat cut, it wouldn't matter who got their diamonds back and who did time: he'd be on Shapiro's carpet first thing tomorrow morning, and he'd deserve to be. He took a step back.

'You.' The man with the knife had seen him. 'Where are you going?' Under the throaty bellow there was an accent lurking but Donovan was no expert on English accents.

'I heard a yell, I thought I could help. I guess I was wrong.'

A ski-mask does more than hide large parts of the face. It emphasizes those parts that do show. When the man in this one smiled it was like the last ten minutes of *Jaws*. 'I like a man who can admit his mistakes. A man who knows when he's made one is less likely to make another, right?'

Donovan nodded silently.

'OK, back the way you came. You were at the front, yes? Well, go tell them what's happening. Tell them no one'll get hurt if they do as they're told. Stay where I can see you. Go on, do it.' He took the knife away from the girl's throat long enough to stab at the air.

'I'm going,' Donovan said quickly. He backed two

or three paces, then turned and jogged up the train.

When he reached the first carriage he stood in the doorway, blocking it. Hard and low he said, 'I'm a police officer. Listen to me and do as I say. There's a robbery going on. They'll be here in a minute. Don't argue, and don't go for the communication cord. Has anybody got a mobile phone?'

Emily Murchison nodded, her eyes round with alarm. She'd been jolted from a doze by the sudden flurry of activity; mentally she was still addressing a sales conference that had finished three hours before.

'Keep it out of sight, they're watching me. Dial this number,' – it was the front desk at Queen's Street, the only one he could be sure would be manned – 'then hold it in front of me. If you see them coming, ring off and kick it under the seats.'

Though Donovan looked like a Hell's Angel on his day off his voice could convey real authority when it had to. Miss Murchison did as he said.

When he heard the tone alter and the mutter of words – it might have been Sergeant Tulliver, who always muttered, or just the distance between the instrument and his ear – Donovan spoke his carefully chosen sentences. He spoke up, in the hope that Tulliver or whoever would hear and understand, and also so that he would be heard by the men in ski-masks.

'My name's Donovan,' he said. 'Everybody keep calm, but this train's being robbed. Steamers – three of them, they've taken a girl hostage, they're threatening to cut her throat. They started at the back of the train so they're almost through: when they've got our wallets they'll stop the train and disappear into The Levels. If everyone co-operates they'll be away from here in five minutes and we'll be in Castlemere in ten. So can we all just sit it out?'

'Good,' said the man behind him, and Donovan shied like a startled horse. He hadn't realized they were so close. But Miss Murchison had: she'd waited as long as she dared, then slid the phone out of sight under the table. It was too late to kick it away from her under the seats; instead she slipped it under the skirt of her coat.

'So let's everybody follow Mr Donovan's good advice,' said the big man, 'and keep calm and co-operate. You.' He pointed the knife at Miss Murchison, whose heart skipped a beat. 'That's a nice scarf you've got. Spread it on the floor, and everybody put on it everything they think we might want. Cash, watches, jewellery, plastic, cheque-books.'

Donovan couldn't risk parting with his wallet: his warrant card was in there. He made a show of emptying it on to the scarf – cash, credit card, everything the robbers would be looking for. They wouldn't be looking for a warrant card. Other policemen had difficulty believing Donovan was one.

'OK?' he asked bitterly when he was done.

'OK,' agreed the man with the knife. He looked at Miss Murchison. 'You next.'

The sales director of Castle Spa, bottlers of soft drinks and mineral waters, was proving equal to the occasion. She produced the mobile phone as if taking it from her pocket. 'I believe these have a certain second-hand value.'

Inside the mask, black wool hemmed with yellow, the thick-lipped mouth beamed. 'They do that. Stick it on the scarf.'

Donovan watched stony-faced, praying to a deity he only believed in for real emergencies. He thought his prayer had a good chance of being answered. The man with the knife couldn't pick the phone up without dropping either the weapon or the hostage, and when his colleagues arrived they'd be ready to leave. They'd shovel the contents of the scarf into a rucksack, pull the cord and jump out as the train stopped. There was neither time nor any reason for them to start playing with the buttons on a mobile phone. But if they do, Donovan was praying, please don't let them hit the last number redial button.

Also on to the scarf went Miss Murchison's purse, her ear-rings, a gold locket with pictures of her parents in it and three heavy gold rings from her right hand; and a wallet, purse and wedding rings in two different sizes from the young couple. At first the wife couldn't get hers off. The man with the knife growled, 'Take it off or I'll cut it off.'

She gave a little shriek and her hands knotted so that she couldn't have got a glove off, let alone a ring. Her husband gave up tugging at it and started to rise, putting his body between her and the knife.

Oh, God, thought Donovan in despair, this is where it goes from robbery with menaces to assault occasioning grievous bodily harm or maybe murder.

He edged in front of the knife, pressed the young man back to his seat, took the girl's hand in his own and raised it to his lips. ''Scuse me.' He put her finger in his mouth, made it slick with his saliva and drew off the ring with his teeth. He wiped it on his shirt and dropped it on to the pile.

All at once they were finished. The booty was bundled into a rucksack and the three men, their hostage still in tow, made for the door. One of them pulled the communication cord and they braced against the expected braking.

Nothing happened. The train continued oblivious through the darkness of the Castlemere Levels.

'Mustn't be working,' said Donovan, dead-pan. Or just possibly, he thought, somebody got a message to the police, who called the station, who called the driver on the radio and told him not to stop for anything.

'I'll make it bloody work. You!' The knife jabbed in Donovan's face. 'You lead the way.'

Stall, thought Donovan. Time's on our side – every minute brings us closer to home. 'The way where?'

'To the frigging driver!' For the first time perspiration was beading the skin round the man's eyes and there was alarm in his voice. 'He sits at the front, yes?'

Donovan did as he was told, led the way past notices threatening plague and mayhem on anyone disturbing the driver and tapped diffidently. 'Excuse me, but—'

A strong hand yanked him away. 'Bugger that!' The big man wrenched open the door and thrust the weapon inside.

The train began to slow. Filling the doorway, the man with the knife looked back at Donovan. If a ski-mask can look puzzled, this one did. Not a word had been spoken.

Donovan pushed past, looked into the cab. The driver was still in his seat, bent over his console, a finger hooked inside his tie. His face was white and running with sweat, his eyes stretched; choked sounds came from between clenched teeth.

'God help us!' With his hands under the driver's arms Donovan eased him out of the cab, leaving it empty. He sat the man on the floor, loosened his tie and belt, took off his own jacket to cover him. 'Try and breathe lightly. The worst'll pass in a couple of minutes.' One way or another, he thought parenthetically.

Behind him the man with the knife was staring at the vacant cab. 'Can you drive this thing?'

Donovan eyed him sourly. 'It doesn't need anyone to drive it, it'll stop itself. Have you never heard of a dead man's handle? Well, this is what it's for. Bursting in like that, you've given the poor sod a heart attack.'

Chapter Three

When the phone rang, the Grahams were busy. 'Let it *ring*!' gasped Liz. 'Do that. God, yes! Do it some more.'

But when it was still drilling its patient, insistent summons two minutes later she relented, pushed Brian off her and reached for it. By way of greeting she growled, 'This had better be good.'

'Oh, it is,' Shapiro said with conviction. 'Sorry to wake you' – the Detective Superintendent was divorced and lived alone – 'but you won't want to miss this. We have a train robbery in progress.'

'Good lord!'

They'd been married ten years, Brian Graham knew that tone: it meant that something more interesting than him had come along. He sighed, reached for his book.

'Where?'

'Coming in off The Levels,' said Shapiro. 'Somewhere about the Mile End Straight. I'm on my way there now.'

'Doesn't the driver know where he is?'

'He's not answering his radio.'

Liz didn't use the train much but it was an easy way to London so she'd done it the odd time. She ran a mental tape of the home straight. 'Which side of the tunnel?'

27

'All the signal box can say is that the train's come to a stop somewhere about the Mile End tunnel and the driver isn't answering his radio. We're not going to know any more till we get there.'

Liz frowned. 'If they can't talk to the driver, how do we know it's a robbery?'

'Ah,' said Shapiro heavily. 'You see the time? This is the last train we're talking about. Remember who was catching the last train?'

Premonition booted the air out of her. Trouble gravitated to Donovan like iron filings to a magnet. 'He got a message through?'

'Brief and garbled,' said Shapiro, 'but what's new?' Liz wasn't fooled: he was worried, too. 'Three men holding a girl at knife-point, relieving passengers of cash and valuables. At that point no one seemed to have been hurt but he rang off rather quickly.'

'He won't do anything rash,' Liz said quietly. 'He won't go to war for the sake of some money.'

Shapiro wasn't persuaded. 'Calling in was rash. If he was caught—' He avoided finishing the thought. 'He mustn't draw attention to himself. He doesn't want them knowing he's a policeman.'

'I don't expect he's planning to arrest them!'

'It's not what Donovan plans that you have to worry about,' Shapiro said grimly, 'it's what he does on the spur of the moment. If he thinks he can get the knife he'll go for it.'

'Maybe he'll get it. Maybe we'll get there and it'll all be over.'

'And maybe they'll kick his stupid head in.'

*

The reason for calling it the Mile End Straight was lost in the mists of time. The line ran straight for seven miles across the Castlemere Levels; the Mile End tunnel itself was half a mile long and three miles short of Castlemere.

The last train, braking steadily while its driver gasped and clutched his chest on the floor, made for the tunnel like a weary beast returning to its lair. There was something inevitable about it. Almost regardless of the emergency, a driver in control of his train would not have stopped in the tunnel. He would have stopped before if he could, continued through if he had to. Almost nothing that would go wrong on a train could get worse so fast that it made sense to try and deal with it inside a hill.

But this train had no driver, was incapable of making value judgements. All it knew was to bring itself to a halt as quickly as was consistent with passenger safety.

Before it was stationary the raiders had the door open. 'We're inside a frigging tunnel. Does it matter?'

'Won't have to,' decided the man with the knife. 'Go ahead, I'll cover you – me and Little Miss Pretty here.' She was still standing in the aisle, quaking and hugging herself, her face that was midway between child and woman streaked with tears. She let out a breathy little shriek as the man pushed her towards the door. 'Careful how you jump down, you don't want to hurt yourself.'

Donovan was calculating percentages. She was a young girl and they were three violent men high on crime and adrenalin. If he let them take her she might be all right, but she might not. If they had a car near here, and if there was no one to stop them, they would disappear with her into The Levels where rape was about the best she could hope for.

If he was going to intervene this was probably the only chance he'd get. When the girl jumped down, for a split second before the man followed she'd be out of range of the knife. If Donovan took him then she'd be safe. Even if they fought, even if he lost, there'd be time for her to hide in the darkness. The raider might have lost his knife by then, or be aware how much time was passing. If he grabbed a fresh hostage it could hardly be anyone more vulnerable.

He was going to do it. He filled his lungs, banished from his mind the likely consequences of failure and moved on to the balls of his feet, ready to jump as the girl jumped.

But the girl didn't jump. Instead she backed uncertainly from the door and a second later one of the ski-masks reappeared. 'There's torches up ahead.'

'So go the other way.' Precisely on cue, as they turned to look the length of the train, lights glittered in the portal behind them. 'Shit.'

Donovan said, 'Maybe you'd better give up the knife. Let the girl take it out: if they know you're not armed it'll take the heat out of the situation.'

'The knife?' The man looked at it as if he'd just noticed it. 'Yes, I could do that.' He held it out, left-handed, not to the girl but to Donovan. 'Here.'

Carefully Donovan reached for it. He was always careful around lethal weapons. But the man didn't change his mind and when Donovan's long fingers closed on the hilt he let it go. Donovan breathed out softly and looked up. 'Good—'

He was looking into the barrel of a small automatic pistol. 'After all,' said the man conversationally, 'I've still got this.'

It wasn't the first time Donovan had found himself looking up the muzzle of a gun but the sight never lost its ability to shock. He felt the strength drain from his muscles, the blood from his face. He breathed, 'You don't want to do that.'

'No,' agreed the man, 'but I will if I have to. I'm not going to jail for the sake of some costume jewellery and a mobile—' He stopped abruptly, mid-sentence, staring at Donovan through the yellow knitted rings. When he spoke again his voice was down to the bare bones of hatred. 'You *bastard*! That's how they got here so quickly – you called them. Now they've sealed the tunnel and they think we're trapped. But they don't know about this, do they?' He stabbed the gun at Donovan's eyes and Donovan recoiled. 'They think all they have to worry about is a knife. They might rush a knife but they won't rush this. All we have to do is find some way of letting them know we have it.'

Donovan had been a policeman for ten years. He knew a threat when he heard one.

The shot echoed round the tunnel like artillery. A thin blue line, marked by torches and rather spoiled by Shapiro's old tweed coat a little right of centre, had advanced a dozen metres under the hill when it sent them diving for the black brick wall.

'Anyone hurt?' rapped Shapiro, hoping no one could hear the rasp in his voice. Even these days it wasn't often that a Detective Superintendent got shot at. But no one had been hit and they fell back in disorder and relief.

Shapiro called Liz on the radio. 'I suppose you heard that.'

'Any damage?'

'No, thank God. Knives – Donovan said they had knives. He never said anything about guns!'

'I don't expect he knew,' Liz said reasonably. 'It's a wonder he got a message out at all, you can't blame him for not giving you chapter and verse.'

'You don't think—?'

'No, I don't,' she answered firmly. 'I think it was a warning. I think if they'd been going to kill him they'd have done it while they still had a chance of getting away. They must know by now they're not going anywhere, that they'll have to pay for anything they do. It may take time but in the end they'll come quietly because they have no choice. Hurting their hostages will only make matters worse.'

A less experienced officer might have believed her. But Shapiro knew not to expect too much sense from criminals with their backs to the wall. If Liz had been right, hostage dramas would always end peacefully, and they didn't. She knew that as well, of course. She was trying to reassure him. She must have forgotten all the times he'd sworn that if he'd had a gun he'd have shot Donovan himself.

'We're going to need support,' he said. 'I'll start the megaphone diplomacy, you get us some fire-power.'

The sound of the gunshot filled the front of the train. It made the girl clap her hands to her ears with a shrill little scream; it made Miss Murchison, who hadn't an hysterical bone in her body, grip the arms of her seat tightly; it penetrated the driver's private world of fear and pain.

Down the train came a series of softer bangs as the doors opened and hasty feet scrunched on cinders. One of the raiders flashed a torch down the tunnel. 'They're getting away!' It was a young man's voice, panic sharpening the native monotone of the lowland Scot.

The big man was older and more pragmatic. 'Let them go. We've got everybody we need right here.' Seven hostages were enough to control with one gun. If it came to a shoot-out, seven targets would be hard to miss.

Shapiro would be at one end of the tunnel, Donovan surmised, and Inspector Graham at the other. Neither would be pushed into doing something for the sake of being seen to. For one thing, they knew he was here, they'd be expecting him to do something clever. While they were waiting they'd try to open a dialogue. But however nasty this got they wouldn't let the robbers go. They wouldn't free men who'd do this to do it again.

A fog-horn croak battled up the long tunnel. 'My name's Frank Shapiro, it's my job to sort this out. You want to talk about how we do it?'

'They've got us. They've got us.' The boy was shaking his head like a caged bear.

'They *haven't* got us, and as long as I've got this they won't.' The big man hefted the gun; not extravagantly, just enough to make the point. That meant he was familiar with the weapon, knew what it could and couldn't do. It could punch holes in anything it was aimed at. It couldn't discriminate between intentional jerks on the trigger and accidental ones.

Had there been no other considerations Donovan would have waited. The longer these men had to think about their situation the more resigned they would become. Only the fact that their blood was up kept them from seeing there was nowhere left for them to go.

But the driver's condition injected a degree of urgency. Donovan was no doctor, couldn't distinguish between a heart spasm from which a man might recover without much help and a coronary attack in which every minute was vital. While he was softly softly catching monkeys a man could be dying. Reluctant as he was to draw attention to himself again, he said, 'You could use the phone to negotiate.'

The eyes burned in the holes of the ski-mask. 'Negotiate? They won't negotiate – they want us to put our hands up and I'm not going to do that. The only thing I have to say they know already: that I have hostages and a gun. That's all they need to know.'

In fact it wasn't. Shapiro also needed to know about the driver, and that so far none of the passengers had been injured. How he would use the information when half of it suggested there was time to resolve this peacefully and the other half that patience could cost a life Donovan had no idea, only that he'd want to know. But he didn't think he could say much more without giving himself away, and instinct warned that if these men knew he was a police officer his usefulness would come to an abrupt end.

He wasn't unafraid for his own safety – he'd been

hurt too often to have any illusions about plugging the holes in his body with a hanky while he got on with the job – but there was more to it than that. In reasonable working order he was the best thing the hostages had going for them. He knew how sieges worked, what the dangers were, how to keep the shit from hitting the fan. Shot, knocked out or bound and gagged he could do nothing. So it wasn't only self-regard that urged him to protect his identity. At least, he didn't think it was.

Hands spread he said soothingly, 'I'm only trying to help.' And in the moment of saying it, like a distant dawn breaking he got the first pale glimmer of how.

Chapter Four

When fishes flew and forests walked, Castlemere Levels was a marsh punctuated by islets. Even after the fens were drained the islets remained in the form of low hills with a distinct shrubby vegetation on top. Such was Mile End Hill. As late as the mid-nineteenth century the land was still so wet that it was easier to drive a tunnel through the hill than make a causeway strong enough to carry a train round it.

Shapiro met Liz on top; but she had to wait for him because she jogged while Shapiro trudged. As she waited, gazing round she saw a clutter of stones like a tumbledown cairn half-hidden by willow-scrub. By the time Shapiro arrived her eyes were aglow. 'I know what he's going to do!'

There was no judging how much time they had. Donovan would be trying to separate the raiders from their hostages but even once the means occurred to him the opportunity might prove elusive. He couldn't force the situation, not against men with guns. But Liz remembered him telling her about the shaft, felt sure he'd find some way of using it. Donovan's brain had the kind of boneless agility usually associated with ferrets in drainpipes.

It was Shapiro's decision but he respected Liz's

intuition. So often, coming at a problem from different angles, she and Donovan ended up in the same place. If she knew by the pricking of her thumbs what Donovan's next move would be, Shapiro wasn't going to say she was wrong. 'Prepare a welcoming committee,' he said. 'I'll get back on the loud-hailer, let them think we're trying to talk them out.'

'The old fool with the megaphone's trying again,' said the third man, easing the rucksack on his shoulders. 'Can't we shut him up?'

The man with the gun shook his head. 'I don't want to waste bullets till I know how many we're going to need.' His eyes, restlessly scanning the carriage, lit on Donovan and his voice hardened. 'What are you grinning at? I'll tell you one thing – if it comes to a shoot-out, you're the first. You brought them here; well, by God, you're not walking away.'

Donovan hadn't realized he was grinning; if he was, it was precipitate. He didn't need the gun to remind him how many ways this could go wrong. These were deeply dangerous men: only the hope that he'd found a way to deal with them played on his face like a shadow of a smile.

Cal Donovan was not a good-looking man. He went from wiry child to stringy teenager to stick-thin six-footer without passing through an attractive stage. The olive skin was drawn over the narrow bones of his face like a medieval icon while, sunk deep in bony pits, his dark eyes had an animal watchfulness that could flare to fevered intensity or sink to sullenness almost without warning. At thirty his self-command was better than it had been five years before but he still walked a tightrope between instinct and prudence, edgy as a cat with eight lives gone. Women, a few, glimpsed a certain tortured beauty; men reacted with the unease evoked by any powerful creature of unreliable temperament.

He spread long-fingered hands defensively. 'Don't shoot me, I'm your last best chance of getting out of here.'

The armed man leaned forward until Donovan was breathing gun-oil. 'Say what?'

By now Jody Perkins was a bright seventeen-year-old working on her Oxbridge entrance. But six years ago she was an active child with boundless curiosity and a Border Collie, and when she went missing on The Levels Donovan and a hundred other people turned out to search for her.

Which is how he knew about the ventilation shaft. They found her twenty feet down the corroded iron rungs set into its wall. Intrigued, she'd climbed that far and then panicked, clutching the ladder while the dog barked hysterically overhead. Constable Donovan was lowered on a rope and brought her up without further incident.

There were two things he didn't know about the shaft: whether the rungs went all the way down, and whether they would carry a man's weight. But this was a good time to find out. They couldn't force a dozen hostages up the pipe ahead of them, would have to make do with him.

Inspector Graham was out there somewhere. He'd told her about the lost child. Would she remember, guess what he'd do and be there to meet them when they emerged? Even if she didn't, men clambering off a dangerous ladder were at a disadvantage in the face of a hostage developing an unexpected hero complex. If they knew he was a copper they might be prepared; but if they thought he was—

'I work for Railtrack, maintenance section. There's an airshaft half-way through the tunnel. As far as I know you can still climb up on to the hill. From there you've got six hours of darkness and forty square miles of wilderness to get lost in.'

For a moment he thought they weren't going to buy it. Eyes hedged round by knitting raked him like claws. He felt their need for hope at war with their natural suspicion of anything that convenient.

Yet the shaft existed, he could show them. And whatever followed had to be better than being trapped in a tunnel. In the end, whether or not they trusted him, they'd go for it. It was probably the only chance they'd get.

They knew it. They also knew the risks. The muzzle of the gun under Donovan's jaw forced his head back. 'Jerk me around, flower, and you're dead. You go first; then if anybody falls it'll be you. First sign of trouble you're going to get buggered by a bullet.'

He bundled Donovan to the door. Then he gripped the girl's wrist.

Donovan took a deep breath. 'She can't come.'

The gun swung his way. 'Don't tell me what to do!'

'She's a wee girl, she couldn't climb on top of the train let alone fifty metres up an old shaft. Even if she doesn't fall she'll slow you up. And if she does fall she'll take everybody below her when she goes.'

He waited. He hoped he'd done enough to convince

them. If he hadn't he was prepared to fight for her, but he didn't expect to win.

After a moment the man with the gun nodded. 'OK.' He pushed the girl to a seat. 'OK, honey, you've done your bit. You stay here.' Speaking to all of them he went on: 'And let's not have an undignified rush for the exit. Stay where you are and wait. I don't know how long it'll take us to get up the shaft, and if I don't know you sure as hell don't. Anybody shows his face before we're gone, I'll put a hole in it.'

They wouldn't use the torch for fear of signalling their intentions. They dropped on to the track, the gunman pushing Donovan ahead of him, and walked back to the mid-point of the tunnel. 'OK, where's this shaft?'

Donovan found it by the down-draught of peaty air. There wasn't enough space between the roof of the train and the vaulting of the tunnel to stand up: he was on his hands and knees on top of the carriage when he felt the movement of air and his groping hand vanished into the void. 'Here.'

Perhaps two metres across, linking a black tunnel and a dark sky, the shaft received no natural light. Now the torch was essential. The last man wedged it in his top pocket so that it cast its beam up through the legs of those above. It gave a shaky fragmented light but enough to show where the rusty brackets were and, once, that the pinnings had gone on one side. Donovan stretched long limbs from the rung below to that above. For a moment he considered keeping quiet but wisdom prevailed. Probably the man with the gun would see it too and know Donovan had tried to kill him. If he didn't see it, as the thing came away from the wall the gun could go off, and Donovan knew where it was pointing.

'The next one's loose,' he said, and the man below said, 'Thanks' – as if he'd pointed out a dodgy paving-stone to a stranger in the street.

It was an arduous climb and, for them all in different ways, an anxious one. Even so, when Donovan reached for another rung and instead felt grass, for a moment he couldn't think what to do next. 'We're at the top.'

'Get out,' panted the man with the gun. They were all out of breath. 'Stay on your knees by the edge. Don't think you can run faster than I can climb these last couple of rungs.'

Donovan told himself he'd never intended to run, had always meant to wait and see if he had back-up before making his next move. If DI Graham was in position with an armed response unit he needed the three men out of the shaft before they realized. And if she wasn't, if no one had thought of the air-shaft, he had to be by the ladder as the man with the gun scrambled out.

It was an awkward manoeuvre with two free hands. If Donovan could catch him off balance and wrest the weapon from him, or send it spinning into the void, the thing would be over. They were two good reasons for behaving himself a little while longer. The effect of a bullet on the human body was a third.

After the oppressive darkness of the shaft the star-dusted sky over The Levels seemed vast. A couple of miles west the lights of Castlemere began; nearer, and also further out across the dark plain, were the scattered lights of farms. The curve of the hill hid from him the lights of the police down by the track and they would have no view of him. Unless the faint column of light from the torch was spotted . . .

'Turn the torch off,' said the man with the gun. 'You: back off a bit.'

Donovan had knelt by the top of the ladder, ostensibly obeying instructions, actually thinking that from there he could act too quickly to be stopped. The man below him must have thought so too. Reluctantly Donovan shuffled a metre sideways.

He looked round but there was nothing to see. No ring of armed police. No DI Graham with her fair hair spread on the breeze like a recruiting poster. No Superintendent Shapiro, broad face beaded with sweat from the climb, taking control in that reassuring, avuncular voice with just a touch of adenoidal accent. Not even a probationary constable or a school crossing patrol lady. He was on his own up here.

OK. So the priorities were to neutralize the gun and raise the alarm. Wee buns. But damn that woman, he thought bitterly: how come she always knew what he was planning right up to the moment he wanted her to?

If he went for the gun too soon the man would merely duck back into the shaft and shoot him from there; and if he waited too long he'd be on his feet and back in control. He waited . . . he waited . . . and then he dived.

He got it wrong. The extra metre made all the difference: instead of bowling the armed man across the turf, Donovan barely reached him, found himself clawing for the gun at full stretch. The man dodged him easily, came to his feet with the gun levelled at

Donovan's face. 'Bad move, flower.' The hatred in his voice was so profound it vibrated.

Donovan had heard of people freezing with fear. He'd assumed it was a figure of speech. He'd been frightened enough often enough that he'd have known if it had ever actually happened. He thought it was probably an excuse offered by people who knew they'd proved unequal to a situation; a sop to cowardice.

Flat on his back, the breath knocked from him, face to face with oblivion, it happened to Donovan now. He froze rigid. His muscles locked round the long bones and would not obey him. He needed to be up, twisting out of the line of fire, jinking for cover. In this light every metre he put between him and that gun halved the chance of a shot finding him, quartered its chance of killing him. He didn't have to get far, he didn't have to get out of range or out of sight, he just had to *get*. Anything he did now would improve the odds.

But he couldn't move. It was as if Lilliputians had swarmed over him with vines the moment he hit the ground. He felt his heart pound and his eyes round, and he couldn't raise a hand to defend himself. A detached part of his brain that was watching curiously, that clearly hadn't made the connection between his impending demise and its own, observed, If this was a novel the light would spring up now and DI Graham would leap into the ring shouting—

'Armed police officers! Drop your gun. Now! Do it now. Do it!'

Yes, reflected that wry remote portion of Donovan's brain watching him sprawl in the weeds moments from his own destruction, that's what she'd say. By the book.

Never mind blowing the bastard's head off while there was still time to save his. Do it by the book, then you never have to worry about justifying yourself. Only about breaking in a new detective sergeant.

For a second the man looked away. But the black eye of the gun remained fixed on Donovan's face, pinning him down, undistracted by the flare of torches, the shapes sprung into focus between them, the distinctive crouching attitudes of people aiming weapons. The man saw them; but stubbornly refusing to acknowledge the cordon and the certainty of capture it represented he turned back to the man at his feet.

Donovan whispered, 'Don't—'

The big man smiled. At least the fleshy lips spread; nothing resembling a smile reached the eyes. The gun twitched fractionally as his fore-finger took up the slack.

The crash of the shot rolled round the top of the hill. A woman's voice shouted, 'No!' into the echo. At last, and too late, Donovan tried to move, to throw himself those couple of metres that might make the difference between emergency surgery and the morgue. He managed to roll just once, then his long body slumped leadenly, face down this time, one arm about his head.

Before the smell of cordite cleared, two officers, one armed with a torch, the other with a gun, hurdled the broken wall and pin-pointed the two men still in the shaft. 'Let's be having you.'

Liz Graham bent over the fallen man, shook her head. It would take a doctor to make the death official but the fact of it was obvious. The bullet had entered above the left ear and taken the right ear with it.

'Damn, damn, damn. I didn't want that to happen.'

'Sorry, ma'am.' The man who fired was making his weapon safe. 'There was no option. He was going to shoot Sergeant Donovan.'

'Well, we couldn't have that, could we?' She sounded like someone putting a brave face on things. 'I suppose.' She looked round. 'Donovan? Where's he got to?'

He was on his knees beside the wall. It had taken him almost till then to realize it wasn't him who'd been shot. Simultaneous with the hammer-blow of sound he had felt, or thought he had, the shock of impact; his body had spasmed and gone weak and he'd felt his senses fade.

But instead of fading out he found himself taking in the smell of damp earth and listening to the conversation. Only then did he understand that he'd miscalculated. His initial reaction, before relief, was embarrassment. 'I'm here.'

'Are you all right?'

'Yeah.'

Liz smiled at the armed officer. 'That's Sergeant Donovan's idea of a full report. All right, let's see what we've got.' She bent again, carefully picked the remains of the ski-mask away from the remains of the face. 'I don't recognize him. Donovan?'

By then the others were out of the shaft, pulling off their own masks. A boy of about nineteen, a man in his early thirties: she hadn't seen either of them before. 'You're not from around here, are you?' They made no reply.

Liz turned back to her sergeant, to acknowledge his success. The expression in his eyes stopped her.

He was looking at the dead man on the grass. It wasn't a pretty sight but they were neither of them virgins: they'd seen uglier things, and much more upsetting ones, than an armed thug shot dead before he could kill someone else.

But Donovan was looking at him with neither hatred, triumph nor even relief, but as if he was seeing a ghost. His eyes were appalled.

'Donovan? Do you know him?'

'No,' he said hurriedly, accent thick as soda farls. 'No, I don't.' And it was the truth. But it wasn't the whole truth. He was looking at a man he'd never seen before; but the face he was seeing, white, half destroyed, the other half wry with the sheer unexpectedness of death, was his own.

Chapter Five

It was three-thirty on Tuesday morning before Shapiro gave up trying to interview the men in the cells. He'd sent Liz home an hour before, and Donovan an hour before that, as soon as he'd made a coherent report.

That took longer than it should have done. It was no wonder that a man who'd confronted his own mortality, who was alive now only because of a woman's intuition and the skill of a police marksman, had been unsettled by the experience. But Shapiro was surprised that Donovan, who habitually pushed his luck until it started pushing back, seemed so subdued. Reaction usually made him surly. Shapiro hoped that if the sergeant got some sleep in what remained of the night, by morning he would be himself again.

There were people, both at Queen's Street and Division, who would consider any change for the better. But Shapiro had known Donovan longer than most and recognized that his moods were the price to be paid for his commitment. He was difficult because he cared too much, because failure grieved him. A whole department of Donovans would have been impossible to command, but Shapiro had been glad of the one he'd got often enough to make allowances.

Unforthcomingness from Donovan he was accustomed to, but criminals under arrest were often oddly loquacious. When a man had been discovered half-way down a drainpipe with somebody else's silver-ware it was too late to be coy. Talking about it, sometimes angrily, often with a kind of dry humour, seemed to ease the stress of watching the next five years go up in smoke.

So he didn't understand why these two were set on silence. They had nothing to lose. They'd been taken in the act, there were dozens of witnesses, the third member of the gang died at the scene so there was no one to protect. Yet they refused to talk. They refused to give their names or addresses or accept the offer of legal representation. The older man spoke, when he spoke at all, with a Yorkshire accent, the younger was a Scot. They weren't violent, abusive or hysterical. Though the boy was clearly shaken, even without the support of his steadier colleague he could not be tricked or persuaded to reveal anything useful. In the end Shapiro had to concede that he wasn't going to make any progress unless their fingerprints were on record somewhere. He collected his coat to go home.

The woman was standing at the foot of the police station steps as he drove out of the yard. He almost didn't pause, never afterwards knew what made him take a second look, then stop and take a third.

A woman calling at Queen's Street at that hour of the morning was not so unusual in itself. As it was mostly men who got into trouble after the bars closed it was mostly women – wives, mothers, daughters – who got the job of collecting them when the paperwork was done. Also there was a small but dedicated band of female winos who, midway through the second bottle, remembered all the slights they'd suffered at the hands of the local constabulary and decided to have it out with them.

Somehow this woman, half-hidden in the shadows, matched neither template. She was hesitant, unsteady even, but he didn't think she was drunk. She was too tidy, too well-dressed for someone who spent half of every night propping up a lamp-post singing 'Nelly Dean'.

And women coming to collect errant male relatives were usually too angry to hover in Queen's Street. Some of them were angry with the police, others with their menfolk, but they'd all had disturbed nights and wanted to get home.

She could be worried about a missing person, a son or daughter who hadn't come home when they should have done. Shapiro put her at about forty, which was the right age to have children at the 'it's-my-life, I'll-stay-out-till-dawn-if-I-want-to' stage. Parents always assumed the worst the first time – Shapiro remembered, Shapiro had been through it. Not with Rachael, who was born sensible, or with David, who worked on the principle that if no one knew when to expect him no one would worry if he was late, so much as with the middle one. Sally looked so fragile and was actually the toughest of the three. A couple of times Shapiro had been worried enough about her to phone Queen's Street at three in the morning.

But that was the natural thing to do, wasn't it? – to phone, not to call in. So it was something more than anxiety that had brought her out in the middle of the night. Something had happened. She'd done something, or had something done to her; she wanted to report it now, not wait till morning, and she couldn't quite find the courage to climb those steps, walk up to the desk and make it official.

Shapiro stopped his car on the yellow lines and got out. She whirled at his tread and her eyes were afraid. Shapiro stopped a few feet from her, before his bulky presence could crowd her, and kept his hands in the pockets of his coat. Solemnly he introduced himself. 'Is there a problem? Can I help at all?'

She looked, wildly, from him to the lit door at the top of the steps. Framed by blonde hair in a shoulder-length bob she had a rather long, strong face whose lines suggested competence and a greater degree of self-confidence than she was currently exhibiting. She wore a camel coat over a cashmere sweater and tweed skirt. There were marks on the coat as if she'd been in an accident.

For a moment it seemed she was going to change her mind, hurry away with her story untold. She looked past him, saw the empty street beckoning, knew or guessed he had no power to detain her; the wrong word from him then and she would have taken to her heels. Her head rocked back, her face racked by indecision.

Shapiro said quietly, 'I *can* help, you know.'

She laughed at that, a single bark of desperate laughter that was no sooner out than turning to a sob. She bit her lips to bring it under control. Then she looked Shapiro in the eye – a gesture whose courage he only appreciated when he'd heard what she had to say – and her voice was intelligent and, in the circumstances, remarkably restrained. 'I do hope so, Superintendent, I could certainly use some help. You see, I've been raped.'

He spent the rest of the night with her. He offered to bring Liz in if she'd rather talk to another woman, but she declined.

Dr Greaves who examined her explained. 'When a woman's been abused by a man it can be enormously reassuring to be treated with respect by another one. In a way it's too easy to retreat into the compassion of women. Unless she's going to enter a nunnery she has to learn to deal with men again and the sooner she starts the easier it'll be. If she can talk to you, Superintendent, that's the best thing for her. She was fortunate it was you who saw her first.'

'Oh, yes,' growled Shapiro, 'it was certainly her lucky night.' He bit back his anger; none of this was the police surgeon's fault. 'What's he done to her?'

'Raped her,' Greaves confirmed. 'It's not the worst I've ever seen. He didn't beat up on her and he didn't do anything aberrant to her. The physical evidence is consistent with what she said – that he came up behind her, dragged her into the bushes, pushed her to the ground and raped her. I've got a good semen sample: you find him and it'll nail him.'

They were supposed to be installing a special interview room, something less clinical that could be used for occasions like this. But more urgent demands kept claiming the budget. Shapiro took her to his office, which if not exactly comfortable had never been accused of being clinical. WPC Wilson made coffee, and over it the woman told what happened. Shapiro offered the occasional prompt but hardly had to question her: she was remarkably professional about the whole business, knew what he needed to know and told him.

Her name was Helen Andrews, she was a divorcee and branch manager of a building society. She had a flat in a big Victorian house at the north end of town.

She'd been to a hen-night – one of her assistants was marrying a solicitor's clerk. They started off in The Ginger Pig and ended up at the bride's home in Castle Mews. When the party broke up, rather than call a taxi Mrs Andrews thought she'd enjoy the walk. It was only half a mile, it was a pleasant spring night and the road was well-lit all the way. She was not a timorous woman, it had not occurred to her to be afraid to walk the main streets of her own town at night.

At the foot of Castle Mount the road up to the ruins peeled away to the left. There was no traffic as Mrs Andrews went to cross. She heard no footsteps, had no intimation of danger; the first she knew was a hand closing over her mouth from behind, then she was hauled back up the kerb, across the pavement and into the broad sweep of shrubbery where the road circled up to the Mount. She was pushed to the ground and gagged with her own scarf.

'Did you see his face?'

The street was only a few strides away, lamplight penetrating the shrubbery in jagged fingers; if anyone had been passing she would have seen them though they would probably not have seen her. He had something white tied over his face, the hood of a sweatshirt over his head: all she could say for sure was that he was light-skinned rather than dark. He wasn't particularly big. He was stronger than her, but most men are stronger than most women. She wouldn't recognize him if he came to her for a mortgage.

She tried to throw him off but failed; after that she offered no resistance. She didn't want to be hurt. 'Was that wrong?'

Shapiro shook his head. 'There is no right or wrong. You survived. You did fine.'

'But the evidence. There'd have been more evidence, wouldn't there, if I'd made him work for it.'

He knew what she was saying. He put his hand on hers on the desk. 'Mrs Andrews, nobody is going to wonder if you're telling the truth because you weren't beaten to a pulp. No judge, no jury is going to wonder if a respectable professional woman walking home from a friend's house suddenly took it into her head to dive into the bushes with a man she didn't know and then scream rape. You behaved very sensibly. Thank God we're *not* conducting this interview in Castle General.'

She fixed him with sea-coloured blue-grey eyes, a cool intellectual gaze forcing itself through the shock and the grief. 'Mr Shapiro, are you saying you believe me?'

Dear God, she's strong, he thought in boundless admiration. She didn't have to come here. She was afraid how she'd be treated but she came anyway. She was willing to say all this, and be doubted, not because she has something to gain but because it's her duty: there's a dangerous man out there and we need to know about it. 'Mrs Andrews, I have no reason to doubt a single word you've said.'

At that, finally, she began to cry. Shapiro went on

holding her hand for a minute. Then he got up, poured her some more coffee, gave WPC Wilson a top-up and sat down again. 'Can you tell me what happened next?'

She sniffed and nodded, but there was little more to tell. The attack was completed quickly, efficiently, with minimal emotional investment: not so much a sex act as a smash and grab raid. He was finished, on his feet and away in the time it took her to get the scarf out of her mouth. She sat in the shrubbery for half an hour, clasping her knees and gently rocking, before she could bring herself to move.

Shapiro took her home. She lived alone: only a grey cat, indignant at being kept out all night, was waiting on the step. 'Is there someone I can call to come over?'

Mrs Andrews shook her head. 'I'd rather be alone.' The assault, and all that followed, had left her exhausted. Mentally she was numb; probably the morning would be harder than tonight.

Shapiro didn't like leaving her, but she wasn't hysterical and she had the right to be alone of she chose. He jotted his home number on her phone-pad. 'If you change your mind, call me. It doesn't matter when. I'll come myself, or send a WPC, or bring you a friend – whatever you want. Just don't sit here feeling desperate.' He thought a moment, useless compassion twisting his face. 'What happened – it wasn't about you, you know, it was about him. His inadequacies, his hang-ups. You're the same person you always were. Nothing someone like that could do to you would make you anything less.'

She wasn't really listening. She thanked him again, edged him towards the door. Reluctantly he went. 'One more thing. Is there anyone you'd like me to talk to? That you want to know about this and don't want to tell?' Telling people who mattered could be the worst part.

Again she shook her head. 'Don't think I'm not grateful, Superintendent. I appreciate everything you've done. When I'm ready to talk to people I will, but all I want to do now is sleep.'

So he left. There was no option: to press any more help on her would be to chisel away yet more of her autonomy, her freedom of choice, that had been the main casualty of the attack.

She hadn't been injured, no more than if she'd tripped on a kerb-stone. When she dusted the leaf-mould off her coat no physical signs would remain of what had happened. But that was no measure of the extent to which she had been hurt. What had been stolen from her was fundamental to who and what she was. It wasn't a vital organ, something she'd die without – the history of slavery proved how far a human being could be stripped of rights and still remain functional. But neither could it be replaced.

With strength and determination she would rebuild her life, but there was no way to excise this night's work. It was there for good. Her confidence, her self-esteem, would never again be what they were before. She knew now that however valuable she was as a human being – however good a friend, a lover, a businesswoman, however much money she earned, however pleasant the life she made for herself – almost any trash from the gutter, as long as he was a man and so physically stronger than her, could take it away.

It would probably never happen again. Rape was

still a rare occurrence, rape by a stranger in a public place rarest of all. But she would always know, from the womb out, what she had previously only acknowledged as a theoretical possibility: that half the population had the potential to reduce her to something of no consequence. That knowledge would shadow all the rest of her days.

Shapiro got home without further incident but he didn't get inside. There was something waiting on his path, something big and black and shapeless. He studied it from the safety of his car, debating whether he should call for assistance. But it didn't move, he couldn't hear it ticking, and he thought he'd investigate further before calling in the Bomb Squad. He wouldn't be the first policeman to launch a major terrorist alert because the laundry had left next door's washing in his porch.

Armed with the torch from his glove compartment he approached with caution. It almost could have been next door's laundry – something bulky bundled up in a bin-liner, the top tied with a bit of string. He knew better than to give it an experimental kick. Instead he used his penknife to make a nick in one of the folds. Nothing came out but a rather sweet heavy smell, just familiar enough to make his heart sink. He widened the nick and shone his torch inside.

Two minutes later he was on the phone to Queen's Street. 'I want SOCO, photographer, pathologist, the works. And screens. I don't want my neighbours watching while we reconstruct *A Student's Guide to Anatomy* with real pieces.

'No,' he added irritably, still shaken by what he'd seen, 'I don't know who it's likely to be inside. From the size, I doubt if it's all of anybody. But I've got a bin-bag full of meat sitting on my doorstep, and since my butcher doesn't do deliveries that makes it a murder inquiry.'

Chapter Six

Within the privacy of a tent erected in Shapiro's front garden, Dr Crowe slit the black bag open and carefully examined what it contained.

It's meat, Shapiro told himself when he felt his gorge rising, just meat. Whoever it once was, whatever their story, that's all it is now. If it was in the butcher's window I wouldn't give it a second look. Somehow that thought failed to appease his stomach.

When the forensic pathologist had finished piecing together the grisly jigsaw he straightened up, peeled off his rubber gloves and thrust his hands deep in his pockets. His plump face fell into thoughtful creases. 'I suppose you want a description.'

Shapiro looked in quiet horror at the shapeless mound on his path. 'Of that? You can tell me what *that* looked like?'

'Oh, yes,' said Dr Crowe, grimly confident; 'pretty much. But that wasn't what I meant. I can give you a fair description of the killer too.'

Startled, the superintendent's eyes flared at him. But though Dr Crowe was still a young man with a rather undergraduate sense of humour he didn't joke about murder. 'How?'

Crowe shrugged. 'It's my job. Do you want to make notes – for a Wanted poster?'

Impressed, Shapiro rooted for his notebook.

'All right,' said Crowe. 'It's a male you're looking for, of course – not very big but very powerful. Huge neck and shoulder muscles, big deep chest. Weight, maybe about eighty pounds. Interesting dentition: undershot jaw, the lower teeth projecting beyond the upper ones. The canine teeth are particularly prominent. Temper, *extremely* unreliable. Members of the public should not approach; even your officers ought to be armed. I suggest one of those poles with a noose at the end . . . '

'Hang on,' growled Shapiro, doubt turning to suspicion, 'hang on.' He hadn't written anything since the weight. He squinted at Crowe, who remained poker-faced; he looked at the remains on his path. 'Eighty pounds: what, five and a half stone? Most *victims* weigh more than that. Before I go on *News at Ten* appealing for calm and information, do you want to tell me what that – thing – is?'

An amiable grin from the pathologist acknowledged that the game was up. 'It *was* a pit-bull terrier.'

Understanding dawned. 'So the *murderer* . . .?'

Crowe nodded. 'Another pit-bull terrier, bigger or perhaps just meaner.'

Appalled, Shapiro stared at the carcase. 'A dog did that?'

'Oh, no,' Crowe said quickly, 'no. They fought to the death, the other dog ripped this one's throat out. Then somebody skinned it. To make it harder to identify.'

'And what was left he dumped on my path,' mused

Shapiro. 'Not even at Queen's Street, but my home. *Why?*'

'That's a bit outside the scope of forensics,' admitted Crowe. 'Have you been clamping down on dog-fighting recently?'

'I wasn't aware we had any to clamp down on.' Shapiro's expression was working through a range of possibilities, from shock to puzzlement to anger to resolution. 'So now we know better.'

Crowe was packing his gear. The body-bag hadn't been needed after all. 'Maybe they're warning you off.'

'I imagine they are,' said the superintendent bleakly. 'However, Shapiro's First Law of Getting Away With It advises against warning policemen off investigating things they didn't know needed investigating until someone warned them off.'

'The whole bloody town's gone mad,' Shapiro said with conviction. They'd gathered in his office at ten on Tuesday morning. He'd had no sleep, and judging from the shadows like bruises under Donovan's eyes neither had the sergeant. Liz alone seemed unaffected. She hadn't had as trying a night as the two men; even so, thought Shapiro irritably, she might have the grace to look tired. 'Ram-raiders,' he enumerated on thick fingers, 'train robbers, a rapist and now a dog-fighting ring. Whatever happened to stealing car radios and mugging old ladies on pension day?'

Even at the end of the twentieth century, Castlemere remained a provincial town with essentially provincial criminals. It wasn't the Vice Capital of anywhere, not even the fens. The local police had had their challenges but they usually came more widely spaced than this.

'How's Mrs Andrews?' asked Liz. She learned of the attack when she came in an hour earlier, still on a high from the success at Mile End. Seeing one of the raiders shot dead in front of her, knowing that her actions would be subject to scrutiny, in no way diminished the satisfaction she felt. But this did: that while she was keeping Brian awake with a blow-by-blow account of how clever she'd been, how clever Donovan had been, how lucky Castlemere was to have them, a decent woman walking home through the centre of town had been dragged under a bush and raped.

Shapiro gave an unhappy shrug. 'I don't know. She wasn't badly hurt; she said she'd be all right; I don't know how she really felt. I was going to ask you to see her sometime but God knows how you'll find the time now.'

Liz took his point. On sheer logistics they were going to be under pressure. 'How do you want to do this?'

'I don't want to pass Mrs Andrews on, even to you – she's had a tough enough time without being messed around now. Will you take the ram-raiders? And as dog-fighting's the sort of milieu in which DS Donovan will pass virtually unnoticed he can have the pit-bulls. All right so far?'

Liz nodded; Donovan said nothing. Standing by the door he matched Shapiro's bent-wood coat-stand for height, build and earnest attention to the proceedings. 'Sergeant?' the superintendent prompted gently.

Donovan blinked, came back from wherever his

mind had wandered. 'Oh – yeah. The dogs. I'll get on to it. What about the train?'

'What about it?'

'Who's dealing with that? We've two guys in the cells, another in the morgue, we've about thirty witness statements to collect – who's doing all that?'

'Me,' Shapiro said glumly. 'I've got Scobie taking statements, and unless the chaps in the cells change their minds they're not going to waste my time on inconsequential chit-chat. Once we get the all-clear over the shooting we can wrap it up. Yesterday's news, Donovan,' he added briskly, 'time to move on to fresh woods and pastures new.'

For a moment Donovan looked about to say something more; then he changed his mind. 'Dogs. I'm on it.'

When the door closed behind him Shapiro said, 'It's shaken him up, hasn't it?'

Liz raised an eyebrow. 'You're surprised? He was that close' – her fingers, all but touching. 'He did a good job there, Frank. I'd like to think those at Division who have him down as a loose cannon might recognize that last night he got a result nobody else here, including you and me, could have. How's the driver?'

'He'll be all right,' said Shapiro. 'It was his heart but they got him to intensive care in time.'

'Also thanks to Donovan.'

Shapiro smiled, the plump cheeks dimpling. 'Yes, all right, Inspector, I've got the message. Now, what about the ram-raiders? Any thoughts on them?'

She considered a moment. 'Well, they didn't show up last night and this morning also passed without incident. The Son of God might sanction another hour or two's surveillance if you ask nicely.' The senior officer at Queen's Street had always been known as God; the recent arrival of a much younger incumbent had somehow called for a new nickname.

Shapiro's expression was rueful. 'I tried already – got a very polite flea in my ear. In short, if I want any more stake-outs I can pay the overtime myself.' He scowled. 'I don't get it. They *should* have gone again by now. What's the problem, is it somebody's birthday?'

Liz refrained from repeating her doubts. 'What we really need is someone on the inside.'

Shapiro raised a quizzical eyebrow. 'Do you fancy your chances undercover, Inspector?'

Liz chuckled. 'If I knew where to find them I'd give it a shot. But I can't get any word on them. Maybe you're right, maybe it is the Tynesiders – that would explain the gossips in The Fen Tiger being as much in the dark as we are.' The hostelry was Castlemere's villains' pub long before the council gentrified the canal basin where it stood. Now weekend sailors brushed shoulders with the local Mafia and never understood the hush that fell when they used the pub phone to report the theft of their outboard motors.

'What about Donovan? Some of his snouts keep their ears pretty close to the ground.'

'Some of Donovan's snouts keep their entire bodies pretty close to the ground! But nobody seems to know much about this. I don't know what more we can do but wait for it to happen again and hope we can respond fast enough to catch them.' Her gaze had dropped disconsolately to the desk-top, lost beneath a week's worth of unfinished paperwork. Now it rose again, speculative. 'Unless we can find the chap in the green fedora. Just for the record, Frank, if we did, how would you feel about an undercover operation? If we could set one up?'

Shapiro was tired, but not tired enough to agree without thinking it through. His eyes narrowed. 'You?'

She shrugged. 'Whoever. In principle, would you approve?'

While he wrestled with it he pulled faces. He looked at Liz. He looked out of the window. He scratched his chin, missing the comfort of a beard to tug enjoyed by millennia of Shapiro men. Finally he said, 'I might. If we could do it cleanly so he wasn't a marked man from day one.'

'A marked man?' Her voice rose delicately on the question mark.

Shapiro smiled wearily. 'Definitely. A woman would stand out like a sore thumb in that sort of set-up. I'm sure there's nothing Donovan could do that you couldn't, but he's twice as likely to be accepted by the gang and four times as likely to be trusted with the sort of information we need. I'm sure you'd make a splendid ram-raider, Liz, but be realistic: your only way in would be as a gangster's moll and nobody'd talk times and routes in front of you.'

'*You* be realistic, Frank,' she retorted, amused, 'I'm fifteen years too old to be a gangster's moll! I take your point; but I wouldn't want Donovan doing it, not with last night still so fresh in his mind. You need a steady hand for undercover work: he needs time to get his nerve back. What about Scobie?'

Shapiro shook his head. 'You also need two brain-cells to rub together. How about Morgan?'

'Maybe. Oh, what's the point discussing it?' she said then impatiently. 'We don't know that the man in the green hat was their look-out, let alone where to find him or how to infiltrate a fifth columnist. Forget I asked; I just can't think what else to do.'

'If it was easy,' Shapiro said gently, 'they'd have got these people in Harrogate, Barnsley, Mansfield, Nottingham or Leamington. We may have to face the possibility that they're too bloody clever for us too.'

Liz was a pragmatist: she knew you couldn't win them all. She could live with that. What galled her was being unable to think up a plan of campaign. She looked away in irritation; when she looked back Shapiro had his eyes closed. 'Frank, you look like death warmed up. Get a few hours' sleep. I'll hold the fort.'

Shapiro opened his eyes and sniffed. 'The reason that senior posts are reserved for older personnel, Inspector, is that having your own office makes it easier to sleep on the job. A couple of hours' catching up on my paperwork and I'll be a new man.'

It was probably a joke, but anyway the chance didn't arise. As Liz was leaving the results on the fingerprints came through. The older of the two men downstairs was Edward Parker, sometime of Leeds; the younger was Martin Ginley of Motherwell; the dead man was Harry Black from Sunderland. Black and Parker had both done time for armed robbery, Ginley had convictions for theft and what used to be called joy-riding until it was noticed how often it led to funerals.

Shapiro scowled. 'Is there nothing left worth nicking in the north any more, that all their blaggers have to come down here?'

He thought that being confronted with their own records might encourage them to open up. But he learned nothing that Donovan hadn't already told him: what happened, who gave the orders, who had the weapons. On the face of it that might have been all there was to tell. But Shapiro knew men, particularly criminals; he knew when he was being lied to, and he knew when he was being told less than the truth. These two were holding something back, and he couldn't think what or why.

Until he was back in his own office, chewing his lip pensively, when Scobie knocked and came in with his arms full of papers and a puzzled expression gathered round his rugby-player's nose. 'Sir?'

'Constable?'

'The hostage, sir. The girl DS Donovan was worried about, who nearly got her throat cut.'

'What about her?'

'I can't find her, sir.'

Shapiro regarded him with more resignation than surprise. 'You mean you've lost her statement?'

'No, sir. She doesn't seem to have made a statement. I didn't take it, nor did Wilson or Morgan. Everyone on the train saw her but nobody remembers seeing her after they left the train. We don't even have a name and address for her.' Scobie watched the superintendent warily, waiting for the explosion.

Instead, slowly, Shapiro began to smile. 'The *cunning* so-and-sos! We all know that a well-prepared criminal is likely to be a successful criminal, but fancy being well enough prepared to bring your own hostage!'

DC Scobie was very good at running after escaping crooks, at bringing them down with a well-timed tackle and bringing tears to their eyes if they attempted to resist arrest. He wasn't as quick on the uptake. 'Sir?'

Shapiro spelled it out. 'She was one of them, Scobie. There weren't three of them, there were four. It was her job to be young, pretty and terrified, and not to struggle or try to escape the way a real hostage might. Black would need all his wits to handle a real hostage, but an accomplice would co-operate. She probably meant to go along when they left the train. But they couldn't take her up the shaft, not realistically; anyway there was no need. As we evacuated the train she slipped away in the dark and we didn't even miss her till now.' He chuckled. 'No wonder the lads downstairs didn't want to talk!'

Unsure what the joke was, Scobie didn't think he'd risk laughing too. 'What do you want me to do, sir?'

'Not a lot you can do, constable, is there? When Sergeant Donovan gets back you could get a full description from him. We'll circulate it, we might get lucky, but it's my guess we'll have to put her down as the one that got away. I doubt we'll see hide or hair of her again.'

Chapter Seven

They stared bellicosely at one another, nose to nose through the wire mesh.

One of them was mostly black with grey brindling on the nose, the broad chest and front legs. The skull was massive and rounded, ragged ears set low on each side. The baleful eyes were oddly triangular, with a prick of reddish light in each. The bolster of muscle that was the neck swelled into the barrel chest without any perceptible join, then narrowed to powerful loins and long, strong back legs. A ratty tail curved up like a scimitar. The grizzled lips fluttered like curtains over yellow tusks and from deep in the muscular throat came a low growl like distant thunder.

The other one said in an Irish accent, 'What do you call him?'

The constable at the kennels was deeply uneasy. He knew he was being pushed into doing something improper, and DS Donovan offering to take full responsibility wouldn't save him if there was trouble. If the dog got loose. If someone reported it. If, God forbid, it bit someone.

Sergeant Barraclough would have had none of it. But Barraclough was on his holidays and Constable Sutton, deputizing for him, laboured under two handicaps. One was the matter of rank. The other was that he owed Donovan a favour for helping him break up a feeding frenzy once when he left a pen unlatched. Others might have helped had they been about at the time but not many would have kept quiet about it afterwards. Donovan never said a word. When' asked about the marks on his arms he said, dead-pan, 'Lovebites.'

'He's a stray,' explained Sutton, 'he's going to be put down. He doesn't have a name.'

'Brian Boru,' said Donovan with satisfaction.

Sutton unearthed a collar that would fit him, a lead that looked as if it might hold him and a muzzle big enough to accommodate those startling jaws. 'If any-body asks—' Donovan began; but he didn't finish the sentence.

'Yes?' the constable prompted anxiously.

Donovan thought for a moment longer. 'Lie,' he said then.

He took the dog to a lock-up behind Brick Lane. Then he fetched Billy Dunne out of the public bar of The Fen Tiger. 'Got something to show you.'

When Billy saw Brian Boru the scant natural colour – nocturnal for the most part, the little man didn't get a lot of sun on his skin – vanished from his tarnished cheek. 'Hell fire, Mr Donovan, what's that for?'

'What do you think? I want to match him.'

Billy was into a lot of things that weren't strictly legal. He could always find a ton of bricks that were surplus to requirements, a keg of beer that fell off the back of a lorry, a reconditioned video that the insurers had understood was past repair. He probably broke a law every day of the week, but as long as he kept his head down and his depredations minor he got away with most of them: police time could usually be spent more profitably than trying to trace Billy Dunne's breeze-blocks. It was more practical to use him than to charge him.

The little man backed the length of the lock-up as if the dog hadn't been chained. 'I don't know about that, Mr Donovan, I really don't.'

'Yes you do, Billy,' Donovan said patiently. 'There's dog-fighting going on round here and you know about it. And I want to know where to take him.'

'It's not *like* that, Mr Donovan,' pleaded Billy. 'It's like – a secret society, they don't admit just anyone. They get nasty if they think people are spying on them.'

'What do you think he's for,' snorted Donovan, indicating the dog, 'company? He's my passport. He's not neutered, he's not registered, if he's got a tattoo it's a skull and crossbones on his biceps. He's an illegal pit-bull and he makes me into a sporting man. They'll be happy to see me. Anyway, what's it to you? I'm not asking you to take me, just tell me where they are.'

'It's not *like* that,' Billy whined again. 'They don't advertise. They don't put a notice in the *Courier.*'

Donovan was running out of patience, which was not a thing he had in endless supply. 'If they did I wouldn't be wasting my time with you. If they did, I wouldn't have to remind you there's only a bit of a padlock holding the dog, I've got the key, and I don't know when he last had a square meal.'

Billy thought it was probably a joke. With any other officer of the law he'd have been sure; with Donovan he couldn't quite be. And he didn't have to risk it. 'OK!

OK, Mr Donovan, I'll tell you what I can. Not where they fight – I really don't know that. But I know where they exercise them. You can't give them a run in the park like a spaniel so they take them to the woods beside the river. You know the place? – there's a little car-park.' Donovan knew. 'I don't know if they're there every night, but I reckon if you went about eleven, with the dog, you'd likely meet someone could tell you what you want to know.'

After lunch Liz was at the Magistrate's Court giving evidence in a case of possessing cannabis resin. It wasn't a major drugs bust, eighteen-year-old Peter Cole had enough joints for himself and a few friends, and he'd been selling them on that basis for about what he paid for them. It wasn't an important matter at all, except in one respect. Peter Cole senior thought he could buy his son's acquittal.

He'd hired himself the smartest barrister in Castle-mere, he'd lined up experts to testify to the defendant's intellectual and scholastic accomplishments, and he'd persuaded one of the group of friends to say that he'd bought the joints and was offering them to Cole. As a juvenile selling drugs to an adult the boy would get off more lightly than an adult convicted of selling to a juvenile.

The only obstacle to this convenient arrangement was that Liz had seen the exchange by the gates of Castle High when she'd been collecting her husband from school one afternoon. She saw who had the joints, who had the money, who ended up with what. Even if the subsequent deal suited both parties she was damned if she was going to watch one daft lad accept the lasting burden of another's conviction for the sake of a new mountain bike.

'Mr Fenton, I know what I saw,' she said calmly, for about the fourth time. 'I knew what I was seeing at the time, and nothing that the defendant, his father or anyone else has said since makes me doubt the evidence of my eyes. Peter was selling, the younger boy was buying.'

'Then you're saying that they're lying,' said Dan Fenton, the light of battle in his eyes – as if this were personal, as if he weren't merely saying what he was paid to, as if he and the police witness hadn't danced till the small hours at the Civic Ball last Christmas. 'That the witnesses who've come here to give evidence before His Worship are telling lies!'

'*Yes*, Mr Fenton,' she said in barely restrained exasperation, as if he were an inattentive pupil who'd just that moment grasped what she was saying.

'And can you suggest, Inspector Graham, why they should do such a thing?'

From the eminence of the witness box she looked down her nose at him. 'I can conceive of a reason, Mr Fenton, yes. But as I have no evidence, perhaps I should limit my testimony to those things I have seen with my own eyes.'

The Magistrates, at least, found her account convincing. She was leaving the court-house with a satisfied smile when she heard a quick tread on the steps behind her and turned. It was Gail Fisher from the *Castlemere Courier*, absent without leave from the Press table. So it was a matter of some urgency. 'I need a quick word – and for once it's me that wants to go off the record.'

Liz smiled. Castlemere police enjoyed a useful relationship with the local paper and the two women had much in common. They didn't agree on everything but rarely argued on important matters. 'How can I help?'

'I heard there was a rape in town last night.'

Caution dropped a veil in front of Liz's face. She considered the implications before saying anything. Then: 'Off the record? Yes. But we're not ready to say anything official yet. I'll call you as soon as we are.'

'Fair enough,' said Fisher. She was a few years younger than Liz, a dramatically attractive woman with a mass of curly dark hair and a liking for long dark gypsy skirts. Many reporters still working for provincial weeklies in their thirties have given up hope of getting anything better. But Gail Fisher had been to Fleet Street – Wapping, actually – didn't like it and came back. The *Courier* was lucky to have her. 'Really, I'm not wanting a story from you. I want to tell you one.'

'Go on.'

'It's not the first time. A friend of mine—' She looked up with a wide-mouthed grin. 'I know what that usually means, but honestly, it wasn't me, it was a friend of mine. She was working late in her office about a week ago. The place should have been empty, but as she locked up someone jumped her in the corridor.'

Liz was staring at her. 'Why don't I know anything about this?'

Fisher shrugged. 'Because that was how she wanted it. He had a scarf over his face, she couldn't even make an intelligent guess at his age. Grey sweats, white trainers, that's all she saw: she didn't see how you

73

could find him from that and she couldn't have identified him if you did. She wasn't prepared to go through the extra trauma of a medical examination, police questioning, maybe her identity coming out, when she couldn't see how it would do any good. She picked herself up, went home, had a long bath and a stiff drink, and then she called me.'

'You could have called me.' Liz's tone was of mild reproof; inside she was fighting anger.

'No,' said Fisher. 'It was a matter of trust – I promised I wouldn't.'

'Then why are you telling me now? I can talk to her, but it's too late to do anything useful.'

'I don't want you to talk to her. I'm not going to tell you her name or where she works except that it's in the Mere Basin redevelopment. But if it's happened before it'll happen again. Once could be random, twice is a habit. I thought you needed to know that.'

'I needed to know a week ago! I needed to know when there was a chance of finding him before another woman got jumped. It's already too late for that.'

Fisher spread an apologetic hand. 'I didn't feel I had any choice. My friend had been raped once – forcing her to report it would be like raping her again.'

Liz nodded slowly, letting the anger go. 'Is she all right?'

Fisher gave an unhappy shrug. 'I don't know. She's on the pill, which is something to be grateful for. I want her to test for sexually transmitted diseases: she says she'll go in a day or two but keeps not doing. She's trying to pretend nothing happened; or rather, that what happened wasn't so terrible after all. She says she's had sex with men she didn't know much better, and she's had sex that hurt more. She says it doesn't matter. She was back at work the next day, but she's scared to death he'll corner her again.'

'Would she talk to me – like this, informally?'

'I don't know. I'll ask.'

'What's she like? No,' Liz added quickly, seeing Fisher about to shake her head, 'I'm not trying to work out who she is, only if there's something particular this man's looking for. The victim last night was early forties, fair, well built, single, a successful business-woman. Is your friend anything like that?'

The reporter's eyes widened. 'Inspector, my friend is *exactly* like that.'

Donovan borrowed a van, chained Brian Boru in the back. It was the only way he felt safe taking his eyes off the dog.

At eleven-fifteen that night the little car-park in the wood overlooking the water meadows of the River Arrow was not a hive of illicit activity. There were just two vehicles there. But that was two more than might have been expected, and neither of them was beating out the rhythm of the Lovers' Lane Rock. One was another van, the second a grey saloon with a small trailer attached.

With the dog on a long rope and a powerful torch in his other hand, Donovan followed the footpath into the trees. The utter darkness of the wood made the torch essential; otherwise he'd have brought a pick-axe handle.

They'd been wandering around for half an hour, wrapping the rope round trees and snarling at one another, and Donovan was about to head back and try another night when shadows moved at the edge of his sight and a man and a dog stepped on to the path in front of him.

A shudder of pure atavistic fear coursed through Donovan's body, as if the devil and his familiar were abroad in the wood that night. He couldn't tell how big the man was, only that he was solid with it; but the dog came halfway up his thigh, a swollen mass of bone and muscle under a coat that rippled in the torch-light. They stood immobile, blocking the path, while Donovan stared and Brian Boru drew himself up to his full impressive stature. The vibration of the challenge in his throat travelled the rope to Donovan's hand. He flicked the torch upwards.

The man covered his face, gestured peremptorily, and Donovan remembered his manners and dropped the beam. 'Sorry.'

''S all right,' the man said, amiably enough. 'Only, people get a bit twitchy, you know?'

'Not as twitchy as me,' growled Donovan. 'I keep expecting the frigging Dog Police to leap out of the trees.'

The man chuckled. 'You haven't been here before, have you?'

Donovan shook his head. 'The poor sod's been living in a lock-up. Somebody told me I could bring him here without being bothered.'

'Right enough. But that's no kind of exercise, drag-ging him round on a rope. Let him run, that's what I do. They can't do much damage out here.'

Looking again, Donovan realized the brute beside him had neither a lead nor a muzzle. He shivered. 'You don't know Brian. He's a desperate dog for a fight. He'll fight his own shadow if there's nothing else going. I like the dog, you know, but I wouldn't trust him an inch.'

'Brian?' The man laughed. 'That's not much of a name for a fighting dog.'

'Brian Boru,' said Donovan indignantly. 'How's your Irish history?'

'Bit of a sporting gent, was he?'

'There was nothing sporting about it. He killed Vikings, as many as he could, any way he could. Nowadays they'd call him the Butcher of Clontarf and take up a collection for disabled Norsemen. But when it's a matter of kill or be killed you have to admire the guy who does it best. It's like the dogs: you can't blame a dog for fighting when it's in his nature.'

'Right enough.' The man fell into step beside Donovan, his dog pacing silently at his heel. Donovan kept Brian's leash short. 'Dogs like these, a good scrap's the best exercise they can have. Did you ever think . . .?'

They walked back to the car-park. The van was gone; the other man put his dog into the trailer. 'Do you have a name?'

'Duggan,' said Donovan. 'Hugh Duggan.'

'First names are enough. 'I'm Mick.' He patted the trailer. 'And he's Thor. Listen. If I hear anything, should I let you know?'

'Oh, yeah,' said Donovan with conviction.

Chapter Eight

'Two rapes with a week between,' said Liz, stirring her coffee vengefully. 'That isn't a habit, it's a compulsion. It won't be long before he tries again.'

'I said that about the ram-raiders.' Shapiro sniffed. 'I'm still hiding round corners to avoid the Son of God.'

Superintendent Giles was not merely twelve years younger than his predecessor, he was a different kind of policeman. He had two degrees. He was computer literate. It was he who found the funding to stake out nine different premises when Shapiro was sure the ram-raiders would strike on Monday evening, and again when he revised that to Tuesday morning. Every time Shapiro met his cool blue gaze he saw pound signs clocking up.

Liz didn't feel like smiling. She wasn't angry with Shapiro: she was still angry with Gail Fisher and her friend, and even that was a kind of referred anger because she didn't know the man she was really angry with. She didn't subscribe to the Victorian view that it was a fate worse than death, but she had better reasons than sisterly solidarity for considering rape a peculiarly vicious offence.

It was a crime perpetrated exclusively by stronger people on weaker ones, as distasteful as a grown man beating a child or a strong one a cripple. Additionally, it tainted a special gift of joy. Like the Bad Fairy, the rapist waved a wand over something meant to be an abiding pleasure and turned it to gall. It wasn't like stealing a woman's purse. It was like stealing her purse, and coming back to steal it again every time she tried to open it for maybe the rest of her life. When it came to rape, Liz had no sense of humour.

'We have to find him,' she said flatly. 'Whatever it costs, we have to stop him.'

'I agree. But is money the answer? With unlimited funding, how would you have saved Mrs Andrews from being raped? You could turn Castlemere into a police state and still not be able to guarantee women's safety from molestation. Even a curfew wouldn't have saved the woman in the office block. It's easy to say that prevention's better than cure but mostly it can't be done. Usually the best we can do is catch those responsible for crimes and hope to restrict their opportunities to reoffend. There'll never be an entirely safe society; and what's more, there never was.'

Liz banged down her empty cup. 'No? Well, consider this. If there was anything out there as dangerous to men as men are to women, the army would be brought in to wipe it out.'

He understood her anger but Shapiro was concerned that it was clouding her judgement. He said quietly, 'And you think of this. The groups at greatest risk of violence in our society aren't women at all. Small children suffer the greatest number of attacks in the home, and young men the greatest number in the street. If you had a son of twenty and a daughter of twenty-one walking home late at night, the girl isn't the one you'd need to worry about.'

For a moment Liz went on eyeing him hotly; then she looked away. The annoying thing was, she knew he was right. 'You think I'm over-reacting.'

'No,' he said honestly. 'How can you over-react to something like this! But we need to focus on the right problem. It's nothing to do with sex. It's about dominance. Rapists are men attacking women because that's how the biology works. But the problem isn't that men can rape women, it's that a few men want to: that the urge to violence occasionally expresses itself that way. Rape isn't an excess of love but a burgeoning of hatred. Rapists don't want what they take, that's only an excuse; if there were no women to rape they'd victimize someone else. What they want is to hurt – physically, mentally, emotionally. All they really want from you is your pain.'

When she first worked for Shapiro, when he was a detective inspector and she a sergeant, Liz was always being made aware of how much he knew that she didn't. It happened less now, partly because she'd made a point of listening then, but still often enough to remind her that though she had her own strengths she didn't have his profound understanding of human nature. She still listened when Shapiro talked because there was still a lot he could teach her.

'All right,' she conceded with a flicker of grace, 'I'll try not to besmirch half the human race with the sins of a minority if you'll think of some way to catch the sod.'

'We're waiting for the results of the DNA test. That may come up trumps.'

Liz eyed him askance. 'If he's done it before, and been caught. But if he's done it before it was somewhere else, and if he's a local man he's only just started and won't be on file. DNA's a long shot.'

Shapiro felt the burden of her expectation. 'Without a description it's still probably the best we have. Unless . . .' On second thoughts he decided not to say it.

Liz finished for him, her lips tight. 'Unless he does it again, and this time he drops his driving licence. Frank, we could go through an awful lot of victims before he does something that stupid. We need to force the pace, push him into making a mistake. What about a decoy?'

Shapiro recoiled as if she'd offered him a bag of pork scratchings. 'To catch a rapist? You're on dangerous ground there, girl. This is a hit-and-run expert, remember. If there's anyone close enough to protect the decoy he won't strike. And if you move the cover back to where he isn't aware of them, he'll be in and out before they can reach her.' He winced. 'If you'll pardon the expression.'

'She'll have two massive advantages over the previous victims,' Liz pressed. 'She'll be ready for it, watching and listening for his first move. And she'll be a policewoman. We're better at self-defence than the average building society manageress.'

The pause meant Shapiro was considering it. He didn't like it but there weren't many options. Doing nothing but hoping for the best was one; this was the other. Finally he said, 'Even in a blonde wig, Wilson's too young and too small to fit the profile. Cathy Flynn would look the part but I don't know how she'd react if he took the bait. Besides, I don't think she'd volunteer, and I'm not ordering anyone to do that. Who's left? We're not exactly knee deep in good-looking blonde Whoopsies aged about forty who can handle themselves in a scrap.' Women Police Constables labour under a variety of nicknames up and down the country. 'Whoopsies' is one of the less pejorative.

'Who says it has to be a Whoopsie?'

'*Donovan* in a blonde wig?' The idea was enough to freeze the conversation in its tracks.

Liz recovered first, shaking the image out of her eyes like soapy water. '*Me*, Frank. I haven't met your Mrs Andrews but from your description, and Fisher's description of her friend, I'm the obvious choice. I'm the same age, build and colouring – if he went for them he'll go for me.'

But he wouldn't agree there and then. He wanted to think about it. Even if he were persuaded he'd need to get approval: Giles held the purse-strings. After the earlier fiascos, clutched might be a better word.

She got home a little after seven. Her husband was in the kitchen washing sugar-beet and flaked maize off his hands. Every morning Liz prepared three buckets of feed for her mare, and if she wasn't there at the appropriate times Brian would deliver them to the stable behind the house. It was the limit of his involvement with the horse, and it took Liz three years to persuade him to do that much.

It wasn't that he didn't like animals. He had a definite fondness for cats. But horses, with their unfathomable thought processes and instantaneous reactions, their iron feet and their sheer size, frightened him. It was in vain for Liz to point out that Polly was a middle-aged lady of sedate good manners, and that the appearance of a bucket was in any event a guarantee of good behaviour. Instead she bought a manger that hooked over the door and could be filled from outside the stable.

She put her arms round his middle and laid her cheek against his back, feeling his bones through his shirt. 'Good day at the chalk-face?'

'3b,' he said wearily, 'have just discovered nipples.' He taught art. Though his pupils ranged from eleven-year-olds to A-level students of nineteen it was always 3b that gave him trouble. Nipples, fig-leaves and those bits of voile, unexplained by the context, that floated in front of classical nudes at strategic moments. As 2b they were too shy to comment; as 4b they were too cool. But every year 3b stumbled on nipples with the thrill of Marilyn Monroe discovering updraughts. 'You?'

'Not very.' She turned him in the compass of her arms so that she could see his face. There was nothing remarkable about it. It was intelligent, kind and sensitive, and boasted a forehead that went most of the way back to his collar. Men who wouldn't have stood a chance if a freak nuclear accident in Market Harborough wiped out most of the male population couldn't see what a good-looking woman like Liz Graham saw in a balding art teacher; and wouldn't have believed that the answer was as simple as love if she'd told them. 'We need to talk about it. There's something I want to do, and I think maybe you have a right to be consulted.'

When he realized what she was proposing his first instinct was to stop her somehow. Not to forbid her, he knew he couldn't do that, he knew by trying he risked more than she was planning to, but by asking her, begging if he had to. His blood ran cold at the very idea.

But he'd been married to her for ten years, knew how important this was to her. She hadn't made detective inspector by pulling flashy stunts, she'd done it by hard work and professionalism. She hadn't dreamed this up on the drive home, she'd thought it through and believed it was the best way to trap a dangerous man who would otherwise remain free. That didn't put Graham's mind at rest, but it told him two things. That if she did it she'd do it properly, with all the support she needed. And that if she didn't do it, because of him, she'd think less of him.

He didn't dare ask how risky it could be. 'How safe can you make it?'

Proud of him, her smile was warm. 'Safer than points duty on market day; safer than clearing a pitch invasion after a four-one drubbing by Rochdale; about the same risk factor as going through Donovan's desk without wearing rubber gloves.'

But he didn't want humour, he wanted the truth. 'Seriously.'

Liz nodded, chastened. She owed him honesty. 'Pretty safe. I'll have a radio so I can have back-up within twenty seconds. If I can hold on to him for twenty seconds the thing's finished, he's behind bars, he can't harm anyone else.'

'What makes you think he'll go for it? I mean, why you? There must be dozens of attractive forty-year-old blondes in Castlemere. How do you catch his eye?'

'We look at what he's done already. Both times he

chose a semi-public place – if either woman had made enough noise she'd have been heard. So maybe the risk of being caught is part of the thrill. Also, he wants a certain type of victim, not just any woman who crosses his path. We can use that. I thought we'd start at Mere Basin. We don't know just where the first attack took place, but he was in one of the office blocks after normal hours so maybe he works there. If so he may notice another forty-year-old blonde coming and going late at night.'

'And if he takes the bait?'

'I yell, and Donovan and Scobie and Morgan dash up and sit on him.'

'You make it sound you couldn't possibly get hurt.'

She was holding his hand, her fingers woven with his. 'You can always get roughed up in this job, you know that. Mostly it's black eyes, occasionally a broken nose.' That took him back: she'd had a plaster over her nose the night he asked her to marry him. He hadn't meant to propose, not quite then, but that plaster brought out his nurturing instincts. 'It's pretty rare for anything to go further awry than that.'

'But it could happen.'

'With three large policemen watching my every move? No. We won't let it get that far out of hand.'

Brian Graham didn't like it any more than Shapiro had done, for some of the same reasons. He didn't give a damn about the overtime budget but he didn't want his wife putting herself in danger. Even a carefully controlled danger; even in a good cause.

On the other hand, every policeman's wife in the country saw him off to work feeling the same way, and Brian doubted if many of them were invited to say how many risks of what nature they should take in the course of their work. He appreciated being asked – she didn't have to do that, she could have said nothing until it was over.

'Donovan. And Scobie's the one with the nose?' His shudder was real enough. 'I don't know what effect they'll have on the enemy, but by God they frighten me.'

Quoting the Duke of Wellington was about the closest Brian came to machismo. His courage took quieter forms; like saying yes to something that filled him with dread when he could have said no. Liz's gaze on his face was fond. 'Brian Graham, you're a star.'

A few minutes later the phone went. When she came back anticipation was warring in her eyes with a little anxiety, and winning. 'That was Frank. We're on.'

Chapter Nine

That night, and again the following night, as the clock in Castle Place struck twelve, she drove under the iron archway and down the steep ramp into Mere Basin. Four canals met in the heart of Castlemere and a six-storey warehouse had been built over each of them on black brick vaults high enough to accommodate a narrowboat chimney and not much more. In recent years the Victorian warehouses had been redeveloped as shops, offices and apartments, and very pleasant it was when sunshine poured through the great square well of the buildings on to the peaty water and gaily-painted boats.

At midnight, however, the shops were shut and the offices were dark and all that could be seen of the two hundred people who lived there were cars parked in the basement garages and the glow of a few lights behind drawn curtains high up in the buildings. It wasn't quite enough to send shivers up the spine, but nor was it the obvious spot for a woman on her own to walk a dog.

In fact Liz was not on her own. Secreted about the Basin were DS Donovan and DCs Scobie and Morgan. Donovan was (of course) on a boat, Scobie was in a car and Morgan was in a little striped tent where the gas company had had the pipes up. To a casual eye the place was deserted.

Except for the tall fair woman with the little white dog who parked her car under The Barbican and walked unhurriedly beneath the building and out towards Broad Wharf. There were lights on the towpath, but Broad Wharf was where they ended. Under the last of them she leaned against a bollard for a few minutes; then she turned round and wandered back. She did this on Tuesday night, and again on Wednesday night, by which time she was heartily sick of the little white dog she'd borrowed; and she didn't attract so much as a wolf-whistle.

On Thursday morning she found a summons from Superintendent Giles on her desk. She knew what he was going to say but she still didn't have an answer.

He was about her age, tall and slender and fair; like a recruiting sergeant for the Hitler Youth, someone remarked nastily when he first arrived. He greeted Liz politely and waited for her to take a seat before asking, 'Any luck at the Basin last night?'

There was only one reply possible. 'No, sir, not so far.'

His smile had a distant quality; not because he was an unkind man, more because the bias of his skills was administrational rather than personal. He liked the words 'organization' and 'method': it was impossible to swap a casual remark with him on the stairs without one or other coming into it. 'The thing is, Mrs Graham, we need results to justify the expenditure. I can't keep four detectives tied up for an hour every night when the only benefit is that Miss Tunstall gets her dog walked.' Miss Tunstall was his secretary.

'It's like any other kind of fishing,' Liz said apologetically. 'All you can do is bait the hook. You can't make the fish jump.'

'Do you know,' murmured Superintendent Giles, 'Mr Shapiro said exactly the same thing about his ramraiders? Any sign of them yet?'

Liz exercised restraint. 'Not so far as I know, sir.'

'No,' he said thoughtfully. To be fair, he wasn't blaming her. He was responsible for making the best use of police resources, both human and financial: in his position she'd have been getting twitchy too. 'A difficult job, drawing out a rapist. When you've only a loose idea of where he might be and none at all of who he is. Well, you did your best, but I think we have to leave it there for now. Of course, if there's another incident and we have more to go on . . .'

Liz made a last effort, knowing as she did that it wouldn't sway him. 'Another incident means another victim. A woman who's been raped can't make good the loss with a cheque from the insurance company.'

'I do realize that,' Giles said, a shade frostily because it shouldn't have occurred to her that he needed telling. He was aware that he had yet to gain the full confidence of these people. They were polite enough, at least to his face, but somehow related to him as if he were not another police officer. As if he were an accountant. 'I don't think you've been wasting your time, Mrs Graham, I think you were right to try. But we can't go on forever. If we can narrow down some of the variables we'll try again.'

She wished she could argue, or even feel sure that he was wrong. Resignedly she nodded. 'Sir.'

Scobie and Morgan were plainly relieved though

they affected disappointment for Liz's sake. Donovan heard her in silence, his narrow face impervious. When she'd finished he looked idly out of the window and, apparently changing the subject, said, 'I've got a dog.'

Liz blinked. 'Have you? How nice.'

'Well, I'm looking after it. Mean big bastard; needs some walking.'

'Yes?'

'Thought I might start taking him up the tow-path every night. Say, about midnight, after everyone's gone home.'

Liz felt herself beginning to smile. 'Sounds a good idea. I quite like a walk about then myself. Perhaps I'll see you around.'

'Maybe not,' he said. 'But I'll be there.'

That evening when he went to feed Brian Boru he found a note under the garage door. It was short on detail but told him all he needed to know. 'Tonight, same time, same place.' There was no signature.

Donovan perched on the work-bench like a dyspeptic vulture, watching the dog. It ate as if against the clock, as if something even bigger and nastier might come along at any moment.

He was planning his next move. To keep the rendezvous, obviously; that was why he'd borrowed the dog in the first place. But alone? With back-up? – remembering that Shapiro wasn't yet aware of his line of inquiry? With the dog? – knowing that without him he'd probably be turned back but if he was there he might have to fight? Brian Boru was not a family pet, but being a thug didn't mean he could hold his own against professionals. His opponents would be fitter, better trained, expertly handled. Brian Boru had only his natural savagery, and in class company it wouldn't be enough. Donovan was aware that if he took him he might have to watch him torn apart. He wasn't a nice dog, but that was a bad end.

Ultimately though it didn't come down to how nice Brian was, or even how nice Donovan was. The dog was his entry to a vicious subculture. He was risking his own neck, and even if he'd liked the dog he wouldn't have prized its skin above his own. Without a dog he'd get nowhere. The animal faced destruction anyway: Donovan thought it likely, if there was any way to ask, that he'd sooner go down fighting than submit to the kindly humiliation of euthanasia.

But taking the dog meant going alone. What he was proposing was illegal. It might be possible to get clearance, in the way that Drugs Squad were allowed to use proscribed substances in their operations, but he couldn't get it before eleven. If he asked Shapiro he'd be told to wait.

Inspector Graham, on the other hand, owed him a favour. If he could cover her unofficial activities she could cover his. He went home to call her from the narrowboat where he lived on the canal.

Even as she answered, though, he thought better of it. Asking favours of a senior officer was a minefield. If she thought he was too far out of line she'd pull him up short. She had to: once she knew what he intended she had to either approve or forbid it. Better if she didn't know.

With an ease born of practice he moved into lie mode. 'Sorry to bother you at home, boss, but I'm going to be out late tonight – I don't know how late but probably till tomorrow. Can we walk the dogs some other time?'

She didn't suspect. 'Yes, fine. I wouldn't mind turning in at a decent hour for once.'

Donovan drove the van out into The Levels, making for the wood beside the river. The van was no more his than the dog was, but there's only one way to carry a dog on a motorcycle and he'd no intentions of stuffing Brian Boru inside his jacket. Before he got there two men in a car waved him over. 'Follow us.' Over the next several minutes they became a small convoy of vehicles, mostly large battered cars with a few large smart ones among them. Once when they paused someone walked back to check he had a dog. If he'd left Brian in the garage his inquiry would have ended in the ditch beside the road.

He tried to remember the way but they wove from lane to lane across The Levels and when they finally pulled into a yard beside a big barn they could have been anywhere inside a five-mile circle.

Mick strolled over, Thor beside him now restrained by a lead as thick as his thumb. He nodded at the back of Donovan's van. 'You brought him then.'

In these surroundings edginess came naturally. 'I don't know about this. Some of these dogs'd make light work of a buffalo!'

Pleased, Mick chuckled. 'Don't worry about the heavyweights – that's Thor's class, nobody'd expect a novice to face them. The freshers fight one another while they learn the game. If he's no taste for it you can take him home and no harm done.'

A shade reassured, Donovan patted Brian Boru's shoulder – twice, before Brian made it clear he should stop. 'He's a desperate dog but I wouldn't want to lose him.'

'No danger, not at this point. Dogs get killed in the big money matches, but to start with the only people interested are the owners and maybe a talent scout or two. If the dog handles himself you might get an offer for him.'

'I couldn't sell him,' Donovan said hastily; which was true enough because he didn't own him. 'Show me what happens.'

They pushed through the gathering crowd of men and dogs. Inside the barn were a number of wooden structures. At one end there were two of them, roped together from sheep hurdles – they could have been calf pens or any other small unit of agricultural containment. 'That's where they try the freshers,' said Mick.

'Freshers?'

'Freshmen – novices.' The man grinned. 'Stupid, isn't it? I don't know if they call them that everywhere.'

In the other half of the barn was a ring about four metres across, built like a section of a giant barrel, chest-high vertical lathes locked together by broad metal bands. Looking closer Donovan saw it was made in four pieces that bolted together – so it could be dismantled and taken between venues, he supposed. Any farmer could provide a few hurdles and a barn but the ring was custom-made and could have no other purpose. It was the pit that gave the pit-bull terrier its name.

Stout chains ran along the sides of the barn with shackles to which the dogs were being tied. Close-coupling prevented them from tearing one another apart for no profit, but nothing could stop them trading threats. As the barn filled the furious barking made conversation a matter of hands cupped round ears. But Donovan noticed an odd thing. The most noise came from the young dogs. The scarred old pros eyed each other in speculative silence, saving their energy for when it would do them most good.

Mick reappeared. 'Bring the dog, I've got him a match.'

Somehow, Donovan hadn't expected to have to go through with this. He'd thought he could use the dog as a passport but avoid fighting him. He'd expected to have a little time to see how things worked, maybe spot a few faces in the crowd, before having to commit himself. Being taken in hand like this was a stroke of luck for a genuine novice but the last thing that Donovan needed. 'Er . . .'

Mick gave his amiable grin again. 'Don't panic, I told you, he won't get hurt. Just a taste for both of you, see if you like it. Same for the other dog – it's his first night too. I've got a fiver on you for luck.'

If there'd been a way out he'd have taken it. But he couldn't leave for the chaos of vehicles in the yard, and a choice between fighting Brian on equal terms and having the crap kicked out of him by angry men faced with the loss of their money, their dogs and their freedom was no choice at all. 'What do we do?'

There was nothing squeamish about Cal Donovan. A childhood on a smallholding in a gritty little mid-Ulster town – it would have been called a village anywhere else in the British Isles – left him with few expectations and finding himself alone at the age of nineteen killed those too. He'd come to England with his brother in the early eighties after losing their parents and sister to a bomb in a chipshop. Within two years Padraig too was dead, taking second prize in a drag-race between a Metropolitan police car and a stolen Porsche. Padraig always wanted to be a policeman while Caolan seemed destined for other things. The Donovans were never mentioned in Glencurran now without someone observing that it's funny how things turn out and someone else muttering about dead men's shoes.

So Donovan had seen things most people hadn't and been involved in things most people only read about, and if they hadn't made him callous he had at least learned pragmatism. Fresh teeth-marks in Brian Boru's bull neck seemed a small enough price for safeguarding his own.

But he wasn't prepared for the undiluted savagery of the next several minutes.

The average dog-fight in the park over who found a bone first is high on sound, fury and flying fur and low on actual damage. By the time the terrified and embarrassed owners have prised the protagonists apart it can be quite hard to find who bit who where.

This was different. For one thing the handlers – not the owners but two men experienced in the job – far from breaking up the fight were encouraging it. Before they released them the animals were foaming with rage, their eyes bulging redly, their muscles knotted. When they were slipped, to a rumble of almost sexual excitement from the men gathered round, they met like clashing armies and the flash of their scimitar teeth through the flying spit, and a little later the flying blood, was like a battle with fixed bayonets.

For a short time neither contender had a clear advantage. They came together like Sumo wrestlers, their combined weight enough to snap a plank when they hit one of the hurdles. The vast jaws snapped and locked and disengaged and snapped again, and but for the fact that the other dog was fawn Donovan would have lost track of which head belonged to which.

After a few minutes' frenzied sparring the contest began to favour Brian Boru. He was no heavier than the other dog, might have been rather taller; mostly what he had was the desire to win. Match fighting, as distinct from the bare-knuckle stuff any dog high on testosterone can try his paw at in any back-alley, was a new experience. But he learned quickly and within minutes had the fawn dog on the defensive, an hysterical note creeping into its barking as it gave ground.

A minute after that a streak of blood appeared on its neck. 'That it then?' said Donovan tersely, readying the lead he could have moored his boat with.

'Not yet,' said Mick, amused. 'Got to give the other chap a chance to get his own back. He might just be a slow learner.'

In fact the fawn dog was a fast learner, had soon realized that being a hard man in the ginnels of The Jubilee didn't qualify him to go head to head with a genuine if untutored talent. He backed round the makeshift pit as quick as he could. Only the fear of exposing his flank stopped him turning tail.

'Ah, jeez,' said Donovan disgustedly, 'what more do you want? He's beat, take him home.'

Mick raised an eyebrow at the other owner. 'Is that what you want – to chuck in the towel? He might still come good.'

He was an older man than Donovan, shorter but powerfully built, a man who worked with his muscles and liked his dog to do the same. But he was as new to this as his animal. He eyed Mick uncertainly. 'You reckon?'

'Sure. He's not getting hurt – I'd give him a bit longer.'

'All right then,' said the man doubtfully.

It may have been the sound of his owner's voice that distracted the fawn dog. He turned aside, looking for a way out. Instead he gave Brian a way in. In an instant the black dog hurled him down, great jaws closing vice-like on flesh and bone, worrying it like worrying a shoe. The fawn dog screamed.

Donovan had Mick by the shirt-front. 'Stop it. Now.'

Mick's eyes flared. 'I'm not going in there!'

Donovan grabbed one of the handlers. The man was leaning on the hurdle, watching the mayhem with every sign of enjoyment. Blood sprayed in a fine arc, spattering his face. It also spattered Donovan's but there was no time to wipe it off. He dug his fingers hard into the man's arm and shouted over the baying of beasts and men. 'Break it up! Before he kills him!'

The man shook him off, unconcerned. He explained like explaining to a child: 'This is what it's about.'

Donovan had a great strength and a great weakness. His strength was that if something needed doing enough he would do it without thought for the possible consequences to himself. His weakness was the same. Almost before he'd decided to, certainly before he knew how or why, he had his leather jacket wrapped around his left arm. The thick lead doubled in his right hand like a truncheon, he vaulted the side of the pit. 'Brian, you bastard, that's enough!'

He expected the dog to round on him, hoped a mouthful of leather would hold him long enough to grab his collar. He hoped its owner would then have the guts to rescue the injured dog. He hoped he'd do it quickly because he didn't know how long he'd be able to hold the blood-crazed Brian Boru.

But Brian didn't go for him, was satisfied with the quarry he had. When Donovan tried to drag him off he found himself hauling at two dogs, the second gripped in the teeth of the first. The fawn dog was on his back now, wailing as Brian chewed on his throat.

In the end Donovan wrapped the short lead round Brian's neck and twisted, tightening it until Brian ran out of air and his eyes glazed. Even then it looked like he'd die with his teeth in his opponent's throat rather than let go. But the mist got into his eyes and his brain, and finally he gave a little choking grunt and shook his head, the fawn dog falling from his loosening jaws. Donovan wasted no time fussing over either of them. He had the muzzle on Brian's bloody face before the dog had a chance to recover his wits.

There was blood everywhere: on the fawn dog's throat and belly, on Brian's face and chest, on Donovan's hands and on his clothes. Deep scratches laced his wrists – not from Brian's teeth, but from the other dog's claws as it fought for its life. Its owner was in the pit now, trying to get his dog up. 'I think his leg's broke.'

'Then bloody well carry him,' Donovan panted savagely. 'And bloody well look after him, or I'll be round your place some night when you're not expecting it and I won't be alone.' He jerked the thick lead mean-ingfully.

It was an empty threat but the man didn't know that. He couldn't carry the dog alone. He organized some help to take it out to his car.

Donovan was still panting – with reaction, fury and deep humiliation at what he found himself party to – trying not to hate the strutting dog beside him who'd done no more than he'd been asked to, when a light tenor voice at his elbow said, 'I like that. I like a man who cares about the dogs. They're not machines, they deserve to be looked after, even in defeat. Did they hurt you?'

'I'm all right,' Donovan said wearily, turning to see who he was talking to. The man's face meant nothing to him, he didn't think they'd ever met. He was a slightly built individual with a pointed face and curly brown hair, probably rather older than he first appeared – mid forties maybe. A pleasant manner for such an unpleasant gathering. An owner? Or maybe a punter; he had a dog with him but it wasn't a fighting dog, not on that lead. Donovan's eyes followed the pale blue shoe-string down from the man's wrist to his pet.

And the little dog, naked except for an effusive topknot and a tassel at the end of its tail, gave Donovan a disdainful yawn, revealing toothless gums.

At seven on Friday morning Liz walked down to the stable, kissed Polly on the nose, then went into the adjoining storeroom to prepare the three buckets and two haynets that would fend off starvation for another day.

Fifteen minutes later she let herself quietly into the kitchen. Brian was still asleep upstairs and she trod softly to avoid disturbing him. She went to the phone and called Shapiro at home.

She must have woken him because he sounded woolly and disorganized for a moment. 'Liz? What time is it?'

'Seven-fifteen,' she said carefully. 'Frank, will you come over? Now?'

That got his brain moving. His voice over the phone was both sharp and concerned. 'What's the matter, Liz? What's happened?'

She didn't answer directly. 'And will you organize a team? SOCO, Dr Greaves – anyone you can think of. Oh,' she added as a fresh thought struck her, 'and did we ever get round to doing what the Son of God said and designating a rape victim support officer?' She began to laugh. At least, it was mostly laughter, though Shapiro could hear something like despair sobbing in the depths of it. 'Oh, Jesus, Frank – it wasn't me, was it?'

Part Two

Chapter Ten

It was four in the morning before the dog-match broke up. Donovan got Brian Boru back to the garage by half-past-five, swabbed both of them with disinfectant, then removed the muzzle and fed the dog. He tucked in like a new Lonsdale Belt taking breakfast for the cameras.

'Make the most of it, champ,' muttered Donovan, 'your fifteen minutes of fame have been and gone.' He intended Brian Boru would never set foot in a fighting pit again. He didn't have to: he'd already achieved all that was required of him. He left the dog to enjoy his victory meal, cutting through the entry that took him home.

At six o'clock it was too late to go to bed and still get to work at a decent hour; instead he made a hot drink and took it into *Tara*'s saloon. He kicked his shoes off and dropped on to one of the long couches to review the night's events. The next thing he knew it was ten o'clock and he had congealed cocoa among the bloodstains on his shirt.

Late or not, he was looking forward to seeing Shapiro. He parked his bike in the back yard and took the steps two at a time, so intent on his mission that he hardly noticed who was on duty downstairs. 'Chief in his office?'

The title was an anachronism now but everyone knew who he meant. 'No.'

Then the atmosphere hit Donovan like a forearm in the kidneys, making him break his step. His eyes filled with alarm. 'What's happened?'

Sergeant Tulliver was on the desk, a solidly constructed man on the run-in to retirement, a safe pair of hands and an unflappable manner expressed in the peaty old Fenland accent. 'Don't know, lad, we haven't been told. Not officially. Unofficially, I think your governor's been in a scrap.'

'DI Graham?' Before the words were out he knew what had happened. She'd gone ahead regardless. Without Scobie and Morgan, because the Son of God had pulled them, and without him because he'd gone dogfighting, she'd pressed on alone with a plan designed to draw out a rapist. It sounded as if she'd succeeded. But if she'd made an arrest the mood should be a lot lighter even if she got thumped in the process. 'Is she all right?'

Tulliver lifted mountainous shoulders. 'I don't know – honest. Dr Greaves has been to see her and Mr Shapiro's there now. But she's at home, not at the hospital. That must mean something.'

Marginally reassured, Donovan hesitated on the second step. Then he swung round and headed back the way he'd come. 'I'm going out there.'

But as he reached the back door Shapiro came in, and for a second as their eyes met Donovan was shocked to see a tired old man wearing his superintendent's overcoat and broad creased face.

Shapiro saw Donovan at the same moment, the dark eyes hollow with dread, the long sinews of his narrow body bow-string taut, the quick staccato movements. The hand which took Donovan's arm above the elbow felt a tremor of apprehension; he walked on without a word, taking the younger man with him. On the stairs, once they were alone, he said quietly, 'She's all right. Dr Greaves has looked her over and there's nothing to worry about. Come upstairs and I'll fill you in.'

Shapiro's office was at the top of the building, looking down on the Northampton canal. There were no boats moored here, the waterway was wide enough to keep traffic moving but not for it to stop. On summer weekends all this stretch was a two-way procession of cabin cruisers and narrowboats chugging along at a steady three miles an hour. But in the week, except at the height of the holiday season, there were only dourly determined anglers and small boys with dogs to disturb the stillness of the towpath.

Today Donovan wasn't interested in the view. 'What happened?'

There was no point talking round it. Shapiro parked his ample seat on the edge of his desk and gazed at his sergeant over folded arms. 'She was raped, lad. This morning, while she was feeding her horse. She's all right – I mean, she's not injured; a mild concussion, that's all. She sent you a message. This didn't happen because of anything you did or didn't do.'

It was the last thing she said before he left her alone with her husband. It made no sense and he put it down to the hysteria she'd held at bay so long, but when she explained he understood.

Donovan's Luck. Before she came to Castlemere it was a standing joke at Queen's Street; or not so much a joke as something they laughed at because it made them uncomfortable. Donovan was lucky in the sense that his share of bad luck fell on others. They used to say that if a maniac sprayed the canteen with a Sten gun, Donovan would catch the one dud round. Donovan's lucky, they used to say, but not for the people round him. He had no family left, and even the people he worked with got hurt. His last DI died of Donovan's Luck.

For two years Liz Graham had seemed immune; for most of that time Shapiro hadn't even heard the words. He expected to hear them again now. That was why she'd wanted the word put about. She'd been the victim of a vicious criminal, not Donovan's Luck. Yes, they'd had an arrangement; and yes, he'd cancelled it. But the attack on her wasn't a consequence of that. It would have happened whether they'd walked the dogs or not. Donovan hadn't let her down; in no sense was he responsible for what followed.

For the briefest of moments, gone so quickly that if he'd blinked Shapiro would have missed it, Donovan seemed to shrink. The blood drained from his face, his eyes glazed and he swayed; just once. A wordless moan slipped between his teeth. Then he sucked in a lungful of air so hard Shapiro heard the unsteady whistle in his throat, and blinked his eyes back into focus. '*Is* she all right?'

Shapiro pushed a chair towards him. 'Bit of a stunner, isn't it? Well, I've talked to her and I've talked to Greaves, and both of them say she wasn't hurt. A bit of a knock on the head, and then . . . But physically, nothing to worry about. Emotionally? – I imagine all right is a bit ambitious in the circumstances. But she's a survivor, she won't be beaten by this. For one thing she's got Brian; for another she's got us. Leave it today, but I think by tomorrow she'll be glad to see you.'

Incredulity drove from Donovan a snort half of laughter and half despair. 'Me? Christ Almighty, she won't want me within half a mile of her!'

Shapiro eyed him with compassion. 'This was nothing to do with you. She was in her own back yard.'

Donovan was shaking his head in a fractional, repetitive gesture of disbelief. 'How did it happen?'

When she'd fed Polly and made up the day's feeds she walked round to the lean-to where the hay was kept. She was reaching for a bale when movement flickered in the tail of her eye and, before she had time to react, a blow to the side of her head sent her sprawling in the litter.

Stars exploded between her and the faceless shape that bent over her. Her first vague notion, that she'd fallen and Brian had come to pick her up, foundered on two rocks: he slapped away the hands she raised to him, and he dropped heavily on top of her, hauling at her clothes and his own, in silence but for the fast rough breathing behind the white scarf tied over his face.

Too stunned for fear or horror, too stunned to resist, she felt his body against hers, his hand pinning her wrists, his swift penetration and mechanical rhythm as if she weren't there at all, as if he were doing this by himself. Before she had taken in the fact that she was being raped it was over: he was off her and gone.

For minutes longer she lay in the straw, separated from her emotions by an impervious transparency like plate glass. She could see through it but it cut her off from everything she knew. Beyond lay the common world of home and work, of people she loved and others she respected and who respected her; but the screen, for all that light went in and out, was solid and she could not do the same.

Then, as the mists began to clear, she worked out what she had to do and began doing it, mechanically, performing the actions though a sheet of glass separated her from the consequences. From habit she checked that the horse was all right. Then she went inside and called Frank Shapiro.

Donovan had some deep scratches on his left wrist. Unconsciously he traced them with the fingers of his other hand. As Shapiro talked, without knowing it he dug deeper with his nails, raking the long weals savagely until the blood started and Shapiro leaned forward and physically pulled his hands apart.

He looked up at the superintendent with his face flayed, the emotions pooling on the surface. 'It *was* my fault. If we'd been out till one o'clock she'd still have been in bed at seven!'

'Then he'd have waited,' Shapiro said patiently. 'There was nothing random about this: he knew who she was and where to find her, if he hadn't got her this morning he'd have got her another time. None of us could have anticipated or prevented this.'

On the face of it they had very little in common: men of different generations, races, perspectives and priorities. But they cared about the same things. It took something like this, and seeing the impotent fury in his own breast reflected in the turmoil in Donovan's eyes, to bring that home. 'But it still hurts, doesn't it?'

Shakily, Donovan nodded. His voice was low. 'I feel

like I want to break something.' Repressed violence surrounded him like an aura.

'Keep it together, lad,' growled Shapiro, 'for her sake. She needs to be able to rely on us. She does not need us under sedation in a back ward at Castle General.' After a moment Donovan nodded again.

'All right.' He gestured at Donovan's bloody wrists. 'Er – how did that happen?'

Donovan stared at him blankly. For a second he couldn't remember. Even when he did it seemed too trivial to dwell on. The morning's events had diluted his triumph to nothing and he threw away his hard-earned information in a couple of sentences. 'I was at a dog-fight last night. I've been offered a job driving for the ram-raiders.'

When everyone else had gone they sat side by side on the sofa, holding hands. Brian wanted to put his arm round her but instinct warned him now wasn't the time. The last man who held her gave her no choice. However kindly he meant it, however much they both needed it, he risked raising echoes of that trespass. He had to make himself wait until she was ready, until she came to him. He didn't know about the plate glass in her head but he knew there was something, some door that only had a handle on the inside.

He phoned to say he wouldn't be at school, didn't say why. He made coffee. He ran her another bath. She'd had one as soon as the doctor finished but she wanted another when they had the house to themselves. He hoped she'd ask him to stay, to help her, to wash her down like a weary horse as he had so often when she'd come home tired, sore and dispirited. But she said nothing. Neither did he; he left her to the steam and the smell of soap, and knew that in the privacy of the locked cell she would scrub the memory of her assailant off her skin but only deeper into her mind. He didn't know what to say or do to comfort her. He made more coffee.

They drank it side by side on the sofa. Her skin was pink and new, as if energetic use of the loofah could erase what had happened. She wasn't crying, hadn't cried from the start. First she was stunned, then shocked, then she was busy dealing with it; now what she felt was a hollow unreality. After a while she ventured, 'You know, this wasn't the worst that could have happened.'

'I know,' Brian said thickly, his hand gripping hers. 'I could have lost you.'

Liz smiled at him. Almost, she seemed the same as always. Almost, that was more shocking than anything else. 'Oh, no. Not for some little shit who can't keep his fly done up: it'll take more than that before you're rid of me.' She leaned against his long side, fitting into the curve of his body. He held his breath and let her settle there, let her drape his arm around her. 'No, I mean—' She struggled to express what she was feeling. 'It's supposed to be. It's supposed to be the most devastating thing that can happen to you – short of massive physical injury, or losing your wits, or losing your husband or child. Well, none of those things has happened to me so this should be the worst. But I don't feel devastated.

'I'm angry, oh yes, I'd like to smash his face in. I feel – soiled. And frustrated, because I had my hands on the bastard and I was too groggy to do anything about it. But I don't feel – diminished. I don't feel he's taken anything away, or even left anything behind that alters who I am. It's like the time I had my nose broken. Of course I resented it. It hurt, and the guy who did it had no right, and for a time it shook my confidence – it was visible proof that I'd failed to control the situation. I felt I'd failed professionally because I let his fist too near my nose.

'But nobody else thought that. There was some sympathy, a few jokes, and three months later my nose was fine and his was up against the bars for eighteen months. Well, this is the same. It's not my fault. I haven't done anything wrong. I was unlucky, but it doesn't say anything about *me*. It doesn't leave me with any fences to mend.

'I *won't* feel humiliated. What was taken from me has no value unless it's given freely. He's none the better for having it, I'm none the worse for losing it. The bruises will fade and I'll still be who I always was. I've coped with worse than this.' She sighed, a little shakily, sought out his eyes. 'Am I shocking you? I think a lot of people *would* be shocked. In a crazy way I almost feel relieved. Because it's over and I'm all right. Because this should be the worst and I know I can handle it.'

He didn't know how to respond. He didn't know if it was normal, even if the word 'normal' had any meaning in this context. Anyway, it wasn't how it seemed to him that mattered. If she'd found a way of dealing with it that didn't put her on the rack, that didn't reduce her to ashes from which she'd have to rebuild herself flake by flake, he wasn't going to argue. He wasn't going to complain because it should have torn her apart and hadn't. He held her against him. '*We* can deal with it. Together.'

She patted his hand where it lay across her belly. 'Mm.'

Brian tried to believe, almost convinced himself, that the tremor that ran through him then was a hybrid of love for her, terror at how near disaster had shaved them and an upsurge of the desire to protect her, though Liz was stronger and infinitely tougher than he. But that friendly pat, like patting her horse, far from bringing them together had driven the tip of a wedge between them. She hadn't rebuffed his support, she'd just put no value on it. She wanted to deal with what had happened alone, declined his involvement as kindly as if he were a child. He could feel her warm fresh skin, smell the soap mingled with the scent of her, but in every way that mattered they were on opposite sides of that handleless door. The shudder that ran through him was presentiment.

Chapter Eleven

Shapiro pursed his lips. 'What do you mean, you've been offered a job driving for the ram-raiders?'

Half an hour before, Donovan's head had been full of it. Between that and the dog-fight he'd had a good night – good enough to make up for some of the times he'd pushed his luck and his authority further than they were designed to stretch.

It was a gamble. The harder he pushed, the more chances he created. He staked his time, his reputation, often enough his neck and occasionally his job, and hoped for enough success to disarm his critics. As long as he came out ahead most of the time, blind eyes would be turned to his precise methods. He didn't compromise the integrity of investigations. He didn't trample suspects' rights and get cases thrown out of court. When a gamble failed he paid the price himself.

But he walked a perpetual tightrope between risks and results. He thought he hadn't enough liquidity to see him through a lean time, was only as good as his record. So two successes for the risk of one was a bonus. It meant he wouldn't face awkward questions about Brian Boru and why he didn't get prior approval for his actions. He'd looked forward to giving Shapiro his report. Now it hardly seemed worth the trouble of telling.

'Er – yeah. At the dog-fight. The guy with the skinned rabbit came over for a chat. Seems that's not his only dog – he's got a couple of bruisers he travels round the fights with. Seems there's a whole network of pits scattered across the country. Ours is new – that's why they came here instead of keep moving south, he wanted to try it out. I'm not sure where it was but given a bit of time to root around I'll find it.'

'And the job?'

'OK. So this guy's making small-talk, about the dogs mostly, but he keeps not going away. And I know who he is, of course, so I don't hurry him. He wants to know what I do for a living, and I tell him anything you don't have to pay tax on. He likes that, and soon afterwards we're talking about what he does for a living. Not in so many words, but he's happy enough for me to know it's not altogether legal. Well, everybody in that barn's into stuff that's not altogether legal.'

'You too,' murmured Shapiro, and Donovan eyed him warily and couldn't be sure if it was a joke.

'Right,' he agreed cautiously. 'Only he's down a driver. Don't know how – lost, stolen or strayed, walked out, got sacked or what. I know he didn't get arrested but I can hardly tell him that. Gates. That's what he calls himself – Tudor Gates.' That note of derision would have been more seemly, Shapiro thought, in someone who wasn't named Caolan. 'So he's looking for a driver and he wonders if I might be interested.'

'What did you say?'

A slow smile slid across Donovan's saturnine features. 'Ah, come on now, chief, what do you think? I told him I'd very likely be available.'

'Why you? For all he knows you can't drive to save your life, you stall at junctions and cry if somebody takes your parking place.' Shapiro's eyes narrowed. 'Or has he some reason to think differently?'

Donovan shrugged uncomfortably. 'I told him I'd done driving work before. As for bursting into tears . . .'

'Ye-es?'

Donovan sighed. 'He saw me stop the fight.' He explained what had happened.

'You got into a pit and separated two fighting dogs with your bare hands,' mused Shapiro. He paused for confirmation, one eyebrow raised, and Donovan gave a rueful nod. 'Now I understand. He's looking for madmen and he found one. What else?'

'The last driver must have split soon after the job at Rubens 'cos they've been sitting on their hands ever since and that's not how he works it. Mostly he hits a town two or three times in quick succession then gets the hell out. Losing his driver spiked that so he's still here. I think he wants to do another couple of raids, quick as you like, and then skip town.' He frowned. 'What?'

Shapiro was smiling; but it didn't last long. It wasn't Donovan he'd had this argument with, it was Liz, so there was scant satisfaction in being proved right. Just for the record though . . . 'Where's he from, your Mr Gates?'

Donovan shrugged. 'North, north-east? English accents all sound the same to me. Even without the green fedora and the curly wig he's as queer as a nine pound note, but he talks like a ship-builder.'

'The Tynesiders. They came here so Gates could fight his dogs, but after one raid they lost their driver. If they hadn't they'd have shown up Monday night or Tuesday morning and my name wouldn't be mud with the Son of God. Is Gates going to call you or what?'

'He wants to see me drive. I'm meeting him at the wood at midday.'

Shapiro looked at his watch. 'You haven't left us much time. Still, it won't take SO19 to arrest a ram-raider in a green felt hat. All right—'

'Er,' mumbled Donovan. 'Do you want to arrest them? Now, I mean.'

The superintendent dropped his nose to look at Donovan over glasses he didn't wear. 'Don't I?'

'If I'm on the inside we can get them in the act. The full crew, not just Gates, and no chance of them persuading a jury they were only recruiting stock-car drivers and I got it wrong.'

Shapiro was tempted. It had seemed a good idea when Liz suggested it but then there was no way in. Now the opportunity had presented itself almost like a gift. A man on the inside could learn more in a few hours than a skilled interrogator in days or weeks. Things dropped in casual conversation – earlier jobs, jobs being planned, contacts, fences. And a water-tight case. And really, not much risk, particularly with out-of-towners. People who knew him found it hard to believe Donovan was a policeman; someone who'd met him at a dog-fight wouldn't even wonder.

'If I said yes, how would you do it?'

Donovan grinned wolfishly. 'Go to the meet, scare them shitless with some handbrake turns, wait to hear

116

from them and call you. Then drive them into an ambush.'

'You may not get the chance to call me. They won't be too trusting for your first outing.'

'I'll find some way to attract attention. Lights. I'll use the wrong lights – headlights if it's daytime, side-lights if it's dark. Chances are no one in the car'll notice. Put out the word that something big and fast and carrying the wrong lights is me – don't stop me, tail me and get on the radio.'

'You won't get carried away and ram somebody's shop-front? In the interests of authenticity, as it were.'

'Try not to,' Donovan promised solemnly.

'All right,' decided Shapiro, 'we'll do it. But look after yourself – these chaps are pros, put a foot wrong and they'll have you.'

'Yeah,' agreed Donovan, unconvinced. 'Funnily enough, he's not a bad sort. Weird, yes, but not – nasty. You know? It's almost as if he's in it more for the fun than the money. I think he gets a kick out of planning it, leaving us with egg on our faces.'

'Check the national computer, see if there's any-thing on him.'

'I will; but I don't think there will be. He told me with great pride the only time he was ever questioned by the police was when he witnessed a mugging. He was quite indignant – said he gave the best description he could, that lager-louts grabbing old ladies' pensions were the lowest of the low.'

'Honour among thieves,' Shapiro ruminated. 'There *is* such a thing, only don't count on it. Just because he has a soft spot for little old ladies doesn't mean he'll feel the same way about you if you blow your cover.'

'About the dogs—'

Shapiro had reached the same conclusion. 'We'll hold off till we have Gates under lock and key. I don't want to make him nervous: a man who enjoys intellectual challenges might put two and two together.'

'And Brian?'

Shapiro's mind went first to Brian Graham, the colour washed from his cheek, holding his wife's hand as a child holds the string of a balloon, for fear it will float away if he relaxes his grip. 'Oh – your dog.'

'I'll need to keep him for a bit. If they come to the garage and the dog's gone they'll wonder why.'

'All right. Try to keep him from killing anything.'

Awkwardly, Donovan said, 'And the boss?'

Shapiro vented a sigh. 'I don't think there's much we can do for her just now. But if we get this business wrapped up we can concentrate on finding her attacker.'

'Do you think she'll come back to work?'

'I don't know, lad. It's a hell of a thing to come to terms with, she may not want to work with people who know. Or maybe by the time she's got over the shock and the anger she'll be wanting her friends. The one thing I'm sure of is she'll have to set the pace herself. We mustn't impose on her our expectations of how she should feel.'

Donovan shook his head in a kind of brooding wonder. 'I can't begin to imagine how she feels. I don't know—' He stopped.

'What?'

Embarrassment made it hard to express himself. A sort of flagellatory urge drove him on. 'Maybe she shouldn't come back. I mean, how are any of us going to deal with that? How do we talk to her – what do we say? Do we act as if it never happened? Do we ask how she's feeling, as if she'd had flu? I don't know how to deal with it.'

'Exactly,' said Shapiro sharply. '*You* don't. This is your problem, Sergeant, you work out a solution. But I'm telling you now, let it become a problem to Inspector Graham and you'll have my reactions to worry about as well. Now.' He checked his watch again. 'Time you were off. And listen: be careful. However much of a card your Mr Gates is, these are not nice people and you're going to be out of touch for a lot of the time. Your first priority is to not get hurt. Don't play the hero. I don't want to find you dead in a ditch.'

Still stinging from the rebuke, Donovan said woodenly, 'Caution is my middle name' – a lie so outrageous that it left Shapiro temporarily speechless.

He went again to the little car-park above the watermeadows. As soon as he turned in among the trees he recognized the high-stepping 4×4 with its bull-bars and its black paint retouched at the front end. They'd been scrupulous about making repairs. Bull-bars or no, it was hard to believe those four headlamps had survived repeated encounters with security grilles; but anything broken had been replaced, anything dented had been knocked out and anything scratched had been repainted at the first opportunity. They weren't going to be stopped for a cracked headlight or because their vehicle appeared to have been in an unreported accident.

Donovan got out of his van, waited for Gates to do

the same. He didn't mind being thought a suspicious sod – in this line it was a good reputation to have.

The little dog got out first. Gates plainly took it everywhere. It reminded Donovan of one of those deeply sinister ventriloquist's dummies that seem smarter and more animated than the man operating them, leaving you to wonder who's pulling whose strings. Maybe the dog had Gates on the end of the pale blue lead.

Gates gave Donovan a smile of recognition that was probably no more than that. But Donovan was naive in many ways and uncomfortable around homosexuals. He relaxed only when the driver got out on the other side of the 4×4. He was about twenty-two, slim and fair, and the look Gates gave him was frankly proprietorial. Donovan mocked himself inwardly. If that was what Gates liked, Hugh Duggan's virtue should be as safe as houses.

Gates introduced them. 'Hugh, this is Andy.' The V-shaped smile on his pointed face broadened satirically. 'Hands off, he's mine. Andy'll be a good driver before long, but he still has some things to learn. Maybe you can teach him. I, on the other hand, drive like an old lady – but I know how I like to be driven.' A tilt of one eyebrow, so perfectly shaped it could have been plucked, invested the comment with sexual overtones. Donovan's expression made him chuckle.

Though they'd spent time together at the dog-fight this was Donovan's first chance to weigh up his prospective employer. For obvious reasons, the lighting in the barn was to show up the fighters, not the punters. Now the policeman made a conscious assessment of the man before him in terms that would mean some-thing to other policemen.

Height, about five-eight; weight, somewhere under ten stone; age – probably mid forties though in the right light he could have passed for thirty. Light brown hair, cut just long enough to curl; high forehead but no sign of balding. Eyes, an odd pale hazel that at times looked almost amber. Face, a narrow heart-shape defined at the jaw by the V-shaped mouth and at the widest point by sculpted eyebrows. Voice – Shapiro was right, it was a well-modulated version of a Geordie patois, all the vowels sounded, many of the consonents slurred. Dress – depended how much he wanted to be noticed: green fedora and burgundy coat if he did, jacket and designer jeans if, like now, he didn't. Con-stant companion, a dog like a skinned rabbit. If he took it to a dog-fight and he brought it to test-drive a wheelman who might be all mouth, Donovan assumed it went everywhere.

With a patient air that reminded Donovan of Shapi-ro's, Gates said a second time, 'Hugh? You want to show us what you can do with this?'

Sulkily, the boy climbed into the back as Donovan took the wheel.

He'd done the Defensive Driving course. It hadn't taught him as much as a Lammas market in Glencur-ran, when herds of steers and tinker-boys on trotting horses could erupt from any side-street at any moment. But he had no great interest in cars – for pleasure he chose bikes every time – so in fact he wasn't well qualified for the job Gates wanted him for. All that got him through the audition was his ability to suspend his sense of self-preservation.

By taking corners at seventy that better drivers would have taken at sixty, and doing it with no sign of fear only a cold wolfish grin, he was able to fool Gates that he had control of the situation when in fact he was barely on nodding terms with it. The great old trees along the woodland rides came hurtling at him from unexpected directions and veered off just in time, mud and leaf-mould spraying from under the big tyres. High and heavy, the vehicle bucketed along the rough tracks leaping from rut to rut like a novice 'chaser. In the back the boy clung to whatever he could get his arms round, sucking his breath through his front teeth like draining a milk-shake.

In the front Gates hung on to his seat-belt with one hand and his dog with the other, his amber eyes flicking between Donovan's face and the track in mounting wonder. Momentarily he expected the car to lose its grip on the amorphous surface and roll, or side-swipe a tree, or hurtle over a thirty-foot cliff into one of the half-hidden sinkholes. But it kept not doing, and the more he studied the driver's face the more confident he grew that it would not. He knew more about men than cars, and a man who could enjoy himself in these circumstances, whose dark face betrayed only grim humour and determination, was a man you'd allow to drive you into hell because he'd probably manage to drive you out again. Had he but known it, Donovan had the job before he threw his first handbrake turn.

Had Gates but known it, Donovan had no idea what the car could and couldn't do. He'd read somewhere that 4×4s performed differently to road cars; in his ignorance he thought they were probably more stable. He knew what he could have done on two wheels, worked on the assumption that he should be able to do twice as much on four. If one of these trees didn't get out of his way in time he'd know better. The icy enjoyment that impressed Gates so much was a hybrid of detachment, because he needed to do this and couldn't have done it if he'd been thinking about the consequences, and real if faintly hysterical amusement because he did occasionally enjoy being frightened half to death.

At length, surprisingly calmly, Gates tapped him on the arm. 'You've made your point.'

As soon as the car stopped the back door opened and the boy swung out, his delicate face flushed with anger. 'You're not going to let him drive? He'll kill us all!'

Gates clucked gently. 'He knows what he's doing, Andy. There isn't a scratch on this car. Tell him, Hugh – you know what you're doing.'

'I know what I'm doing,' Donovan echoed obediently. His eyes swivelled back to Gates and sharpened. 'At least, I'm going to. I want to know exactly what I'm getting into. I've earned that.'

Gates considered for a moment, then nodded. 'All right. Let's go back to our place, I'll tell you what we do and how we do it. Only one thing, Hugh. If you come back with us now, you're in. Too many people have too much to lose for you to start getting cold feet.'

Donovan looked at Gates, at Andy, at the tops of the trees emerging from a nearby sinkhole. Then he nodded. 'I'm in.'

Chapter Twelve

Gates travelled in Donovan's van, the dog on his knee. Donovan didn't wish to seem inquisitive but even if he weren't a police spy there'd be things he'd want to know. 'How many are involved?'

'Six is the optimum figure,' Gates said willingly enough. 'We can do it with less but it takes too long. Any more and you start tripping over one another.'

'Six in the 4×4?' Donovan couldn't see it. It would take them but there'd be no room left for swag.

'Oh, no. We use two cars: the second to get me away – I'm the look-out – and for back-up if things go wrong. It hasn't happened yet, but I'm a Scout at heart, I like to be prepared. For the record, a breakdown would be considered your cock-up. I take it you're familiar with engines? Check that one over, make sure it's reliable.'

Donovan was better with engines than behind the wheel. He gave a brief affirmative nod. 'That what became of your last driver? He wasn't much of a mechanic?'

'He was an excellent mechanic,' Gates said sadly. 'What he wasn't so good at was taking orders. Above all I need to know that if I tell someone to do something, or to do nothing, that's what he'll do. Can I count on you that way, Hugh?'

Donovan met his sidelong gaze, saw the leprechaun twinkle, recognized that beneath it the man was in deadly earnest. 'I'll do what I'm paid for.'

Gates was satisfied with that. 'Fine.' He pointed a manicured forefinger. 'Turn right here, we're home.'

Lost at the end of a lane bounded by high banks was a cottage. A sign offering it for rent was propped against the side wall. When they left it would go up again.

'Cosy,' sniffed Donovan.

Gates smiled. 'We have to stay somewhere and we'd attract more notice in an hotel. As far as the estate agents know I'm alone here.' He gave the dog on his arm a quick hug, added coyly, 'Apart from Chang.'

'Where do you keep the big ones?' asked Donovan. 'I don't want to open the bog door and find myself eyeballing two pit-bulls.'

'There's a piggery at the back, I've got them in there.' An enthusiast, his pixie face brightened. 'Do you want to see them?'

'I already did.' The younger of Gates's dogs competed in a graduate match that left its opponent in much the same state as Brian Boru left his. The older dog made a kill.

Gates chuckled at the look on Donovan's face. 'I'm not sure you're cut out for the fighting game, Hugh.'

'Convince me,' grunted Donovan. 'I was only there because I met this guy in the wood and he took a shine to Brian. Which reminds me: I'll have to be back in town by six to feed him.'

'Move him down here with us. Andy'll come with

you, give you a hand, make sure you find your way back. You can collect your gear at the same time.' He climbed down from the van, headed for the back door of the cottage.

Donovan followed slowly. 'I wasn't thinking of moving in. I have somewhere to live.'

'Then think again,' Gates said pleasantly over his shoulder. 'I thought I made it clear: we're a team. We live together, work together, and when we're finished we move on together. What's the problem? You said you live alone, you've no commitments, there's only the dog to consider and he can come with us.'

Donovan had to remind himself that he was playing a part, he wouldn't have to do anything he agreed to. 'I'm used to being on my own, is all.'

The warmth in Gates's smile appeared to be genuine. 'So now you can get used to being part of a family.' He led the way inside.

If anything, the cottage was more run-down inside than out. Mostly the furniture was old and worn; where things had worn out entirely they'd been replaced with new cheap ones that were even nastier. The place smelled of neglect. Somebody's old mum had lived here, Donovan surmised, with a cat for company and somebody fetching her shopping once a week; enough to keep the old soul alive, not enough to keep the lane from getting overgrown. When she died, or went into a home, the cottage was rented while the family decided what to do with it.

'Go on through,' Gates said, 'say hello to Charlie while I give Chang his lunch.'

Charlie was a heavily-built man in his thirties shoe-horned into a little-old-lady-sized chair, chewing on a pen and studying the back page of a newspaper. Dono-van supposed he was picking racehorses, but what he was doing was the crossword.

'I'm the new driver,' Donovan offered, along with his assumed name. He looked round critically. 'There doesn't look to be room for six.'

'There isn't,' Charlie agreed in another of those impenetrable northern accents. 'There isn't room for six legless dwarves suffering from insomnia, let alone six working men who like to get some sleep from time to time. Don't go looking for a room, the best you'll do is a chair and a blanket. If there really were six of us you'd have to take turns at the chair.'

Donovan frowned. 'How many are we then?'

Charlie shrugged. 'You've met them. The coach, the boy and me. And you. And maybe Patsy, when the dust settles. For the moment Patsy's too scared to put in an appearance.'

Donovan tried to milk the information he needed without seeming nosy; it wasn't an easy task and he may not have wholly succeeded.

'The others left with your last driver, did they?'

Charlie gave a snort of grim humour. 'In a manner of speaking. He's dead, two of the lads are behind bars and Patsy's on the run.'

A terrible weight of foreboding settled on Dono-van's head. He didn't want to ask; he didn't want to know. But he needed to, and besides too little curiosity would be as suspicious as too much. He said carefully, 'Last job go a bit wrong, did it?'

Charlie shook his head. 'Not the last one we did for the coach: don't worry on that score. Trouble was, he was away for the day – a dog-fight in East Anglia. All we had to do was stay out of trouble, and they couldn't even do that, the silly sods. Wanted a day in London, didn't they? You'll never guess what they did on the way back.'

Wanna bet? thought Donovan bleakly.

'A train robbery!' exclaimed Charlie, still unable to credit the absurdity of it. 'A goddamned frigging train robbery.'

Liz got as far as the bottom of the front steps and stopped, exactly where Mrs Andrews had and for much the same reason. She didn't want to do this. She didn't have to do it. All that had got her this far was the abstract notion that she ought to.

It would have been easier coming in the back way. If she headed straight for the stairs, with luck she would see no one who'd expect more than a polite nod until she was safe in CID at the top of the building. On the other hand, those she avoided meeting now she'd have to meet later. It would be nice to think that she'd taken all the hurdles she could at one outing, that after this she could come and go without either feeling or causing embarrassment. She had nothing to be ashamed of, was damned if she was going to tip-toe round the place as if she had.

So when she was ready she took a deep breath and marched up the steps into the front office like an Assistant Chief Constable paying a surprise visit in the hope of finding the Duty Sergeant asleep with his feet on the desk.

They'd have been less startled if she *had* been an Assistant Chief Constable – if she'd been an Assistant

Chief Constable in full ceremonial regalia complete with sword. There were three of them: Sergeant Tulliver, WPC Wilson and PC Stark who was bringing the Incident Book up to date. They did a matched set of double-takes, looking up as they heard the door, down again as they recognized her, then up once more in surprise at seeing her here and now.

Refusing to run, making herself face them, Liz sketched a smile. 'Bet the Incident Book makes good reading this week.'

For a moment none of them knew what to say. But she felt a wave, not of embarrassment nor even sympathy so much as respect, that gave her hope. The ice was cracked; soon it would break.

PC Stark said quietly, 'About the same as usual, ma'am. Some pain, some grief, and a lot of police officers doing work nobody could pay them enough for.'

Liz felt her heart swell. This wasn't going to be the torture she'd feared. She'd been right not to put it off. The support she needed, from people who knew about being hurt and humiliated and having to carry on regardless, was right here. She nodded. 'So what's new?' She headed for the stairs.

WPC Wilson came quickly round the counter, her face pink. 'Er—'

'Mm?'

But whatever the younger woman had wanted to say stuck in her throat. She coughed but couldn't clear it.

'The chief's upstairs,' said Tulliver, covering her confusion with his own. No one could get used to Shapiro's promotion. 'Shall I call him?'

'No, I'll stick my head in when I get up there.'

Wilson swallowed. 'Ma'am – what happened. If there's anything any of us can do, please say.'

Liz's smile broadened. 'I will. Thanks.' There was almost a spring in her step as she climbed. She was conscious of having emerged from an encounter she'd been dreading not merely unscathed but strengthened. More than just relief, she felt the stirrings of confidence.

Shapiro was in mortal combat with his paperwork. His expression was belligerent, his eyes slashing and stabbing like lethal weapons, his pen flashing spiky comments in margins and ending his signature with a vicious full stop. He flung the vanquished in a tray for a clerk to mail or file as appropriate. But still the foe waited in serried masses, an endless army of paper that grew even as he despatched it.

In fact this was nothing new. Shapiro's paperwork always mounted until either those waiting for it made a fuss or he couldn't find room on his desk for his elbows. What was different was the savagery with which he was attacking it, and that had less to do with the task than what he was using it as a diversion from.

Before she decided that twenty years as a policeman's wife was enough, Angela used to discourage him from working on Saturdays. She liked to have the family together for Shabbos, and though she appreciated that crime didn't keep kosher she would have raised a disapproving eyebrow at the triviality of his present occupation. Except that she'd have understood why he couldn't sit at home and think when anger was threatening to blow the top off his head. Paperwork wasn't an antidote, but the mindless tedium at least blunted the pain.

The step in the corridor outside his office was so familiar that for a moment he gave it no thought. A moment later his head jerked up and his eyes widened. 'Liz?' His voice rose as if he'd been cornered in his office on a Saturday morning by an axe-murderer.

From habit she tapped as she opened his door. 'On your own, Frank?'

Shapiro stumbled to his feet, ushered her in. She looked drawn, her skin pale and touched with grey. Even her bright hair had lost its glow. But in her eyes she was herself. A little bruised, a shade jet-lagged, but the authentic Liz Graham with her sharp mind and her cool head and her strong sense of purpose.

He spread a blunt hand at the littered desk. 'Paperwork,' he explained unnecessarily.

Liz nodded. 'The secret is to keep on top of it. As the bishop said—' She stopped. The unspoken punchline hung in the air between them, grey as ashes, heavy as lead.

'Oh, Liz.' Sorrow thickened Shapiro's throat.

She lifted her head abruptly and her eyes slapped him. Her tone was impatient; only someone who knew her as well as he did would have detected the tremor. 'For pity's sake, Frank, don't let's start analysing every word we say! I'm *not* going to have an attack of the vapours at every veiled reference to sex. I'm all right. Lots of unpleasant things happen in this world, and most of them happen to police officers. Pilots say it's not a bad landing if you walk away. Well, I'm walking, Frank. Tap-dancing may take a bit longer.'

Her courage struck him to the heart. Feeling his

eyes fill he blew his nose vigorously. In the course of a long and eventful career he'd met a wide variety of professional tragedies. He'd seen colleagues injured, maimed and killed; he'd seen them succumb to the stresses of the job and lose their nerve, their wits, their wives and everything they'd worked for. He'd known officers who had killed themselves and a few who'd killed other people.

But to the best of his knowledge he'd never known one who'd been raped. He tried to think of it as just another in the long list of injuries which criminals inflict on defenders of the law, but failed. It wasn't. You could laugh, ruefully, about the odd broken bone sustained in the course of duty; but the assault on Detective Inspector Graham couldn't be defused by a bit of healthy badinage.

The enormity of it left him rudderless. He'd known this woman for twelve years. They worked closely together, shared a deep respect as well as a genuine friendship that had survived various disagreements, conflicts of priority, even of principle. Now, because of a lightning attack behind her house, he'd no more idea what to say to her than Donovan had. Resentment at that seethed in his breast, only contained by the knowledge that he mustn't – absolutely must *not* – let her see that it made a difference. She'd never let him down, never once; he wasn't going to have her think that anything a barbarian could do to her could affect her relationships with friends and colleagues.

'Right,' he said briskly, stuffing his handkerchief in a trouser pocket. 'Now, what are you doing here?'

'Two things. Informing you that I'll be available for duty on Monday.' She gave a little self-deprecating

132

smile. 'And making sure that when I arrive on Monday morning I won't get as far as the back door and bottle out.'

'Monday?' Shapiro was dismayed. 'Liz, that's too soon. Did Dr Greaves agree to that?'

'Dr Greaves gave me a thorough physical and the only damage he could find was a slight concussion. I've an appointment at the hospital later today, to make sure there aren't any souvenirs, and after that my diary's free. Now, I could sit at home feeling sorry for myself; I could go buy a wig and a long black coat like your granny wore so I could venture out in daylight without being recognized; I could spend the day with a counsellor and be reassured that it's perfectly normal to feel a whole lot of things I don't feel at all; or I could get on with my job. Which of these do *you* think'll make me feel most like a human being again?'

She wasn't as calm about this as she wanted him to think but perhaps that didn't matter. Perhaps pretending to be in control led to regaining control in fact. He had two concerns: whether she was competent to work, and whether the stress of trying would be harmful. On the first he had no doubts. She wouldn't be at her best and brightest, but Liz Graham in third gear still outperformed most people in top.

The second criterion was harder to judge. All his instincts told him she needed cosseting, needed time and space to rebuild in. He thought getting out in the sun with her horse, or on to a Greek beach with her husband, would speed the healing. But he couldn't trust her instincts on every issue but this one. He scrutinized his hands folded on the desk, gave a protracted sniff. 'My grandmother was a woman of impeccable fashion sense who owned a hat shop.'

Liz had known Shapiro as long as Shapiro had known Liz. She knew when she'd won an argument without him handing her a coconut. She vented an unsteady sigh. Girding herself for battle with him had stiffened sinews which softened with the victory. 'Monday then.'

'If you're sure it's what you want.' His gaze was compassionate but still troubled. 'Before you decide, think how you're going to deal with it when this becomes public knowledge. Because it will. You know this town: gossip'd get about somehow even if all the people moved out. I can tell you, the way I tell all rape victims, that every effort will be made to protect your identity, and I don't believe anyone at Queen's Street would betray that, but we have to be realistic. Because of who you are this isn't a normal rape case and you shouldn't count on anonymity. Sooner or later some sick sod you're in the process of arresting will throw it in your face. You need to know how you're going to react.'

She hadn't considered it. The rules to protect the privacy of rape victims worked so well she hadn't wondered if they'd work for her. But he was right: rumour was no respecter of law and the piquancy of a sex attack on the town's senior policewoman would lend it wings. By Monday all Castlemere's criminal fraternity would know what had happened. Most of them would have too much class to refer to it. But not all. It would happen; if not Monday, then soon.

She forced her voice on to a level. 'Professionally, I hope. You're right, sooner or later someone will. I'll try and think up a good put-down first. But how I deal with it is less important than the fact that I *will* deal with it. I have to, if I want to go on doing this job in this town. Whether it's Monday, a week on Monday or six months from now: it's not going to be any easier whenever it comes. That's why I'm here today. Some things get harder to do the longer you put them off. That's why I'd like to get back to work at once, even if it does give me some rough moments. I'll cope. You know that.'

He did; but it would still be like a knife turning in the wound. He wanted to protect her but he couldn't protect her forever. She wouldn't let him; apart from that it would be a bad idea. The rest of her career hung on what the next several days would bring.

But the next several days would be easier if the inquiry seemed to be making some progress. That meant discussing it. By her presence here Shapiro assumed she was ready to do that. 'You told me yesterday morning pretty much what happened. But you were still in shock. Has any more detail come back to you since?'

The thing was in her mind constantly, running and re-running before her eyes like a jerky, meaningless snatch of film. Yet focusing on it, thinking about it in a deliberate and coherent way, was unexpectedly hard. Liz made the effort, creases netting her eyes. But nothing new emerged. 'I really don't think so.'

Shapiro's face screwed up like an old apple. 'I need to get some sense of why *you*? Because you're another good-looking forty-year-old blonde professional woman? We know that's what he likes – is it just co-incidence that he picked you? Has he seen you in your garden and thought "That'll do nicely"? Or was it more

135

calculated than that? Did he know about the operation at the Basin – is that where he saw you, only he realized you had company then so he found out where and when he could get you alone?

'You see what I'm getting at? In the first case he's just a bastard, in the second he's a clever bastard. He knows who you are – precisely who, he knows you're involved in this investigation. He knows you tried to trap him, this was his reply. That makes the attack on you personal.

'Either he followed you home or found out where you live so he could ambush you when you least expected it. That's not just nasty, it's arrogant; and that means he's not doing this because of some primordial urge he can't resist, he's doing it for kicks. He's not at the mercy of his hormones, he won't be pushed into taking risks and making mistakes: he can wait until he can have what he wants at little or no danger to himself. He's going to be a sod to catch.'

'Well, Frank,' Liz exclaimed impatiently, 'I had actually worked that out. Something to do with the fact that he's already raped three women and we still don't know anything about him! I *know* it's going to be hard. It's always bloody hard. We've still got to bloody do it.'

'Of course we have,' he agreed mollifyingly, wanting to pat her shoulder and knowing she'd probably slap his hand away. 'And of course we will. I'm just looking for anything you can tell me that'll help. Every prison library is run by some clever bastard who thought he'd outwitted us. That's where this man's going to end up – stamping "Property of HM Prison Service" on cheap editions of Charles Dickens.'

Dropping her eyes Liz sketched an apologetic

shrug. 'I'm sorry, Frank, I don't mean to jump down your throat. I know it'll take time – God knows it always has when it's been me doing it! Don't feel you have to humour me: if I'm behaving like a silly mare you'd better tell me. By Monday I have to be back in full working order.'

'No,' he said gently, 'you don't.'

'Yes,' she said firmly, 'I do. And for what it's worth, I think he knew exactly who I was. To come to my house, to my own back yard – that's not like waylaying someone on the public street or in an office-block. That's as personal as it gets.'

'That's what I thought,' Shapiro admitted. 'Makes it worse, somehow, doesn't it?'

'Not for me it doesn't,' she gritted. 'So he knows where I live – I already knew that. Now let's track the bastard back to where *he* lives.'

Chapter Thirteen

All the time he was getting enough gear from his boat to look he was moving out, Donovan was waiting his chance to get word to Shapiro. But the boy shadowed him too closely. There was no time to use the phone, to pass a message to a neighbour or even drop a hint that might be acted on. Finally, in desperation, he wrote a note that he put in an envelope with the keys and dropped through the hatch of the *James Brindley* on the next mooring. What he wrote – 'Got a job offer, have to split, love to Liz' – would make no sense to Martin and Lucy Cole. But they knew where he worked, would have the wit to forward it to Queen's Street where Shapiro would understand what it meant.

Andy took a covetous look round *Tara* as they left. 'I can see why you don't want to muck in with us.'

Donovan shrugged. 'It's not mine, I've just been looking after it. Keeping the squatters out. Everything of mine's in the bags in the van.'

Brian Boru thought he was going fighting again: his eyes glowed with anticipation. Donovan didn't have to force him into the van, the dog dragged him out by the chain and clawed at the tailgate. He thought his life had improved immeasurably in the last few days.

Gates met them outside the cottage, greeted Donovan politely and Brian effusively – Brian's answer was to lift his lip just enough to show the tip of a fang – and had a quiet word with Andy while Donovan was unloading the van. He couldn't hear what they were saying but he could guess. 'Did he try to contact anyone?' 'He left a note when he dropped his key off. But I saw it, there was nothing in it.'

They settled Brian in the piggery – he couldn't see the other dogs, the exchange of threats and menaces as they heard one another didn't last – then went inside.

'There isn't much room,' Gates said wryly. 'If it's any comfort, we don't live like this all the time. It was the best I could do that was both handy and private.'

Coffee was simmering on the stove. Gates poured four cups and they joined Charlie in the little sitting-room. There were four chairs, which would have been enough if Chang hadn't claimed one of them. The nude dog and Donovan regarded each other with mutual dislike.

'Chang, Chang,' admonished Gates, patting his knee, 'come over here and let the nice gentleman sit down.' It was the first time in his life Donovan had been described as a nice gentleman. Either, in fact, let alone both.

'In the circumstances,' Gates went on, sipping his coffee, 'you'll forgive a certain reticence about who we are and where we're from. If this works out and you stay with us, I'll fill you in on all the details. For now, I expect what you really want to hear about is the next job.'

Donovan had to decide how much he knew about the last one. It was in the papers, of course, both the nationals and the *Castlemere Courier*, and as someone with a professional interest he would naturally have taken notice. On the other hand, he'd better not refer to facts which had come from SOCO or the national computer. He said, 'I take it that was you last Sunday?'

Gates nodded. 'Went like a charm. And next day everything fell apart because my driver fancied a trip to London and ripped off the other passengers on the way back.'

'Charlie said. Jeez,' whistled Donovan, 'I didn't think anybody robbed trains any more.'

'They don't,' Gates said succinctly. 'At least, not very successfully. I hope Charlie also said it was done without my knowledge and approval?'

'I did, coach,' said the big man obediently.

'So you understand the importance I place on rules,' said Gates. 'Because of what happens when people don't keep them. One man died and two are behind bars because they did their own thing. Well, I can do nothing about that except make sure it doesn't happen again. There are four of us now: it's enough if we pare the safety margin. I'll drive the second car, you three load the goods. But three isn't very many, and Andy's a bit new to it, and Hugh – have you done this before?'

'Driving. Not thieving.'

'You wouldn't have to do it this time if I had my way, I'd sooner keep you behind the wheel. But loading up would take forever with just two.'

'That's OK,' said Donovan, 'I'll leave the engine running, I can be back behind the wheel in a couple of seconds. What are we after – what do I concentrate on and what do I leave behind?'

'Electricals. Concentrate on the stuff in boxes at the back of the shop rather than the window display.' He flicked a little elfin grin. 'Ignore boxes printed with the word "toaster" and go for videos, TVs, stereos, electronic games. One advantage in going short-handed: we'll put you all on the front seat and drop the back one to make more room.'

'How do you work the look-out thing?'

Gates nodded his approval: the new driver was asking all the right questions. 'Me and Chang check out the area ten minutes before you arrive. If there's a clear run I'll get out of sight, back to my car. If there's a problem – a police patrol, too many people about, the council's ripped up our escape route to look for a gas leak – I'll take up a position where you can't miss seeing me and wait till you've passed.

'When you come in, Hugh, look for me. I'm obvious enough, if I'm there you'll see me, and if you do keep driving. Do nothing to attract attention, just carry on through town and make your way back here. If it was only a glitch we can try again later – later in the day, next morning, whenever. But I like everything in our favour before I commit us. I'd rather cancel a dozen times than have to shake off a police escort once.'

'I'll vote for that,' Donovan said with appropriate fervour. 'So where are we going, and when?'

'How long have you lived round here, Hugh?'

Donovan saw no point in lying. 'About eight years.'

'Then you know the town – where the various

shops are, the emergency exits and so on. What do you reckon to Stevens Electrical as a target?'

As the biggest electrical retailer in town, Stevens was the obvious choice. They would have state-of-the-art goods worth many thousands of pounds in stock every day of the year. Their shop window was wide and low enough for the 4x4, and there was room in the street to swing and hit it square on. However . . .

Donovan tried to explain his reservations tactfully to a man who took pride in his planning. 'Jagger Street's in the old part of town: turn off and you're into narrow streets as crooked as a dog's hind leg. There are only two exits on to decent roads – Castle Street, that comes back to the square, and Bedford Road. As soon as the alarm goes the cops'll block 'em both; and if we turn up a side street they'll have all bloody day to catch us.'

Gates watched him enigmatically. 'You mean I've got it wrong?'

Donovan shrugged. 'I'll do what you want. But you asked my opinion and that's it. Stevens is a good target in a bad place. If you don't like taking risks you'd best go somewhere else.'

'Such as?'

'Hell.' Donovan wondered if a police officer had ever before been asked to nominate a local business for a ram-raid. But there was no way out. 'What about Owens?'

'Owens in Bridgewater Street? That backs on to the by-pass?' He chuckled at Donovan's expression. 'Sorry, Hugh, I'm teasing. I came to the same conclusion. That's what we're doing. Owens.'

'When?'

'When we're ready.'

In the event it didn't take till Monday for the unpleasantness to start, and in the first instance it wasn't directed at Liz.

On Saturday afternoon Castlemere United were entertaining Norwich City in a match whose outcome was never in serious doubt. The three-one scoreline may have been ungenerous to United's share of play, but only those members of the sub-capacity crowd who were related to the home goalie felt they wuz robbed.

Football duty was popular with the policemen of Queen's Street, so it wasn't often that WPC Mary Wilson found herself directing fans in and out of the Rosedale ground. But an epidemic of spring flu threw the carefully worked out rosters back into the melting pot, and WPC Wilson accepted the task philosophically.

Right up to the moment when, separating two groups of opposing fans before their exchanges degenerated from friendly insults into something heavier, she found a pair of thick hands gripping her waist and a pair of thick lips pressed against her ear whispering, 'Was it you, darling? Good, was it? Want some more?'

She was so startled that she let her chance to identify the speaker escape. By the time she spun he'd already disappeared into a crowd of Castlemere supporters wearing United scarves and adolescent grins that, as men in their twenties and thirties, they should have outgrown by now.

'Who said that?' Her eyes flayed them. Most of

them had no idea what she was talking about; others chuckled knowingly and backed away, hands up, before her furious gaze. It could have been any of them. If no one owned up and no one pointed the finger she was helpless to proceed. Even if she'd identified the culprit she wasn't sure he'd committed an offence.

Except that he'd offended her. Anger spurred her on. The sensible thing would have been to let them away with no more than a withering stare. But the impertinence outraged her sense of decency and she was not prepared to let it pass. 'Go on, go home,' she sneered at them. 'Go home and tell your wives and your mums what a good afternoon you had. Be sure and tell them the best part, too. Only don't be surprised if they don't bray just as loud as you, you damned donkeys!'

By the time the ground was cleared, the away fans homeward bound and the police detail back at Queen's Street, Wilson had cooled down enough to regret her outburst. If Superintendent Giles had been in the station she'd have confessed to him. He wasn't, but Detective Superintendent Shapiro was.

He heard her out in silence, showing less emotion than he felt. When she was finished he said, 'Why are you telling me?'

She shrugged awkwardly. 'In case there's a complaint, so someone'll know what it was about.' She gave a wry smile. 'And because confession is good for the soul, sir.'

'Avoiding actions that need confessing is even better,' Shapiro said pontifically. Then the austerity melted. 'Don't worry about it, Constable, you sound as though you did all right. If they'd said it in front of Donovan he'd have decked them. Besides, who's going to come in here to complain? They must know we're itching to arrest someone.'

Happier, she started to leave; but then she turned in his doorway, her young face creased in bewilderment. 'Why would they do that, sir? Why would they make a joke of it? Whether or not they thought it was me.'

Shapiro sighed. 'Because they're young men, Constable Wilson, and young men have almost nothing in common with the rest of the human race. They'd been to a football match, yes? They'd spent all afternoon merrily bawling insults in one of the few situations where that's acceptable behaviour. They'd probably been drinking, and anyway they were high enough on wit and the sound of their own voices.

'So they came out of the ground looking for something else to shout about. One of them saw you and told his mates this rumour he heard about a policewoman getting raped. After that it was only a matter of time.

'It doesn't make them evil. It makes them stupid. It makes them childish. When they're together they lose about ten years apiece and revel in the kind of behaviour that any one of them, alone, would recognize as crass and be thoroughly ashamed of. They're probably ashamed of themselves now but it'll be another two or three years before they're mature enough to admit it. In the meantime it's easier to giggle than own up to being wrong.'

She nodded, and twitched a little grin, and left; but Shapiro felt like a man with a river lapping at his doorstep who thinks he hears the rumble of distant thunder.

It was WPC Flynn next, and she was altogether less resilient than Mary Wilson.

There'd been a Sunday morning market on Castle Mount since time immemorial. It enjoyed a reputation for roguery and shy dealing but it was hardly deserved. You were less likely to find stolen antiques than cheap clothes, mass produced ornaments, gaudy toys and cracked eggs.

It was a pleasant enough duty on a fine Sunday and WPC Flynn was wandering among the stalls looking for ideas for her mother's birthday present. A couple of regulars nodded a greeting and there was no indication of anything amiss until someone touched her elbow and said quietly, 'Check out the Undercover Agent.'

There is a glamorous side to underwear retailing, but it isn't the one seen on market stalls where string vests, combinations and really serviceable knickers may be found. The sight of winceyette nighties fluttering in the breeze reminded her passingly of her mother's birthday.

But what she saw as she pushed her way through an unexpected mass of winking, chuckling men made her forget again. Hoisted on a pole like a royal standard were a pair of voluminous navy-blue bloomers. A sign tacked to the pole announced: AS SUPPLIED TO CASTLEMERE POLICEWOMEN. SPECIAL OFFER: ONE PAIR ONLY.

With or without the law on her side WPC Wilson would have shut the stall down there and then. She'd have demanded receipts for every item displayed, queried the invoices, insisted on cross-checking with the supplier, and generally engaged in the sort of police harassment that lets everyone know just where the lines are drawn.

But WPC Flynn was a less robust sort of person and instead of wading in with righteous indignation she froze, staring at the placard in horror, and then blushed crimson. The chuckling turned to hoots of unrestrained hilarity. By the time PC Stark, who was checking out the motor supplies stall on the far side of the Mount, tracked down the rumpus she was fighting back tears.

'So what did you do, Constable?' Superintendent Giles asked him later.

'I confiscated them, sir,' Stark replied, staring stonily over his superior's head. 'To prevent a breach of the peace, and in case they were evidence. In order to do so without straining my back I considered it necessary to stand on the trestle holding the rest of his stock. Unfortunately' – the merest flicker of an expression – 'it broke, sir.'

Giles nodded slowly. 'That *was* unfortunate, Constable. I trust you didn't hurt your back after all?'

Beginning to suspect that the new superintendent might have hidden depths, Stark allowed himself the ghost of a smile. 'No, sir. Quite a soft landing, sir. Got a bit of mud on my uniform, but as luck would have it there was a lot of cloth lying around so I cleaned myself up with that.'

'Well done, Constable,' said Superintendent Giles.

Chapter Fourteen

Even if she refused to change her plans, which is what he expected, Shapiro thought Liz should know about the weekend's events before she turned up for work on Monday morning. On Sunday evening he called at her house.

She was ironing. Irrationally, he was surprised. He'd rather imagined that her clothes leapt out of the washing machine as well-ordered as the ideas springing from her head. Of course it was nonsense. Everyone's laundry, and everyone's thoughts, need knocking into shape before they're fit to be seen. The secret of good dressing, both sartorial and mental, is to do it in private.

But if there was nothing unusual about a woman ironing there was something distinctly odd about *what* she was ironing. She was ironing everything. Almost everything she owned was draped around the living-room, on the backs of chairs, on hangers hooked over doors. A couple of the shirts were Brian's, and there was a table-cloth and a dozen handkerchiefs, but otherwise the clothes were hers. She must have emptied every wardrobe and every drawer. She must have been stood here half the day to fill so many hangers.

Brian had showed him in. Now he retreated to the

kitchen with a helpless little shrug and no attempt to explain.

Shapiro realized, of course, that what Liz was doing had nothing to do with ensuring she had a tidy outfit for tomorrow. It was obsessive, ritualized cleaning. She could have chosen to clean the house from top to bottom, to paint the woodwork or to prune the roses within an inch of their lives: essentially it would have been the same. What she was doing was making a fresh start. The recent past was polluted by the actions of a stranger, and she with it; she was trying to draw a line under that by making the things with which she most nearly surrounded herself fresh and new. She couldn't sear the past out of her skin but she could sear it out of her clothes.

He said quietly, 'You want to tell me again how you're perfectly all right?'

The hand she waved at the room was not quite steady, nor was her laugh, but the effect was not of a psyche slipping out of control. She said, 'Don't misunderstand, Frank. This isn't madness, this is therapy.'

'I know.'

Her eyes were tired. 'You do? You want to try explaining it to Brian?'

'How is Brian?'

She put down the iron. After a moment she pulled the plug out, signalling the ritual complete. 'Hurt. Worse than me, I think. He wants things he can't have. He wants me to break down so he can gather me in his arms and console me. He wants me to behave like a woman wronged in a Victorian novel. But I'm not like that, Frank. I never was, he's no right to expect it. Brian's my husband, my lover and my best friend. But

149

this is my problem. I have to tackle it the way that feels right to me; and it'll be done with when I feel it is. I'm not only not going to let it beat me, I'm not going to let it affect me any more than I can help.' She gave him a wan smile. 'I can't guarantee I won't succumb to occasional fits of strangeness – like this one – in the process; but hell, Frank, I could sing hymns on the interview tapes and still be less strange than some of the people we work with.'

'There are,' he agreed darkly, 'some very strange people about. Some of them aren't even policemen.' He told her about Wilson and Flynn.

She took it better than he'd expected, even managed a grim little chuckle at the placard pinned beneath the waving bloomers. 'Come on, Frank, you're not expecting me to be upset about that?'

'Cathy Flynn was.'

'Cathy Flynn's about as much use as a chocolate teapot. She ought never to be allowed out of the office.'

'She was upset on your behalf. They both were.'

'Well, they needn't be,' Liz said firmly. 'A week from now it'll be old news. Unless we make an arrest, in which case the joke's on him.'

Shapiro sighed. 'Liz, I have nothing but respect for the way you're coping with this. There's something very special about someone who can come through this kind of personal and professional trauma with their sense of proportion intact. So this is an observation, not a criticism. The effect this is going to have on policing this town is not exclusively in your hands.

'It's a matter of public knowledge now – God knows how it got out, we knew it would but I never guessed it'd be so soon – and as we might also have guessed there's a section of our citizenry that thinks it's funny. This may be only the start. If Superintendent Giles finds he can't deploy any of his women officers without starting a riot he may feel he has no choice but send you on leave till the dust settles.'

The way her hands fisted and her eyes sparked, he thought that if Liz had still been holding the iron she'd have thrown it at him. 'No, damn it!' she cried. 'If I can cope with the situation, so can Cathy Flynn and so can the Son of God. I will *not* be swept under the carpet to avoid embarrassing other people! I've done nothing wrong, Frank. I don't intend to be penalized for this.'

He had every sympathy; but he also recognized the realities of the situation. 'There's no question of that, Liz. But the bottom line is keeping the peace, and if that means sending you on leave you may have to go. We're not talking of retirement, we're talking of a week or two away while things settle down. Apart from anything else, it's tough for the Whoopsies to do their job while a bunch of little kids in men's clothing are ogling them and wondering if it was them.'

'Well, let's consider the Whoopsies by all means,' Liz said nastily. 'It's going to be pretty tough on me too – I just consider that it's part of my job. And part of theirs.' She frowned. 'Anyway, how does it help if I go to Bognor for a week? Or will you make a public announcement so nobody'll leer at the Whoopsies any more?'

'I know you're upset,' he chided her gently, 'but do try not to be crass. No, I'm not going on *Police Six* with it. What I might do is give Gail Fisher an interview confirming the basic facts and asking that anyone else who's been attacked and hasn't reported should come forward now. I could add that our officer who was attacked has taken some leave and gone away for a week. That should take the pressure off.'

Liz shook her head in bitter disbelief. 'Frank, I don't know why we're even discussing this. I'm fit to work, I want to work, I'm being paid to work – and you want to send me to the seaside because Cathy Flynn was upset by a pair of bloomers? Send *her* to Bognor, she needs it more than I do.'

Shapiro was inclined to agree. He felt himself starting to grin. 'Oh, Liz, why can't you be a lazy time-serving git like other coppers and take a free holiday when it's offered?'

But she wasn't smiling. 'You know why, Frank. Because after a week on the beach I'd need another. And after two I'd never get back.'

'So I should tell the Son of God you wouldn't welcome any such suggestion?'

She nodded incisively. 'Tell him I'd fight it tooth and nail.'

When Shapiro had gone she looked round the room, hung with clothes like ungainly Christmas decorations, in a kind of wonder and with the fragile beginnings of amusement. Whatever had she been thinking of? She put them away, keeping out only what she'd need for the morning.

Brian said, 'You're still going in, then?'

Again she nodded. 'I have to.'

'No,' he said carefully, 'you *want* to.'

She turned to him, held his gaze. His kind eyes were the best feature of an otherwise unremarkable face. She looked there for some understanding of how

152

these events were affecting her, their implications for the medium and long-term future. Shapiro understood. He might not like how she wanted to handle it but he understood that her needs took priority over her inclinations. That she had to work backwards from where she wanted to be and make choices that would help her get there. She looked for some appreciation of that in Brian's eyes, and could not find it.

'I want,' she said fiercely, 'the same as you do – that this never happened. But that's not an option. As second choice, I want to have the damage repaired so that things are as good as they were before – between you and me, between me and my colleagues, between Queen's Street and the town. That *is* possible but it'll take hard work and it has to start with me. And I have to start tomorrow, before the cracks widen too far.'

The pain in his eyes was like another assault on her. 'Oh, Liz,' he said softly. 'I wish you'd tell me how you really feel.'

Despair flared in her like temper. 'I *have* told you!' she cried. 'You just don't listen.'

His sensitive hands reached for her shoulders but she shook him off impatiently. 'You see?' he murmured. His misery was like his soul, gentler than hers, not less passionate but less demonstrative. His heart would break with barely a crack. 'You're pushing me away. It's not *him* doing that, it's you. You seem to think I'm a detail you can sketch in when you've sorted out the important things with Frank Shapiro. But *I'm* important, Liz. I'm half of our marriage, you can't push me aside while you decide what to do. You owe me better than that. You owe us better.'

153

'And don't you owe me something?' she snapped back faster than thought. 'Support, maybe? Time and space? You must know how difficult this is for me. Why are we talking about *your* feelings when it's me that's been raped?'

She should have slapped his face: it would have been less hurtful. He recoiled, in fact, as if she had. He backed away. He knew he couldn't win a head-to-head with her when her hackles were up. He thought if he let it drop now, came back when she was calmer and they talked about it rationally, they might make some progress.

He was turning to leave the room when he suddenly saw himself through her eyes. That wasn't discretion, it was cowardice. If he let that be her last word it would never be erased; Damoclean, it would hang over them forever. He wheeled back, surprising her.

'How dare you accuse me of not supporting you?' he demanded in quiet fury. 'I have always backed you to the hilt. I've watched you do things, take risks, that knotted me up inside – things no man should have to watch his wife doing – rather than be accused of standing in your way. My career has always played second fiddle to yours. And you have the nerve to ask for my support!

'Can't you see I'm not a by-stander in this? I'm a victim too. Our marriage is the most important thing in my life, and what that animal did struck at its very heart. Of course I have feelings about it, and they matter, and if you're as blasé about all this as you pretend why can't you spare just a little interest and concern for them?'

'Blasé?' she shouted in outraged astonishment.

'Because I won't dissolve in tears on your manly bosom and let you decide what's best for me? Get a life, Brian! I'm running up a down escalator here, I don't know that I can reach the top, but I'm damn sure that if I don't give it all I've got I'll get dumped on the floor.

'I'm sorry if I haven't treated your feelings with due deference. I thought that since mine were having to get by on a lick and a promise yours could, too. But then I only had some man I don't know from Adam humping me. You had an animal strike at the very heart of the most important thing in your life. Hell, Brian, I'm really sorry I wasted all this time wondering what was right for me!'

They didn't go in for slanging matches. Disagreements between them were usually settled amicably. They had exchanged the odd cross word over the breakfast table, but nothing that needed forgiveness later. They had never had a real stand-up, drag-out fight before; perhaps, without something of this magnitude to prompt them, they never would have. They were two reasonable people, they didn't fight about things that could be settled sensibly.

But there were no reasonable answers this time, and neither was entirely rational. Nerves strung to top C, they hadn't enough composure for one, let alone to share.

'How can you even think you're fit to work?' Brian snorted derisively. 'If you can't exercise self-control in your own living-room, how the hell are you going to cope with a bunch of people who're full of their own woes and don't give a damn about yours?'

'With the support of my colleagues,' Liz shot back. 'Them I can count on.'

He sucked in a sharp breath at that, as if the barb were a physical one she'd struck into his flesh. 'I can't cope with this,' he admitted then, his voice trembling. 'I can't cope with you like this.'

'Then perhaps *you'd* better have a week at Bognor,' snarled Liz. 'Send me a postcard, let me know how your feelings are getting on.'

He had nothing more to say, nothing left to fight her with. He did what, in retrospect, he might have been wiser to do before – left the room, went upstairs.

Liz watched him go with a maelstrom of emotions in her breast. She felt anger, bitterness and a horrid kind of triumph because she'd stood her ground and he hadn't. But she also felt let down. She felt she'd let *him* down. She thought he'd said stupid, insensitive things; she thought *she'd* said some pretty unforgivable things too. She thought she should probably go after him. But she didn't.

Chapter Fifteen

There was nothing wrong with the 4x4. Donovan tinkered anyway, mainly for the pleasure of feeling oiled components slide under his fingers. He was a sensual man.

It was the oil that saved him.

When Donovan painted his boat he got so much paint on him that days later people would say, 'Green again this year? And yellow window frames?' When he changed a type-writer ribbon he looked like an extra on the *Black and White Minstrel Show*. And when he danced cheek-to-cheek with an engine he got oil all over his face.

Behind the cottage there was just room between the rusted outbuildings for the 4x4, Donovan's van and Gates's run-about. Washing against the back fence like a dark tide was a belt of woodland. There was no telling from here how deep it was or how far it went; it had a neglected look, surplus to requirements and forgotten. It was like a piece of primeval forest that had somehow escaped axe and plough, and would probably continue to do so having neither practical nor aesthetic value.

Donovan heard movement in the undergrowth and momentarily his heart quickened; but nothing in there was likely to give him a problem. The others might feel threatened by sounds of surreptitious movement in the bushes, but Donovan was fairly sure it wasn't a police dragnet closing in. Perhaps it was badgers – the woods round here were full of them.

It was neither policemen nor badgers. The green hem of the wood twitched as something pushed through and Donovan found a girl watching him over the remains of the fence. 'Who're you?' she demanded warily.

She'd stood close to him for long enough that she should have known. He recognized her, though the woolly jacket was torn and dirty now and the frizzy hair was tied back with a bandana. She looked older, not so squeaky-clean, not so likely to scream and shed terrified tears at the sight of a knife, but she was unmistakably the girl from the train.

But remembering faces is something policemen are trained for. Thieves tend not to look that closely at the people they're robbing. Also, Donovan had been clean then and wearing a collar and tie while Hugh Duggan's jeans, sweatshirt and person were all liberally anointed with oil.

The voice would be the hurdle. Donovan's accent, unremarkable in itself, was rare around Castlemere. Was it too late, he wondered, to assume a speech impediment? Probably, he'd talked to Gates for too long without. Maybe the best he could do was say as little as possible in front of the girl. 'Duggan,' he grunted. 'You?'

'Patsy,' she said. She waited for a reaction; when he didn't oblige she lost interest in him, her eyes sliding away across the yard. 'Tudor around?'

Donovan indicated the cottage.

The girl skipped over the fence, agile as a forest animal, passed him without a look. Preoccupied, she'd filed him in her mind as someone tall, taciturn and oily and left it at that. With luck, next time they met she'd remember him as the man from the yard, and after that as Hugh Duggan and nothing else. Donovan breathed a little easier.

He leaned on the bull-bars and eyed the wood. If this started getting nasty, that was the way he'd go. Five metres beyond the fence he'd be in deep gloom. In two minutes he could lose himself so completely it would take an army to find him.

But he didn't want to quit this close to success. The worst was over: she'd have remembered him by now if she was going to. Later she might get the nagging feeling of having seen him somewhere, not know where and decide he reminded her of someone on TV. Even if she did place him, all was not lost. So far as Patsy ever knew he was a railway engineer who knew about the air-shaft.

And in consequence led her companions into a police ambush, following which he swapped his job for one of the vacancies thus created. These people didn't stay free by believing in coincidence. They were cautious, suspicious. If the girl remembered him she'd tell Gates, and Gates would—

What? Beat the truth out of him? Not Gates; even if he'd been big enough it wasn't his style. Charlie was big enough but didn't seem the violent type either. No, if Patsy chanced to remember, and as a cautious man he felt the risk was too great, Gates would quit Castle-mere as soon as he could pack. Donovan had the registration numbers of his cars but they were certainly false and would be changed at the first opportunity. To ensure a head start he'd probably shut Donovan in one of the outbuildings. It could take him hours to free himself, but he didn't think he risked anything worse.

So after a little while he stopped looking at the wood and went back to his engine. A while after that he went inside and cleaned up. But he didn't clean up too thoroughly.

Charlie was still puzzling over his crossword and didn't look up. 'Patsy's back.'

'I saw her outside.'

'Coach is pointing out the error of her ways. Best not to say anything.'

Donovan shrugged. 'None of my business.'

When he saw her next her face was rebellious, streaked with tears, and patched with hand-sized splashes of red that would darken into bruises. She threw herself into the chair beside Charlie's. 'Look what he's done to my face,' she said sulkily.

Charlie spared her no sympathy. 'Harry's dead and the boys are in jail, and you want me to worry about you getting your face smacked? Grow up, Patsy.'

'Don't blame me for what happened,' she said indignantly, 'it wasn't my idea.'

'No, it was Harry's. The flash ideas were *always* Harry's,' the big man said wearily. 'But he was a driver, ideas weren't his thing. If no one had gone along with his flash ideas he'd be alive now.'

The girl turned her back on him. The only other person in the room was Donovan. She regarded him critically for a while – too long, he felt his skin beginning to crawl. 'You any good then?' It sounded as if, whatever he said, she'd argue.

It was hard to equate this spiteful little witch with the terrified schoolgirl on the train. He'd risked his life to protect her; now he couldn't imagine how he'd been fooled. He shrugged. 'Ask the coach.'

'Ask the coach, tell the coach, kiss the coach's arse,' she mimicked bitterly. 'Does nobody round here have a thought in his head except what Tudor puts there?'

Finally Charlie looked at her. 'Yeah,' he said heavily. 'Harry did.'

The stairs creaked and Gates was watching them from halfway up, the light eyes astute, the small V-shaped smile speculative. When he had their full attention he said quietly, 'What about the 4x4, Hugh? Are you happy with it?'

'It'll do,' grunted Donovan, still rationing his words in front of Patsy.

Gates smiled. 'It had better – we need it first thing tomorrow. We hit the shop at seven. There'll be enough traffic about by then that we won't stand out, not enough to get in the way.'

Donovan felt a chill like a cool breath move up his spine. Twelve hours and this would be done. As long as she didn't remember for the next twelve hours it wouldn't matter what Patsy remembered after that.

Gates spelled out the plan in detail. Even so there wasn't a lot to remember. Andy in the run-about would drop him in Bridgewater Street at ten-to-seven. Eminently visible in white overalls with a paint brush in his pocket, Gates would linger outside Owens, ostensibly waiting for someone, actually checking for problems. At seven Donovan would arrive. If all was well

Gates would be out of sight by then, back in his car parked round the first corner, and he'd wait till the raid was complete. If the job went wrong, anyone who got there ahead of the police would get a lift; anyone else would be on his own. If it went well they'd meet back at the cottage.

'Whatever else you do, Hugh, don't bring the police. If you think you're being followed, lose them; if you can't lose them, lose the car and get away on foot. But if you are picked up, keep your mouth shut. You're on your own – I shan't be able to help you – but I'll keep your money for when you're able to spend it.'

He chuckled at Donovan's expression. 'I'm only saying if the worst comes to the worst. It won't, it never has yet, but I want you to understand what the priorities are. Not getting caught is first, together with keeping quiet if you're unlucky. The haul comes a poor third – what we miss one day we can make up another as long as we're all OK. But God help anyone who brings trouble to my door. I am *not* the price of your freedom. Betray me and somehow, some day, I'll make you pay.'

It wasn't the most lurid threat Donovan had ever heard but it may have been the most sincere. He gave a disdainful sniff. 'I don't grass.'

'Good. Because I don't make hollow threats.'

It was a long evening, with nothing for Donovan to do but avoid talking to Patsy, and a longer night in which the contours of the chair he sprawled in became ever more deeply impressed on his bones. He got no sleep until exhaustion finally claimed him about half an hour before Gates shook him awake. 'Time to move.'

He really was a very cautious man. Before he left the cottage he wanted to see everyone ready to go, dressed in their ram-raiding outfits and in the 4x4 with the back seat down and the engine on. 'I'm not going to twiddle my thumbs in town while you wrestle with the starter!' But the engine caught first time. 'Then let's do it. Good luck, everyone.' He waved a white arm from the window as Andy drove him away.

For ten minutes they sat in the front of the 4x4, listening to the throaty purr of the engine and growling at one another. All had cause to be on edge. Two of them were worried in case the police showed up, the third in case they didn't.

At six-fifty Donovan slammed the 4x4 into gear.

When they reached the by-pass, under the guise of washing fly-specks off the windscreen he turned on the lights. There were no police cars in sight but any of these drivers could be a policeman. Maybe the 4x4 had been spotted already; maybe he'd drive into an ambush. If not he'd have to kill a little time till help arrived. There was a telegraph pole set in the pavement not far from Owens, he didn't think Shapiro would mind him side-swiping that to jam the passenger door shut. He reckoned he could stop Charlie and the girl climbing out over him while Shapiro saw to Gates and the boy.

If Shapiro showed up. If somebody noticed these damn great headlights blazing away in the spring sunshine.

Even if they didn't, Queen's Street would quickly learn of a giant 4x4 wrapped round a telegraph pole in Bridgewater Street.

If they missed Gates at the scene they'd pick him

up at the cottage or fleeing the area. One way or another, Donovan thought it would work out.

Right up to the moment that he turned into Bridge-water Street and there was a knot of people on the pavement between the telegraph pole and Owens Electricals.

'Bloody hell,' said Charlie tersely.

They hadn't considered the possibility of something happening which would both prevent the raid and stop Gates warning them. Had some beat copper with his eye on a stripe used his initiative and stopped the small man in white overalls loitering outside the electrical store? Had Gates stepped back for a clearer view up the road and missed seeing a speeding van? Donovan thought he glimpsed blood splashed on the kerb.

'Slow down,' said Charlie, 'and keep going.'

There must have been a dozen people clustered outside the shop: men in suits, a couple of office cleaners and some schoolboys, craning forward and jostling as if something exciting had happened. Donovan could see nothing through the crush of them – no pointy hats, no white overalls – but if he'd been intending to drive through the window he couldn't have done it without killing someone.

Charlie reached across the girl and gave the wheel a fierce shake. 'Slow *down*, you stupid sod! You want them looking at us instead? Something's gone wrong, we'll work out what later. Slow down, stay calm, get back on the by-pass, and when you're sure we're not being followed head for the cottage. There's no need to panic – you haven't frigging done anything yet!'

The moment when he might have done something

had passed along with the telegraph pole. When he turned down the first side-street there was no sign of Gates's car. He made himself breathe again, eased the 4x4 back to a sensible speed; after a moment he fumbled the light-switch off. He didn't want anyone noticing now. 'What do you reckon went wrong?'

Charlie was still watching him mistrustfully. 'Anything – nothing – we'll hear soon enough. The main thing that went wrong was that you damn near blew it. I thought you said you'd done this before?'

Donovan's embarrassed shrug was by no means fabricated. 'I have, so. It's this business of looking out for people who may or may not be there that's new to me.'

There was no pursuit. He took the scenic route to be sure and reached the cottage around seven-thirty. The run-about was already in the yard.

Andy was in the kitchen. There was no sign of Gates. 'Well?' demanded Charlie.

The boy's delicate features twisted in disgust and something else which Donovan couldn't put a name to. 'The stupid bloody dog, wasn't it? Tudor would bring it with us. He tried to leave it in the car, it went to follow him and he shut the door on its foot.'

There was quite a long silence. Then Charlie said, not in a critical tone, more as if he wasn't sure he'd got it right, 'You mean, we scrubbed a job worth thousands of pounds because the dog caught its foot in the car door?'

Andy nodded, the fair hair flopping over his brow. There was a sort of grim amusement in his voice. 'There was blood everywhere. The dog was screaming, Tudor was crying, we were drawing a bigger crowd than a three-ring circus. All I could think of was to shovel them both back in the car and go looking for a vet. Tudor wouldn't leave the dog so I came on to tell you what happened. I'm going back in a couple of hours to pick them up.'

Charlie sighed. 'I can see the coach'd be upset. Still . . .'

'Stupid bloody dog,' Andy said again. Then Donovan realized what the odd inflection was. It was jealousy.

Donovan went outside and stood by the cars sucking fresh air deep into his lungs. He was thinking of those police officers who spent half their lives in this sort of situation, under cover, associating with people who'd crucify them if they found out. Donovan had been doing it for less than a day, risking not much more than a severe talking-to, and already he'd nearly blown it. He looked at the wood and wondered again about Plan B.

Fear of failure stopped him going. This was his idea, Shapiro went along because he said he could make it work. Circumstances beyond his control were one thing, if it got dangerous he'd cut and run with a clear conscience; but nothing had happened. He was in. Charlie was worried about his competence, not his bona fides. If he quit now there'd be no more chances. If he couldn't handle this he was just another small-town policeman and before long people would start expecting him to behave like one.

Donovan had always fancied his chances at under-cover work. He looked the part, sounded it; he even moved like someone who was up to no good. But you also needed nerve to stay in deep cover when every instinct was telling you to up and run. Donovan had thought he had that, too; until that moment late on

Monday night when he delved deep into his reserves of courage and suddenly, unexpectedly, hit rock bottom.

The shock of that was as real now, as incredible and yet unavoidable, as in the instant when he froze on top of the Mile End Hill. He still couldn't believe he'd lost it so abruptly, so comprehensively. He could still taste the bone-sucking horror, the numb panic – he was going to die, he couldn't help himself, and *he wasn't ready*! In a moment the blithe assumption that he could take whatever fate dealt him, if not with equanimity at least with self-command, fell to dust. Fear unmanned him. If he wanted to go on doing this job he had to deal with it, and the only way he knew was head on. More hung on this than merely making an arrest. If he couldn't bridle his nerve now he'd have to rethink his entire career. He turned back to the cottage.

Patsy was standing at the kitchen door. He went to walk round her but she moved too, blocking his way.

'What?'

Her eyes searched his. She barely came up to his shoulder but she stood close, peering into his face. He could feel her scrutiny like claws in his skin. Her brows, almost colourless, were drawn together by the intensity of her stare. Behind her eyes there was a tense uncertainty, as if she knew something was wrong and didn't quite know what. Donovan didn't dare look away. He thought there was still a chance he could brazen it out. He said again, impatiently, '*What?*'

But as they stood toe to toe he saw the cores of her eyes change, the queries harden to exclamation marks as suspicion grew to conviction and the implications began to dawn on her. Her voice vibrated with accusation. 'You were on the train!'

Chapter Sixteen

Shapiro wondered if he should make an announcement about Liz's return, decided she'd resent the fuss. In retrospect, though, he wished he had. A word of warning to the Monday morning shift and the first thing she heard as she came up the back steps need not have been an argument between two constables as to whether she should resign.

DC Morgan was not an argumentative man. He came from the same fenland stock as Sergeant Tulliver, shared with him the native's peaty vowels and morose expression. People tended to ask what he was worrying about when he wasn't worried at all. He was an easygoing man who made sure of being good enough at his job but not so good that his superiors got any ideas about promoting him.

Another fenland trait that waxed strong in him was a clannish loyalty. He could be roused to a fierce protectiveness by an attack on his own.

It was a measure of Liz's success that she'd come into this insular community and within two years had its native sons considering her one of them. Her career had been an odd mixture of fighting for acceptance where it should have been automatic and finding friendship in unlikely places.

Morgan said gruffly, 'That's like saying anyone who gets his ribs kicked in had better quit because people know he can be beat. 'Course they bloody do. Nobody ever mistook me for Superman, never once, no more than they took you for Wonder Woman, Cathy Flynn! It isn't necessary, or even desirable, that they should. We need their support more than their adulation.' This may have been the longest statement ever volunteered by DC Morgan.

'That's easy for you to say, Dick Morgan,' snapped WPC Flynn, who was sufficiently ashamed of her performance the previous morning to be on the defensive. 'It's not you that's taking stick over it. Last time Donovan got himself pulped, did anyone put up witty posters about it? They did not. It's because she's a woman, and the attack a sexual one, that the men of this town think it's funny. As long as they know one of us was raped and don't know who, every policewoman in town is going to be fair game. If it was me I'd *want* a transfer: a fresh start somewhere it wasn't common knowledge. In everyone's interests.'

When no one replied, for a moment she thought she'd convinced them. Then she sensed Liz standing behind her and spun in a startled flurry of embarrassment.

'But mainly,' Liz said quietly, 'in the interests of those who can't deal with a bad joke without thinking it means the end of law enforcement as we know it.'

She didn't often pull rank on junior officers; she didn't often have to. She expected, and got, the respect of those ranked both below and above her. It had taken Queen's Street a little time to get used to the idea of a woman DI – a lot of sentences petered out in hums, hahs, mumbles and coughs until she specified, calmly but firmly, that the feminine form of Sir was Ma'am and the more they said it the easier it would come. Now they knew one another better she allowed some latitude – Donovan invariably called her Boss, which was meant as a compliment, and Guv was an institution among detectives. But it didn't extend to permitting a WPC who was reduced to hysterics by the sight of a pair of bloomers telling her where to work.

Flynn blushed scarlet. 'Sorry, ma'am. We weren't—'

'Expecting me? So I gather. You should know by now, I enjoy surprising people. And just for the record, I'm not going anywhere. Anyone who finds me an embarrassment had better learn to live with it.'

Half-way upstairs she heard a quick, heavy tread and Morgan fell into step behind her. He sounded contrite. 'Sorry, ma'am. We shouldn't even have been discussing it.'

Liz turned to face him. 'You weren't discussing it. You were doing what I expect of you – backing my judgement.' She flicked him a little grin in case he didn't know it was a joke. 'I like that line about needing support more than adulation. I must remember that, it'll look good in a report sometime.'

'Well, don't use it in front of the chief – I pinched it off him in the first place,' Morgan admitted. Chuckling, they climbed the last flight.

Liz barely had her diary out when Shapiro joined her, and by then he'd already spoken to Morgan. 'Well, that didn't take long.'

She gazed at him levelly. 'No; and it really upset me too. See that? I'm quivering like a jelly.' The hand she held out was steady as a rock.

Shapiro sniffed. 'Am I over-doing the Caring Work-place bit?'

She smiled. 'Just a smidgin.'

He nodded. 'So what are you doing today?'

Liz tapped her diary with a forefinger. 'I'm in the Crown Court at some point. Sharon Burke's applying for bail.'

'I could do that.'

'You could blow my nose for me as well, Frank, but I wouldn't thank you for that either. I want to do Burke because we've a better chance of keeping her in cus-tody if I do. If you go it'll look like a big bad policeman oppressing a poor defenceless woman. If I do it, it won't.'

'Who's sitting?'

'Cushy Carnahan, he's a soft touch for a female defendant at the best of times. By the time Dan Fen-ton's piled on the agony about how this poor woman was bullied for most of her married life and only retali-ated when she felt to be in mortal danger, he'll have lost sight of the fact that she drugged her husband's cocoa and set fire to his bed when he was too groggy to leave it. I'll remind him. I'll also remind him that she was arrested boarding a Channel ferry with her Italian toy-boy and her husband's nest-egg.'

'I take it you've not got a lot of sympathy for the notion of delayed self-defence, then.'

The look she gave him was scathing. 'Self-defence is when you have your back to the wall and no alterna-tive. If Burke couldn't stop her setting fire to his pyja-mas he also couldn't stop her packing her bags and starting a new life with the Latin lover of her choice. She didn't have to kill him. And if she gets bail we'll

171

never see her again. I wonder if Mr Fenton's thought that if he's good today his fee may go on gondola rides?' Liz closed her diary and sat back. 'What else is new? Any progress on the rapes?'

He wished he had something to tell her. 'Not yet. I've got Scobie visiting known offenders but nobody's in the frame yet and to be honest the MO doesn't sound like any of our local perverts.'

Liz shook her head. 'I don't think this man's on record. Anywhere. I think it's something new with him. More than anyone else, sex offenders stick to a pattern, as if the pattern's more important than the sex. If a rapist had been targeting blonde middle-aged women anywhere in the country we'd know about it by now.'

'What's the alternative? That he's tried squash and golf and now he's taken up rape?' Shapiro wouldn't have joked about it, however wryly, with anyone else. But Liz was a colleague before she was a victim, and he'd already been warned about tip-toeing round her.

She grinned – a shade rueful but a definite grin. 'There's a first time for everything. Maybe he's just a beginner.'

Shapiro dropped his gaze apologetically. 'Sorry to get personal but you're the best witness we have. Would you say he was a youngster – a bit of a novice?'

She wasn't offended. She thought for a moment but had no doubts about the answer. 'Actually, no. He knew what he was doing. He wasn't a big man – I've told you all this, haven't I? – but there was a confidence about him. He didn't get violent because he didn't have to: he had surprise on his side. He knew what he wanted, he wasted no time, he took it and then he left.

Like a military operation. To me that doesn't seem like a kid still coming to terms with his sexuality. I got the feeling – no more than that, but it was a definite feeling – of someone about my age.'

'Old as that, eh?' Shapiro murmured sardonically.

'You know what I mean – past the first flush of youthful indiscretion, still this side of senility.'

'What about a psychiatric case?'

'No,' she said immediately, with a certainty she could not have explained. 'No, he was in control all right. Control was what it was all about.'

Shapiro nodded slowly. Then he looked at her. 'I will get him, you know. Whatever it takes. If the DNA's good enough I'll go for a mass screening.'

The hiss as she caught her breath was sharp enough to hear. 'Hell, Frank, I don't know if that's a good idea.'

'There's precedent.'

'Yes, but not all good. You can't supervise big numbers with total accuracy. Remember the time the culprit persuaded a friend to give a sample in his name? – confused the whole investigation.'

'So we're careful,' said Shapiro doggedly. 'And we could limit the numbers, if you're sure about his age. Men between thirty and fifty, say, excluding those above fourteen stone. He'd be in that group.'

'So would most of Queen's Street. So would Brian!'

'And most of Queen's Street, and Brian, would gladly give a blood sample to eliminate themselves from the inquiry. So will most other men. Then we take a closer look at the ones who don't – who're too busy, or too squeamish, or away on holiday – whatever.'

She stared at him, impressed and appalled in equal

measure. 'Have you any idea the man-hours you'd be getting into? You're talking of expenditure in excess of one hundred thousand pounds. You'll never get it approved.'

He raised one eyebrow. 'Have you any idea how stubborn I can be if the need arises?'

She had. She thought he could probably make it happen if he wanted it enough. 'There's a civil liberties aspect to this.'

'We're giving men the opportunity to clear themselves,' he said shortly. 'Where's the infringement of liberty in that? Besides, *rape* is a civil liberties issue.'

'Tell me about it.' For perhaps a minute Liz said nothing more; but Shapiro could see her thinking and knew the conversation wasn't over. Then she said, 'It's too big a sledge-hammer.'

'Three rapes inside three weeks is no nut!'

'It isn't Armageddon either. This is our town, Frank, I don't want to see it split. Making people take sides on this is too high a price even for catching a rapist.'

'We should wait for him to do it again? Or we could tell women to stay off the streets unless they travel in packs. Do you like what that'll do to the town?'

'Frank, I don't like any of this,' she said forcibly. 'But I don't think all-out war on half the population is the answer. Damn it, neither did you before Friday! I think the answer is detective work.'

'I have nothing to go on!' exclaimed Shapiro, bitter with frustration. 'The DNA'll help us put him away if we get him, but screening is the only way it'll help us find him.'

'What about a TV appeal? I doubt we'll persuade him to give himself up but we might reach someone who knows him. Women friends in particular might be anxious enough about their own safety to pick up the phone. We'll need a confidential line, this is too delicate to expect them to talk to an officer.

'But if we stress that we're just asking for ideas at this point, that we expect to get dozens of names and clear most of them right away, maybe women who've felt uneasy about a date will get to wondering and call us. After we've eliminated the improbables you could ask the others for blood samples.'

Shapiro had to concede she was right. Mass screening a town the size of Castlemere would be a logistical nightmare. It was a last resort, they weren't that desperate yet. He hadn't considered it after the rape of Mrs Andrews. He'd have to watch that. If Liz could keep the thing in perspective he had no excuse for not doing.

'Yes, all right, I'll see what I can set up. God, I hate going on telly!'

'Maybe I should do it,' said Liz.

Shapiro looked at her quickly but couldn't be quite sure that she was joking. He gave a disapproving sniff. 'You concentrate on keeping Sharon Burke behind bars. And catching my ram-raiders. I don't wish to gloat,' he added untruthfully, 'but it is the Tynesiders: Donovan made contact.'

She didn't begrudge him his small triumph. 'Where's Donovan now?'

Shapiro shrugged. 'I saw him on Friday when he was on his way to meet them. Saturday I got a message via his neighbours – coded, he must have been being watched when he wrote it, but saying there was another job in the offing. But it hasn't happened yet –

nobody's reported a big black 4x4 parked in their front window – so I assume he's still with them.'

'You don't think something could have gone wrong?' She meant, that he could be in trouble.

'I don't think so. They've no history of violence against the person. Remember Mrs Cunningham? They made sure she and the baby were safe before they went ahead. If Donovan makes a hash of it I think the worst that'll happen is that we'll lose them.'

Liz knew, because she knew him, that Shapiro was deliberately understating the risks involved to save her worry. 'Bunch of pussy-cats, hm? Only took up ram-raiding because the flower-arranging classes were full?'

'Listen,' he said in mock indignation, 'he's all right. It's making money they're interested in, not thumping coppers. They're businessmen. I'd rather deal with professional criminals any day than enthusiastic amateurs who learned the job from watching television. Like those madmen on the train. Like the sod who dumped a dead dog on my path. Did I tell you about that?'

'Yes, Frank.'

It made no difference. He told her again.

Chapter Seventeen

'Oh, no,' said Donovan with all the conviction he could muster. 'No, you're mistaken.'

But no doubt gathered in Patsy's bitter eyes to reward him. Her voice was flat with certainty. 'I *knew* I'd seen you before, and that's where. You were the guy on the train. The one who knew a way out.'

OK, Donovan thought rapidly, just because she knows that doesn't mean she knows everything. His voice dropped to a whine. 'Jesus, Patsy, don't tell the coach. I took this job in good faith. I didn't know it was you people on the train till after I got here. It was too late to back out so I kept my mouth shut. You'd have done the same.'

'I wouldn't have lied to Tudor. Not if I wanted to keep my face.' The bruises still rankled.

'I didn't lie. When he offered me the job I'd no reason to tell him, later I couldn't. It doesn't change anything. I was hired to drive, the fact I was on a train you robbed isn't relevant. I didn't try and stop you, I just tried to stop anyone getting hurt. Especially you. I thought you were in danger. I stuck my neck out for you.'

Moral blackmail was wasted on her. 'If you've nothing to hide, why can't I tell Tudor?'

Because he's brighter than you, Donovan thought grimly, he'll work it out and I'll spend the next six hours tunnelling out of a shed. 'Because it'll make everyone jumpy and cost me a job, and there's no need. What're you afraid of – that I'll tell the cops? Is that likely?'

'I don't know you,' Patsy said obstinately. 'How should I know what you're likely to do?'

'Well, I'm not going to do anything that'll put me in jail, now, am I? You can trust me that far.'

That may have been a mistake. Even at Patsy's age women have heard men say 'trust me' so often, and been let down, that the words automatically arouse suspicion. Her chin came up; it was the only way she could look down her nose at a man six foot tall. 'I don't have to trust you at all. Tudor can if he wants to.'

Donovan managed to shrug as if it didn't matter. 'OK. Then I'll get my cards and he'll get out of town. That'll cost him time and money, and he won't blame me: he'll blame the shambles on the train and the only one left from that is you.'

That reached her; he saw her waver. The icy certainty that would have sunk him began to crack. 'You said you worked for the railway.'

'So I did, till they laid me off. I didn't owe them any favours, that's why I helped your friends escape.'

'Did what?!'

'It's not my fault the Old Bill knew about the airshaft as well! Be fair, I did my best to get them out.'

Patsy was trying to remember everything that had happened, everything that had been said. It was a week now and the details were fading. His explanation seemed to fit. 'Harry said you called the police. On that mobile phone.'

'Harry was wrong. The woman who owned it called them.'

'He was ready to beat your head in! Why didn't you say?'

'So he could beat her instead? Call me old-fashioned but I'd sooner not see guys beating up on women. I tried to help you, too. OK, you didn't need it but I didn't know that. I could've got hurt helping you.'

'Yes.' She was still thinking, still torn.

'Look,' he said reasonably, 'tell him if you're scared not to. Maybe it's for the best. But you'll be in trouble and I'll be down the road. Or you could forget we ever met. Who's to know? No one'd expect you to remember everybody on that train; you probably don't remember anyone else. For all our sakes, forget you remember me.'

Gates would have seen through it. But Patsy was thinking with her face and she was tempted. 'I don't know.' She turned abruptly back to the kitchen.

If Gates had been there she might have gone to him. But he wasn't, and she had an hour to think about it before he returned. An hour to anticipate his reaction. An hour for Donovan's suggestion to start sounding quite sensible.

Donovan was trading snarls with Brian Boru when he heard the car return. He stayed where he was. Patsy would screw him now or not at all. If she did, if Gates worked it out and opted to terminate his employment with a degree of prejudice, he could come looking for him.

But it wasn't Gates who came into the pig-sty, it was Charlie. 'Coach wants to talk to everyone inside.' Donovan scoured his face for subcurrents but found none. He followed the big man into the cottage.

Gates was still in his painter's whites, the front splashed with blood. He was pale and his cheeks carried the silvery tracks of dried tears but his voice was calm. Of the dog there was no sign.

'I want to apologize for this morning. My mistake put you all in danger. I don't accept sloppiness from you and you shouldn't have to take it from me. In the event all we've lost is time, but I let you down and I'm sorry. It won't happen again.'

There was an embarrassed silence before Charlie asked what they were all wondering. 'What about Chang, coach?'

Gates gave a watery smile. 'I shut the car door on his foot, all the little bones were broken. I told the vet it didn't matter what the treatment cost. But he said with so much damage you couldn't expect it to heal perfectly, that he'd always be lame. He thought it mightn't heal at all and he'd have to amputate. I didn't want that. Chang was special, I wanted to remember him at his best. I had the vet put him to sleep.'

A quiver of presentiment fluttered in Donovan's belly. Not that he had more than a passing interest in the fate of Gates's unpleasant little dog. But that was the point; it was *Gates's* unpleasant little dog, the man thought the sun shone out of its bare behind. But he destroyed it when it was no longer perfect. It was a timely reminder that Tudor Gates wasn't just an effeminate little man with a pleasant manner: he was the ring-leader of a criminal gang. His hobby was dog-fighting. He hurt people who let him down. He destroyed things that no longer pleased him.

Gates was regarding him oddly, puzzled that the dog's fate should affect him so. He looked quite touched. He patted Donovan's arm. 'He had a good life, you know. Now we have to look forward. How does everyone feel about having another go tonight, after the shops close?'

The Burke case was called before the Crown Court rose for lunch. Liz arrived with ten minutes to spare. She didn't need any more: she was familiar with the papers, knew how Mr Fenton would set out his stall and how she'd try to upset it. After that it was up to Cushy Carnahan, and he had as soft a spot for police-women as for female defendants.

She expected to win but it wouldn't break her heart to lose. As a fledgling detective she had taken defeats personally, as a reflection on her competence. But she'd grown out of that. She fought her cases but accepted that their resolution was in other hands. If Sharon Burke skipped the country it would be the system's failure, not hers.

So there was nothing about the case which would explain the sensation under her breastbone like a food processor chopping swedes. The case, the place and the people here were, with minor variations, the same as always. Even the defendants were depressingly familiar.

But if it wasn't any of them that was different then

it was Liz. She hadn't expected to feel so – exposed. So far as she knew, no one here was aware she'd been raped. There might be some speculation, but all Castlemere's policewomen were having to contend with that. If she couldn't cope she'd no right to criticize Cathy Flynn.

So she would cope, food processor or no food processor. How she felt wasn't branded on her forehead, any more than what she'd been subjected to. All she had to do was go through the motions. If she'd been going to panic she'd have done so before this. It was already too late for anything to go badly wrong.

A touch on her shoulder made her start but it was only the defending counsel in the Burke case, checking that she hadn't had a change of heart. 'I'm prepared to push for this woman. She's had a rough time, I don't think she ought to be treated like a criminal.'

'Murdering your husband is a criminal offence,' Liz reminded him gently.

'If it *was* murder.'

'It was murder unless it was self-defence, and it wasn't self-defence if she had an alternative. When Burke drank the Valium in his cocoa she had an alternative.'

Dan Fenton gave a tight smile. 'Let's not try it in the corridor, it offends the judge. I just wanted to be sure we're still at odds on this.'

'I'm afraid so, Mr Fenton, yes.'

He smiled again, more generously. 'Well, it's not the first time, I don't expect it'll be the last. I'd like to think we might still manage a twirl at the Civic Ball come Christmas.'

They'd cut a dash at the Town Hall last Christmas. Fenton was not a big man, neither as tall nor as broad as he seemed to think important lawyers ought to be. He compensated by assuming the attitudes and gestures of a big man, and attacking everything he did with gusto, whether defending a murderess or dancing the Gay Gordons. At the Town Hall he made a memorable figure in his white tuxedo and scarlet cummerbund, cheeks flushed with wine, thinning hair flying on the turns, as he danced the feet off every woman present who was sound in mind and limb and aged under sixty.

It was, thought Liz, the last determined expression of youth by a man who any day now would have to admit to being middle-aged. His wife had already crossed the threshold, watched from one of the little gilt chairs Davy May had set out with microscopic attention to nonchalance beside the dance-floor. Liz plopped down beside her when she made her escape. 'Mr Fenton's in good form,' she panted.

Amy Fenton nodded knowingly. 'I don't even try to keep up with him any more.' And she added, but somehow less as an afterthought than a summary: 'Dan likes to do everything well.'

All lawyers prefer winning cases to losing them, but Dan Fenton liked to win more than any barrister Liz knew. He did win most of the time. He deserved to – he put everything he had into it, time and effort and body and soul. Sharon Burke could hardly have put her defence in safer hands. Fenton and Cushy Carnahan together made a lethal cocktail.

Remand proceedings are about the shortest event in a court. Defendant's name is called, the prosecution asks for a continuing remand – a short one if he's in custody, a longer one if he's on bail – the defence agrees, the bench grants it and it's time for the next case. A couple of minutes apiece is usually sufficient.

A contested bail application takes longer. The prosecution outline their case in order to demonstrate the risk that witnesses may be interfered with or the accused do a runner. Defence counsel sets out to show what a decent citizen his client really is and how, but for the vagaries of fate, he'd be in line for beatification.

Finally it's the decision of the man on the bench, and he can't win. If he agrees to custody he risks jailing an innocent person. If he allows bail and witnesses are intimidated or the defendant repeats the offence or absconds, it's all his fault.

The responsibility had turned Cushy Carnahan into a wizened old man before he was sixty. He clutched the edge of the bench as if afraid that the tide of conflicting expectations would wash him away and followed sally and counter-attack from under brows drawn low by concentration, time and gravity.

Mr Fenton rose to make his application, thumbs lodged in the armholes of his waistcoat. Sharon Burke, he said, was an unhappy woman driven by circumstances to one terrible act of violence. Being ground to dust by a sadistic husband over a period of years had reduced her to such despair that she believed she was literally fighting for her life. There were no witnesses and no danger to anyone else. It would not be merely an act of mercy to release such a woman to the support of friends and family, said Mr Fenton, it would be an act of justice.

Liz opposed the application on the grounds that the fatal attack on Burke could not have occurred during a violent exchange as he had been rendered helpless by tranquillizers. Mrs Burke had an association with a foreign national and was arrested trying to leave the country, raising clear doubts as to whether she would remain within the jurisdiction of the court if granted bail.

Fenton rose to question her. 'Detective Inspector Graham, are you aware that my client suffered numerous attacks by her husband during the twenty-two years of their marriage, requiring hospital treatment on five occasions in the last three years?'

'I'm aware that Mrs Burke was treated by Accident and Emergency at Castle General for injuries which could have been caused deliberately. But she didn't make a complaint so we were unable to establish whether Mr Burke was responsible.'

'She told friends that her husband beat her.'

'But not us, sir. On the two occasions we asked about her injuries she said they were her own fault – that she was clumsy, she cut herself with the breadknife; another time that she fell down the back step.'

'Inspector!' exclaimed Fenton derisively. 'You *believed* her?'

'Belief wasn't the issue. We couldn't act without a complaint.'

'So because you failed to gain Mrs Burke's confidence you consider there's no evidence of domestic violence, even though the poor woman was in A & E so often she knew the staff by name! And without a formal history of abuse you're unwilling to accept the painfully obvious truth that Sharon Burke was the victim of a violent marriage and suffered repeated episodes of mental, physical and sexual thuggery until she could take no more. Isn't that the truth, Inspector?'

'The truth is a matter for the jury to decide. My job is to ensure that they get the chance, and I believe Mrs Burke's release on bail could be prejudicial to that.'

Dan Fenton frowned. He'd known the police would object to bail but hadn't expected to have a fight on his hands. Most witnesses are made docile by their unfamiliarity with the situation. That's less of a factor with professional testimony, but he still wasn't used to losing arguments with people in the witness box.

It wasn't the first time DI Graham had given him trouble. He realized she was only doing her job, but if she wanted to make a name for herself he wished she'd do it some other way. He liked women, but better as secretaries and dancing partners and wives than opponents. His eyes hardened while his voice grew soft. The judge wouldn't like it but he too had a job to do.

'Inspector Graham, you seem to have a distorted picture of my client. She's not a bullion robber with an executive jet waiting. She doesn't have a numbered bank account in Switzerland. She's a woman of fifty who's known nothing but brutality all her married life. Yes, she killed her husband. She's never denied that. In immediate terror for her life, reeling from his latest assault, in a state of shock and despair she snatched at the chance to save herself further punishment.

'You say that once the attack on her was over she was no longer entitled to act in self-defence, and of course that's right. I'm sure you'd have handled it better. You'd have left the house, called your solicitor and the police, and begun proceedings to protect yourself from this violent bully you'd been unwise enough to marry.'

He was pushing both his luck and the rules of criminal pleading. Another member of the judiciary might have asked him to save these remarks for a more suitable occasion. But Fenton's reputation allowed him to get away with things for which a more junior barrister would have been taken to task.

But there was a limit to how much latitude he could expect so he kept moving, to say all he wanted to before he was stopped. 'But it's not you we're talking about, Inspector, it's Sharon Burke. Sharon has no financial independence. She left school at sixteen, married two years later. Her friends thought she'd done pretty well: Burke made a good living in the building trade, they had a nice house, took foreign holidays, ran a good car. It sounds a decent enough life, Inspector, doesn't it?'

His voice rose to a dramatic stridency. 'But then what can you – an intelligent, educated woman with a good job, social position, a decent home life – possibly know about humiliation? About being something for a man to wipe his feet on? Has she told you he raped her? Not occasionally, when he was drunk, but routinely, once or twice a week, any time he felt like it. His idea of foreplay, Inspector, was knocking her down.

'Can you imagine what that does to a woman's self-esteem? Can you imagine how hard it is to go on believing that you're an important human being with all the rights and privileges that go with that? Police, solicitors, court orders – these things exist for other people's benefit, not yours. Can you imagine how it must feel to be used like that?'

Afterwards Liz would say it happened too quickly for thought, that a moment came when the path divided and she had to choose with only instinct to guide her. In fact it wasn't like that. She seemed to have all the time in the world to weigh the alternatives, and decide what mattered to her. She'd had enough of discretion: it was more in her nature to fight back.

Even then she didn't rush. She glanced at the bench, where Judge Carnahan was red with indignation at what Fenton was doing but seemed somehow impotent to stop it. She glanced down at the Press table, saw Gail Fisher watching her with puzzlement growing to concern. She looked at the back of the court where the police officers, frozen in horror, didn't dare meet her gaze.

Then she looked back at the defending barrister. 'As a matter of fact, Mr Fenton,' she said, very calmly and quite without ambivalence, 'I know exactly how that feels.'

Part Three

Chapter Eighteen

Brian Graham had 3b for the first hour after lunch on Mondays. The lesson he'd prepared on design contained no nudes but the name of Charles Rennie Mackintosh was causing the usual hilarity when Mary McKenna put her head round his door and signalled him outside. 'Can we have a word in my office?' The same glance at the time-table that told her where he'd be also told her who he was teaching so she brought a student teacher to take over the class. The last time 3b were left alone for more than a few minutes they whitewashed the blackboard.

So this was going to take a little time. Puzzled, Brian followed the principal to her office and took the seat offered him. He'd left the door open; she closed it.

She had red hair and a forthright manner, and she came right to the point. 'Brian, you should have told me about Liz. We could have juggled the schedule, got you a bit of time off.'

He dropped his gaze as if she'd caught him out in some mischief. The colour rose in his throat. He mumbled, '*Me* take some time off? I couldn't get *her* to take some time off.'

'So I gather,' said Ms McKenna drily.

Brian caught the echo of import in that, made

himself look at her. He knew he was behaving stupidly, as if he had something to be ashamed of. But when he looked up McKenna's eyes were compassionate.

He didn't understand. 'How do you know about it?'

There were two questions there: the obvious one, to which the answer was that another teacher's husband was a witness in another case that morning, and the important one. McKenna had never flinched from dealing with difficult issues and now was no time to start. 'Brian, if you thought it was a secret I'd better tell you Liz made what amounts to a public statement in court this morning. I don't know any details, just that. Do you want to go home, see if she's all right?'

It was a kind offer but it went to his heart as straight as a well-aimed arrow. Liz wouldn't be at home, and she would be fine. He didn't need any details to know that this situation hadn't been forced on her. She hadn't been backed into a corner: Liz Graham didn't allow herself to be used like that. Liz Graham didn't do anything she didn't pretty well want to. She'd done this because she chose to: out of pride or anger or tactics, regardless of its effect on anyone else. On him. Liz would be all right: Liz was the strong one, the bruiser. She'd come through this with her head up, bloodied but triumphant, as she came through everything. Brian felt he'd had the legs cut from under him with a chain-saw.

He didn't trust himself to speak, just nodded. He collected his jacket and drove home. He sat by the phone for an hour before he picked it up.

*

'Well,' Superintendent Giles said manfully, 'you've put the cat among the pigeons now.'

'Yes,' agreed Liz. There was no point denying it.

'Can I ask why?'

She sketched a shrug. 'It seemed a good idea.'

'At the time.'

'Yes. And since.'

'Why?' He wasn't arguing, he genuinely wanted to understand.

'The situation was becoming impossible. Everyone in Castlemere knew a policewoman had been raped: until they found out who, the innuendo was going to affect every woman here, me included. The damage was done already; I thought if confidentiality was no longer possible the next best thing was to put the facts on record.'

'You thought all this,' Giles murmured astutely, 'between Fenton asking the question and you answering it?'

Liz conceded his point with a tiny grin. 'Not exactly. It was one of those seminal moments: I had either to tell the truth or lie. I suppose it made me think about how we were handling it. It seemed right then; I still think it was right.'

The superintendent pursed his lips. He had very clear eyes; now the blue in them was cool. 'If Fenton deliberately put you in that position to help his case I'll complain to the Bar Council.'

Liz shook her head. 'Coincidence, sir. There was no way he could have known; unless someone here told him and I don't believe that. I was damaging his case, he wanted to shut me up. He expected me to have to say no.' Again the little smile. 'It ruined his day when I said yes. Now he has to explain to Sharon Burke why she's going to be in custody for the next six months while the CPS gets its case together.'

'And' – Giles looked for words that made no assumptions – 'what are you going to do next?'

'You mean, will I tidy the place up by going into purdah for a while?' Her voice took on an edge. 'No, sir. I've done nothing to be ashamed of, I'm damned if I'm going into hiding.'

'How does your husband feel about it?'

Liz blinked. 'Brian?'

'Brian. He does know?'

'I shouldn't think so, not yet. He'll still be in school.'

Superintendent Giles regarded her thoughtfully. As policemen go he was a New Man: he valued the contribution of women officers to a police service which sometimes needed an infusion of compassion and sensitivity. He regretted that the only way women seemed able to get on the promotions ladder was by sacrificing those very virtues and starting to behave pretty much like men. He sighed. 'I shouldn't count on that, Inspector.'

Dead on cue, Miss Tunstall tapped and put her head round his door. 'Sorry to disturb you, sir. But I've got Detective Inspector Graham's husband on the phone, and he sounds rather upset.'

She found Brian at the kitchen table with three mugs in front of him, each half-full of the coffee he kept making but was too agitated to finish drinking.

She dropped into a chair opposite him, slinging her bag over the back. 'We'll have to make this quick, I'm needed back at the office.'

He literally gasped. She really had no idea what she'd done, what either of them was doing here. 'Liz, talk to me! Damn the office. Tell me what's going on. What happened, why you did it. What you were thinking of!'

She wasn't surprised he was upset. He was a private man, she could imagine how the news of this getting out would affect him. But there was nothing she could do to shield him. The situation was not of her making: she was sorry he was having problems but he'd have to rise above them just as she had. Now the facts were a matter of public record the gossip would soon wither and die.

She swallowed her impatience and told him how it had come about. 'It seemed the lesser of two evils. Things couldn't go on as they were. Every woman at Queen's Street was under pressure – I had to do something to protect them.'

'You didn't think maybe it's their job to protect you?'

Her eyes were wide with censure. 'No, Brian, I didn't. I'm the senior woman officer in Castlemere: I didn't get there by dumping my problems on my juniors.'

'Fine,' spat Brian, white-faced with fury. 'Well, we've established what's best for you and what's best for Queen's Street, and once we've got the traffic wardens' vote we can be quite sure all the legitimate interests have ben catered for. What about me, Liz? Do I figure *anywhere* in this? You must have asked yourself how going public was going to affect me. Didn't you? Please, Liz, you must have.'

The extent of his anger and distress amazed her.

She honestly didn't understand why he felt betrayed. Shapiro when she told him, and Giles when she told him, had been taken aback but respected her right to set the pace on this. It was a difficult situation, there were no perfect answers, but they were prepared to back her decisions simply because they *were* her decisions and no one else had a better right to make them. She didn't understand why her husband didn't feel the same way. 'Brian – *does* it affect you?'

It would be hard to find a gentler man than Brian Graham. It showed in everything he said and did, in the low voice, the self-effacing humour, even the way he walked. His virtues were the modest ones of kindness, dependability, generosity of spirit. Violence appalled him.

But he came as close then as he ever had to slapping her. His long hands fisted at his sides and it seemed to take an effort of will to keep them there. His bony skull rocked back, eyes shut as if in pain. His voice was a desperate whisper. 'Liz, what do you *mean*, does it affect me? Everything you do – everything that happens to you – affects me. You told a crowd of strangers that you'd been raped. You didn't ask me first. You didn't even tell me first. If Big Mac hadn't pulled me out of class I might have heard it from 3b!'

'It was going to come out sometime,' she said reasonably. 'It seemed better to pick my own moment.'

'But why didn't you *warn* me?'

'I didn't know what Dan Fenton was going to say! My only choice was between lying, glossing it over or telling the truth. I told the truth. I really don't see the problem.' The tragedy was, she really didn't.

His breathing was ragged. 'The problem? The problem is that tomorrow I'm going to have to face a bunch of kids who know my wife's been raped. Half of them are going to be embarrassed, the other half'll be over the moon. Christ almighty, they think they've put one over on you when they find out your first name! When they have this for ammunition they'll snipe and they'll snipe, and they won't stop until either I break down in front of them or I do some corrective dentistry on them with the board rubber. How can I teach like that? What if one of them knows who attacked you – an older brother, an uncle, a father even? Your honesty may have made your job easier but it's made mine damn near impossible.'

Unused to criticism from him she reacted with more speed than grace, leapt to her feet so quickly the chair spilled from under her. 'Brian,' she exclaimed in exasperation, 'don't be so pathetic! Of course it's difficult. Do you think it isn't difficult for me? But there's only two options: lie down under it or get up and kick back. You lie down if you want to but it's not my style. If the alternative to keeping my head down and telling fibs is everyone knowing, then so be it.

'I've been raped once. Well, my wits were fluttering round the eaves like a flock of starlings so I wasn't best able to prevent it. But I'm not concussed now, and I'm not submitting to any more violations. I won't be hustled out of sight by the kind of prejudice that expects the victim of a sex attack to pay the price – and pay it again and again for as long as anyone remembers. Women leave town to avoid that, but I'm not doing so. This wasn't my fault, not in any way at all, and I'm not going to act as if it was.

'Now you can deal with that, Brian,' she said

fiercely, 'or you can take that holiday in Bognor while the fuss blows over, but that's how it's going to be. I've earned the respect of this town, and I'm damn well going to have it. Not sympathy – I don't want sympathy – I want justice and respect. I'm going to stand up for my rights. Not just for me: for the other women who aren't strong enough to; and even for you, Brian, and all the other-halves who're worried about what the folk at work might say. And if you haven't the guts to stand with me, then God damn you!'

She didn't wait for a reply. She snatched up her bag and flung out to the car, and the wheels spat grit.

Half-way to Castlemere she found herself regretting some of that. Not what she'd said, because it was important and not just to her, but how she said it. She had a lot of anger to dispose of, she couldn't afford to do it at work, but Brian wasn't her enemy and he hadn't deserved what he got. She'd have to apologize. For two pins she'd have gone straight back and done it then. But she glanced at the clock on her dashboard and decided it could wait till this evening when they'd both be calmer and could perhaps move on from regrets to working out a compromise. She'd get away from work around five, they could talk properly then.

In fact she finished at seven, and when she got home Brian's car was gone from the drive and a drawerful of clothes from his chest. There was no note. She sat on the bed in stunned disbelief. She couldn't think where he might have gone. She couldn't think of anyone who might know. When she was forced to accept that she had no way of finding him, she cried – brokenly, desolately – for the first time since the attack.

Chapter Nineteen

DC Morgan was also in court on Monday morning, giving evidence before the magistrates in a case of handling stolen goods. The defence counsel asked for it to be called early to enable her to appear elsewhere in the afternoon; which would have been all right, Morgan thought morosely, if she'd reciprocated by getting on with the damn thing. Instead she challenged every word he said, and had her witnesses repeat themselves endlessly, with the result that Morgan was there from ten-twenty until noon. The eventual conviction was scant reward: no one was going to send a grandmother to prison for handling a frozen leg of lamb. Probation was the best Morgan had expected. Mrs Thelma Dickens, doyenne of petty crime in that sink of iniquity known as The Jubilee, gave him a wink as she left the court.

As a result Morgan wasn't at his desk when Keith Baker phoned at ten-thirty. The switchboard asked if anyone else could help but Baker said he'd call back later – it was nothing urgent, just something DC Morgan had been asking about. By the time Morgan got the message, however, Baker was half-way down a cow with a drenching tube. It was mid-afternoon before they finally made contact.

'That dog you were asking about,' said the vet. 'I treated it this morning.'

Morgan pricked up his ears. 'The Chinese thingy?'

'Crested Dog, yes. Painter brought it in. Shut its foot in a car door. Funny business.' Baker's answer to pressure of work was to talk like a telegram, omitting pronouns and conjunctions and anything else that didn't earn its space. 'Funny dog for a painter to have; but then he was funny sort of painter. More your interior decorator.'

'Did you fix it up?'

'Could have done. Would have done. Didn't want me to. Didn't want a lame dog. Had me put it down.'

Morgan frowned, disappointed. 'Then he'll not be back.'

'No – paid his bill before he left. Cash. Funny little sod – tried to tip me. Point is, though,' he went on, returning to the purpose of his phonecall, 'I got a look at the car that picked him up.'

Shapiro pushed the facts about like pushing cold food round a plate with a fork. 'They were on a raid this morning: the look-out was in white overalls for visibility. But his dog got hurt and he went to find a vet instead. So they're still here and still in business. We knew that, of course – Donovan would've been back if they'd left town.'

'Probably,' Morgan agreed cautiously.

'The car Baker saw – that's not the 4x4 so it's the look-out's car. That means it'll be in the target area for some minutes before the raiders arrive. We have the number, we know what the look-out looks like – pity about the dog but even without it he's pretty distinctive. We know the sort of goods they're interested in, and the times of day that suit them.'

He was thinking aloud. Morgan was good for thinking aloud to: he never interrupted, never got to the punchline first, but if questioned afterwards could repeat the salient points as proof that he hadn't nodded off half-way through.

Shapiro went on. 'Well, they missed their chance this morning. They must be getting anxious about hanging round here so long: my guess is they'll go straight to the next slot – tonight, an hour either side of seven – get it done and get out, hope for better luck elsewhere.'

He was convincing himself. He hoped he wasn't raising stout walls on marshmallow foundations. But Castlemere hadn't been good to them, even before the dog's accident they'd lost their driver somehow and had to waste time finding another. In fact they'd been unluckier than they knew, but hopefully they wouldn't realize that for a little while yet.

'All right,' he decided, 'I'll go see Mr Giles – grovel a bit, threaten a bit, whatever it takes to reinstate the stake-out. If we can watch those half dozen shops for two more hours we'll get them, I know we will.'

'If they go tonight,' said Morgan lugubriously. 'If nothing else goes wrong.'

After thirty years as a detective it took a lot to make Shapiro feel like an irrepressible optimist. Morgan was worth keeping around for that reason alone.

'Same time, same place,' said Gates, 'just the other end of the day. I'll be in place by ten-to-seven, you hit

Owens at seven. I'll go as a golfer – Andy, put the clubs and the big umbrella in the car.'

They went over the timings yet again. 'Two minutes,' insisted Gates. 'I don't care if they've got the Crown Jewels in there, you've only got two minutes so concentrate on the good stuff and get out when your time is up. Unless there's a police patrol nearby, two minutes isn't long enough for them to respond to the alarm. If it goes well, we'll meet back here at seven-thirty.'

When the time came they produced their ski-masks, Donovan started the 4x4 to prove it hadn't died during the day, then Andy drove Gates away. The raiders waited the statutory ten minutes then set off.

This time it went wrong before they reached the end of the lane. As Donovan went to turn out the little red car turned back in, flashing its lights waspishly. Donovan, reversing all the way to the cottage, had his attention fully occupied but Charlie could see that Gates was spitting tacks. He couldn't guess what had gone wrong this time but plainly something had, and this time Gates wasn't blaming himself. Charlie couldn't see how it could be his fault but he crossed his fingers just the same.

The cars pulled up side by side in the yard, disgorging all five occupants, tense and quarrelsome. Gates was ruddy with anger. 'Pack up, we're leaving.'

'What happened?' If Charlie hadn't asked Donovan would have had to.

'They were waiting for us! The town was full of coppers! They *thought* they were being discreet. They thought since they weren't in uniform no one could possibly know who they were. But there was no missing them. All the places we'd thought about hitting? – they were watching them. Electrical showrooms and jewellers. We did a quick tour, without getting too close, then we got out fast. They didn't spot us.'

'I don't understand,' said Charlie emptily. 'How could they be waiting for us?'

Gates was incandescent. 'How? Charlie, isn't it obvious? Somebody talked!'

Patsy took three quick steps back, out of range of his hands. Then her eyes flew to Donovan.

'Don't look at me,' he said rapidly, 'I've been chaperoned since I got here, the only way I could've talked to anyone is by telepathy.'

Gates stared at him, the elf eyes sharp as flint; then he nodded. 'I know that. I don't think it was you, or anyone here. Thanks to Harry and his bright ideas, two of our people are sitting in police cells right now. I imagine the pressure proved too much for one of them. Martin, probably – kids can't take it like a grown man.' He shook his head in angry disbelief. 'He can't have told them much or they'd be here. But he's said enough for them to watch the places we'd want to hit at the times we'd want to hit them.'

Charlie cleared his throat. 'Maybe not. We've done this a lot of times now – maybe they finally worked out how.'

He was too big to slap but Gates rounded on him with the same viciousness that Patsy provoked in him. 'You ever hear of police budgets, Charlie? You really think this one-horse town can afford to guard every shop we might be interested in? No, they were told.' His eyes circled the yard like cold fire, settled on the girl half behind the car. He started towards her and she shrank before him. His voice was a soft menacing monotone. 'I warned you what would happen if you let me down. I warned all of you.'

'Me, Tudor?' Her voice soared and cracked, and she stumbled backwards, trying to keep the vehicle between them. 'I haven't done nothing. I never told nobody.'

'You robbed that train. That's where our troubles began. But for that we'd have been finished here days ago. Harry'd be alive, nobody'd be in jail, nobody'd be talking to policemen.' His hands went to his narrow waist, tugging at the buckle of his belt.

Stripped of the social polish he was just another thug, cleverer than some, nastier than plenty. In the face of failure the elegant manner, the well-modulated voice, the air of gentle irony all deserted him and the man who bet on which dog could rip out another's throat was revealed.

'You've been trouble since I first clapped eyes on you,' hissed Gates, stalking her leopard-like between the cars. 'You were another of Harry's bright ideas: I should have told him to stick to driving then, if I had he'd still be here. But he wanted you in and I gave way. I thought, What harm can it do? But you poisoned him. Did you think I didn't know?' His voice turned to savage mimicry. ' "Oh, Harry, you're the best man here. Oh, Harry, you could be so much more than just a driver. Oh, Harry, why don't we do something of our own while Tudor's away? Do what I say, Harry, and I'll let you shove it up me some more!" '

The girl screamed at him in terror, 'That's not true! I *never* told him to go behind your back. Sure I liked him, but I was happy the way things were. The train was Harry's idea – I just went along for the laugh.'

'Then why aren't you laughing now?' Almost close enough to grab her, the little man moved on the balls of his feet like a dancer, the belt in his hand swinging free. 'Laugh, Patsy. Go on – laugh.'

It was as if no one else was there, just the two of them engaged in some sadistic game. Andy watched with a malevolent satisfaction that was clearly, if unconsciously, sexual. Charlie's broad face screwed up unhappily and he raised a hand in protest but somehow lacked the resolve to intervene.

Which left Donovan. Different rules apply under cover but he still didn't see how he could stand by while a vicious little crook flogged a young girl. OK, the girl was also a vicious little crook, but what she was mattered less than what Donovan was. All that crap about the King's Shilling: funny thing was, it mattered. You didn't take the money then make excuses not to do the job. You didn't do only those parts of the job that were easy and safe and got you home by six every night. You did, in so far as you were able, what needed doing, and accepted the long hours and the risks that came with the package.

And you didn't stand by and watch someone commit an assault occasioning grievous bodily harm. That was funny, too. He'd known the girl was a threat to him, thought it was because she remembered him from the train. But it would have made no difference if she'd forgotten him, had never seen him, if he'd never been on the train. What was going to betray him was his own sense of duty.

So he slipped behind Gates and reached over his

shoulder to catch his wrist as he raised his hand. 'Don't do that.'

Charlie stared at him in horror, Andy in resentment, Patsy in shock. Gates spun dervish-like, wresting his arm free, his face aglow with indignation. Coals sparked in the amber eyes. Like a foul-mouthed child he yelled at the top of his voice, 'Take your fucking hands off me!'

Donovan had just enough time to think, 'He really is mad. He's got no more control than a kid in a tantrum.' Then Gates's right arm whipped back, and the narrow strap split the air and opened Donovan's cheek to the bone.

Shock cushioned him from the pain. He was aware of the skin parting as under a blade; clapping his hand to it he met the start of blood. For a moment he could only stand and pant, fighting light-headedness. When that receded anger came. He fastened both hands in Gates's clothes and lifted him on to his toes. 'You little shit! Take my hands off you? I'll turn you over my knee and spank you.' He dropped him then, thrusting him away like week-old rubbish. 'Or I would if I didn't think you'd enjoy it.'

Charlie separated them, one big hand on Donovan's shoulder, stopping short of laying the other on Gates but interposing his solid body. 'Come on, now,' he rumbled mollifyingly. 'Let's cool it, shall we? Enough's gone wrong without us laying into one another.' He looked at Donovan's cheek, winced and groped in his pocket; but all he came up with was a used tissue and a toffee-paper.

Forced to stand back, Gates too was appalled at what he'd done. In his pocket was a newly laundered handkerchief. He took it out and proffered it. 'Hugh, I'm so sorry.' His voice had dropped a full octave from that banshee wail to a murmur of apparently sincere regret.

Donovan regarded him sourly for some moments but finally took the handkerchief. 'What, no lace?' he growled. When he touched it gingerly to his cheek it came away dyed in his blood.

The murderous rage had passed but Gates had not forgiven Patsy. His eyes on her were cold with hatred. 'This was your fault. Pack your gear and get out. If you show your face again I'll bury you.'

People come into crime in all sorts of ways – by design, carelessness or accident, for the money, for the kicks. Mostly it serves up more problems than solutions, but it fast becomes a way of life and the way out is not the way back. When Harry Black brought her in it was the nearest thing to a family Patsy could remember. Difficult as it was to imagine a way of life so bankrupt, so bereft of meaning, that dossing in tumbledown cottages between ram-raids was a step up, that was where Patsy had come from. And she didn't want to go back. So Gates's threat shook her in a way that his hands never had, that even the lash of his belt would not have done. Patsy couldn't face being alone again.

Whether it also shook loose a last chip of memory, like the last slate that hangs on for days after the storm before falling, or whether she remembered earlier and couldn't think what to do about it, there was no way of knowing. But her eyes flared at him and she shook her head urgently, the electric hair dancing. 'Tudor, no! You can't send me away. It's not my fault! I didn't grass you up, he did!'

Donovan looked up balefully over the bloody rag but there was no question about it: she'd finally decided where her loyalties lay. She was practically poking him in the eye.

Gates's gaze was caustic with disbelief. 'You – poison! He took that for you.' He jerked a hand at Donovan's cheek. 'That would have been your face if he hadn't stepped in.'

She shot back, 'He isn't who you think! You think that dog in the shed makes him one of us but he's not. He isn't even Hugh Duggan. His name's Donovan, he was on the train, and Harry reckoned it was him called the police.'

Chapter Twenty

So sure was she that it was Brian ringing the doorbell,
Liz didn't even hurry to answer it. She wiped her face,
composed her mind – a little, it would have taken too
long to do the job properly – and fixed at the front of
it what she wanted to say. She certainly owed him an
apology, probably more than that, but something less
than her soul. Where they went from here would have
to be discussed, but whatever she'd said she didn't
want to go alone. He was an ordinary man in many
ways – too often she had put him aside while she
dealt with urgent and important matters – but she was
amazed at the size of the gap his absence left in her.
That was the first thing she had to say.

It wasn't Brian. Gail Fisher of the *Courier* stood half
sideways on the step as if expecting a rebuff. Liz
blinked. She wasn't surprised that Fisher knew where
she lived; she was astonished to see her here. 'I'm
sorry, Gail, I've nothing to add to what I said in court.'
A brittle note conveyed her displeasure.

'I'm sure.' Fisher nodded quickly. 'That isn't –
exactly – why I'm here. Can we talk for a moment? I
won't stay, I don't want to embarrass you, I just thought
I ought to warn you about – well, what I've done.'

Liz sighed, took her to the living-room. 'I didn't just

come floating down the Arrow on a bubble, you know. I'm not going to be amazed to see what I said in open court quoted in Thursday's *Courier.*

'Well, that's the point,' said Fisher. She seemed ill at ease, perched on the edge of the big sofa as if poised for flight. 'You won't have to wait till Thursday – I've given something to the dailies for tomorrow morning. I've also recorded a piece for the local radio: it'll be in their news magazine at nine tonight.'

If she'd thought about it Liz would have anticipated as much. She'd known she was crossing a Rubicon, hadn't expected or even wanted the reporter to shirk her obligations in order to protect her, like a child or an imbecile who couldn't take responsibility for her own actions. Once Liz had decided on her course, the sooner everybody knew the facts, the better.

She nodded slowly. 'Thanks for telling me. I'll call my father – he's the only person who matters who doesn't already know.'

Fisher swivelled quickly in her seat, her body bent forward. 'Inspector – Liz – I'm so sorry about what happened. The last thing I want to do is make things harder. I'm on your side: you do know that? Most people will be on your side. I don't think you'll regret what you did.'

Liz smiled tightly. 'Let's hope not.' The rape was different: that was a crime. She had no intention of discussing personal business, like the danger that what she'd done had destroyed her marriage.

As she was leaving, Fisher took her hand and held it a moment. Not a woman to whom casual intimacies came naturally, Liz was about to take it back; but the current of sympathy that travelled across the bridge stayed her a moment. She pressed the other woman's hand in reply. 'Thanks for coming. I know what to expect now.'

'Maybe; maybe not,' murmured Fisher.

Charlie lashed Donovan's hands to a pipe under the low roof of the byre. Agitated by the sudden flurry of activity the dogs could be heard whining and scratching at the wall of the adjoining pigsty.

Donovan didn't stand peaceably to be hung up like washing: he struggled and swore until Charlie knocked the fight out of him with a single punch under the ribs. He dropped doubled-up on the floor; Charlie lifted him and finished the job. His face close to Donovan's he murmured, 'You're in deep shit now, son.'

Gates was watching Donovan's face, waiting for the pain in his belly to be enough for him to worry what came next. When he saw the hurt in his eyes turn to fear, Gates began to speak. 'You're a policeman, aren't you?'

There was no point lying. He'd known Gates would work it out if he had anything to go on. Donovan nodded, setting off ripples of complaint in his wrists and midriff.

'And that's your name – Donovan?'

'Detective Sergeant Donovan. I'd show you my warrant card but I left it at home.' The ache under his ribs meant it took him two breaths to get it out.

Gates gave a tiny smile. 'I'll take your word. You work with Mr Shapiro then.'

Donovan was startled. 'You know him?'

'My homework includes weighing up the opposition. I've been to his house – I left him a souvenir.'

For an Irishman of Donovan's generation the words had only one meaning and it wasn't a pottery castle inscribed 'A Present From Portrush'. His racing heart missed a beat. 'A bomb?'

Gates laughed, a tinkling laugh merry with natural cruelty, like a child pulling the legs off a spider to see how many it needs to run away. 'Of course not. It may have been a bit of a bomb*shell* – you don't expect an anatomy lesson on your path first thing in the morning.'

'The skinned dog – that was you? *Why?*'

'I was cross with him. I got back from a dog-fight at three in the morning to find I'd no crew left – except for Charlie who was anxiously rehearsing ways of breaking the news! I wanted to hit back. I had Andy collect one of the night's losers and we took that round to him. I kind of hoped it might give him paws for thought.' The pun was wasted: no one so much as smiled. Gates gave a martyred little sigh.

Donovan was trying to think. 'You know he's looking for you? When he missed us in town he'd go back and talk to your friends again. He could be here any minute.'

'Yes, he could,' agreed Gates; 'if someone talked. But then, perhaps I did them an injustice. Perhaps all Mr Shapiro knows came from you.' He held his head on one side like an intelligent budgie. 'In which case, as long as he doesn't hear from you again we're safe.'

'He didn't hear from me this time. I'd no chance – damn it, you *know* that! It had to be someone else.' But Gates just smiled.

Donovan tugged but the belt securing his hands

only tightened. He glanced bitterly round the crew. Charlie wouldn't meet his eyes. In the doorway the girl sniffed and turned away. Andy leered at him with expectancy.

Gates seemed avuncular by comparison. The all-consuming rage had not returned, for which Donovan was glad: beside himself with fury he could kill as easily as spit. As long as he was in control he would put his long-term interests first.

But still Donovan didn't expect Gates to cut him down, help him put Brian Boru in the van and wave him goodbye. He'd thought if it got this far he might take a thumping before they made their escape. Well, no one had thumped him yet, not really. But somehow he wasn't reassured.

Gates said, 'Charlie, take Patsy and the car and get on your way. Head north up the motorway – they won't expect that. Me and Andy'll follow in the 4x4. We'll meet you at the second services. Get me a Danish and a *cappuccino* – we'll be there before it's cold.'

The big man looked quickly from Gates to Donovan and then at the floor. 'Um—'

Gates gave an understanding smile. 'Don't worry, we'll be right behind you. I just want to say goodbye to Sergeant Donovan.'

'He's getting rid of you, Charlie,' Donovan said, fast, before Gates could intervene or Charlie could leave and pretend he hadn't heard. 'He wants rid of you because you've got the wit to keep him off me. You're a thief, Charlie, that's all – if you'd been caught today that's all you'd have been charged with. If they catch you tomorrow the charge'll be the attempted murder of a police officer.'

'Shut up, Sergeant,' said Gates pleasantly.

'Or what?' snorted Donovan. 'You'll make me sorry? You're going to beat the shit out of me! I know that, you know it – Charlie knows it too, don't you? You don't like it, you don't need it, but unless you stop him now you're going to get a piece of it. When you're caught it'll make about four years' difference to your sentence.'

The big man raised unhappy eyes to Gates. He wasn't a fool, just a man who sometimes found it convenient to fool himself. He knew why Gates wanted him to leave. If he'd meant only to rough the policeman up he'd have done it in front of them all, as an example. If he wanted privacy it was because he meant to go further than that. 'Coach?'

Gates explained clearly and gently. 'He's a spy, Charlie. I can't let that pass and he knows it. He knows he's going to get hurt. He thinks he can split us by appealing to your better nature. You can't blame him: in the same circumstances anyone would lie. I want you to leave because showing him the error of his ways will take a few minutes and it'll be safest if you and Patsy go now.'

Charlie didn't need it to be true, only tolerably convincing. He didn't want a show-down with Gates: all he needed was a sop to his conscience and, if the worst happened, some ammunition for his brief. So he had every incentive to believe. Head down he shouldered past Gates and out into the yard.

Donovan saw his last best chance disappearing and yelled after him – 'Charlie!' – his voice soaring.

Gates murmured, 'Andy,' and the boy hit Donovan again where Charlie had. It wasn't a comparable blow but it was enough to take his breath away. By the time he had it back he could hear the car's engine dwindling down the lane.

'Just us now,' said Gates softly. 'And the dogs.'

Andy brought them from next door, a chain in each hand. Neither was muzzled, restrained only by collars like plough-harness, the chains making wild music as they pulled and tossed. But this wasn't a match situation, and though they were excited to be on the move the dogs weren't looking for a fight.

'And the other one,' said Gates.

Andy secured his brace to a handy bracket and left again. Donovan heard mingled snarls and shouts and hoped for the best, but Andy returned with Brian Boru.

Gates was watching Donovan's face. 'You've seen pit-bulls at work, you know what they can do to one another. I imagine you've also seen what they can do to people.'

Donovan's lip curled thinly but he said nothing, damned if he'd give Gates the satisfaction. He'd gone into this knowing he could get thumped; if he got bitten instead it might mean tetanus shots instead of X-rays but it would be the same freckled Irish nurse at Castle General dressing his wounds and lecturing him on his lifestyle. He thought he could take anything Gates could do to him.

Gates saw him think it and the V-shaped smile was brilliant. 'What – you think I'm *bluffing*? Winding you up for the pleasure of seeing you sweat? I'm sorry, Donovan, you were right the first time, when you told Charlie I was going to damn near murder you. Well, nearly right.'

He pivoted on his heel, gazing at the dogs. 'See

those, Donovan? Those are three of the best fighting dogs in Britain. I include your Brian because I know potential when I see it. I'd put serious money on any one of them to beat any other dog on the circuit.

'But anything palls eventually, even dog-fighting. And then you start wondering, is that all they can do? Dogs have been used to hunt elk, and lion, and bait bears and bulls. And hunt men. Could my dogs do that? Could they tackle the cleverest, most dangerous game of all?' Again he looked to Donovan for some reaction; again his only reward was the dew gathered on Donovan's lip.

He shrugged lightly. 'In theory they could. Dogs with no training at all have turned on and killed human beings so a trained fighting dog should have no problem. A quarry with no jaws to speak of, puny muscles, throat and belly exposed – it ought to be a foregone conclusion. But for the psychology. In their heads, dogs take the orders and men give them. Half their training has been about obedience, about accepting men as their pack leaders. Now I'm asking them to forget all that and kill a human being in cold blood.'

Donovan had been a policeman long enough to hear a lot of threats: if he'd taken them all seriously he'd have been a nervous wreck. Most threats were like a dog growling, an attempt to avoid rather than start a fight. Like dogs, people who wanted to hurt you didn't waste time on threats – they went straight for the throat.

'All right,' he said with a kind of world-weary nonchalance, 'What do you want?'

Gates blinked. 'Want?'

Donovan licked dry lips. 'What is it you want? My

216

chief could be here any time so you're not doing this for fun. There's something you want, something you think I can get for you. What is it? Tell me, let's see what we can do before one of them dogs gets loose and bites somebody.'

Gates was genuinely delighted. 'You do, don't you – you really think I'm saying this to frighten you! Why? For a safe passage? I don't need you for that, there's no one out there. Maybe Mr Shapiro will get here eventually; but I'll be long gone and so, I'm afraid, will you.'

Donovan shook his head, the black hair dancing in his face. 'Come on, Gates, talk to me. I know you're pissed off, I don't expect to get out of this scot-free. You want me to say I'm scared? OK, I'm scared. I'm going to get hurt here, I don't know how much; damn right I'm scared. But kill me? You don't need that any more than Charlie does. They get you for killing a copper, they throw away the key. You'd have a bad time in jail.'

'I'm not going to jail,' Gates said calmly. 'That's why you have to die, Donovan. If it was a question of punishment I could settle for less, but you're a danger to me as long as you live. From a wheelchair, from an iron lung, you'd tell Mr Shapiro things I don't want him to know.

'I'm sorry to be brutal but it's too late for us to start considering each other's feelings. I have to kill you; that being so, I intend to find out what these dogs can do. It's a chance I may never have again. I want to see how they solve the problem of killing a man.'

He gave an apologetic little shrug, as if he wasn't sure of the etiquette, the right thing to say next. 'It shouldn't take long. Supremacy isn't an issue: once they accept that you're fair game it'll be like killing a sheep – quicker, because you won't be running away. A few minutes should do it. The terminal wards are full of people who wish they could get it over that fast.'

Finally Donovan believed. Gates meant exactly what he said. He wasn't bluffing, he wasn't out to trade, he wasn't going to change his mind. This was where it ended: in screams and in blood. Donovan had seen it, knew what it was like when those jaws ripped into living flesh. A few minutes? – maybe. But minutes like those defied measurement on any clock.

His mouth was so dry he had trouble getting the words out. 'Untie me?'

'Don't be absurd.'

But Donovan wasn't thinking of escape, only of getting it over. He knew now that Gates wouldn't be satisfied with kicking his lights out, that he meant to kill him and to kill him this way. But Donovan didn't want to hang by his hands while the dogs leapt for him, tearing his flesh. With his hands free he still couldn't make a fight of it but on the ground he'd die quicker. 'For God's sake, man! How much do you reckon I owe you?'

Gates had no compassion. He didn't mind how long it took, how much trial and error. But he was concerned that the dogs might be inhibited by the fundamental difference between men and all their natural prey: that men go upright. If they could drag him down they would make their kill, but Gates was worried they would continue to consider the man taboo as long as he hung over them. This was a unique opportunity

– he couldn't try again if he got it wrong. He nodded slowly. 'All right.'

He needed to protect himself until the dogs took over. There were some tools just inside the door, rusted past identification except for a pitchfork. Distastefully brushing away the cobwebs he took it up. 'Cut him down, Andy. Leave his hands tied.'

Donovan staggered as the weight came off his arms but the pitchfork brought him up short. Numb with fear, it never occurred to him that the quickest way out of this was simply to keep going. He backed off, his bound hands before him, his eyes flickering between Gates and the puzzled fretful dogs. His breathing was ragged and under his clothes his body ran with sweat.

Accustomed to handling unreliable animals, Andy edged cautiously round him. Both he and Gates seemed to expect Donovan would *do* something. But fear disarmed him. All he could do was back away and hope to hang on to the contents of his stomach.

'All right,' Gates said softly from the door. 'Slip the dogs.'

'One at a time or all together?'

'All of them,' said Gates with a shudder. 'You won't want to go back in once the action starts.'

But Andy didn't share the older man's dread. He was a skilled handler, better than many men who'd been doing it longer, and he took pride in that. These dogs were part of him, their strength, their fury and their triumphs were all his. He wasn't afraid of anyone while he had such allies. He hooked the chains off the collars and the dogs milled round his legs. His lip curled disdainfully as Donovan stumbled back till the wall ended his retreat.

The dogs padded after Donovan with more curiosity than aggression, smelled his fear but couldn't work out what it meant. Sunk protectively in the fleshy folds of their faces, agleam with unexpected intelligence, their eyes pinned him to the wall.

Andy gave a chuckle. 'They don't know what to do. Come on, you useless lot, a man's nothing but a big rabbit standing on his back legs – he'll come apart just the same. Come on, do what you're trained for!' He aimed an encouraging boot at a muscular backside.

The shouts, the insults, the fear and excitement building in the byre struck a chord of familiarity in the dogs. Oh – *that* was what it was about, was it? They understood that, understood all about fighting – they just weren't sure what it was they were meant to fight. The milling became increasingly energetic and agitated, the animals snapping and snarling at each other in their confusion.

Then one, bolder or meaner than the others, reached a decision. Circling behind the pack he pirouetted on his back feet and launched himself into the air with all the strength of his powerful, agile body.

Fifty metres away in the darkness of the wood the badgers surfacing from their setts paused a moment in their business and raised their heads, startled by a man's screams echoing round the little cluster of buildings that had stood for so long silent.

Chapter Twenty-one

After she'd spoken to her father, Liz sat in the dark, debating whether she should listen to Gail Fisher's broadcast. She had no wish to. She knew Fisher wouldn't deliberately make things worse, but the bare facts were sensational enough. Liz had managed to keep her feelings under control thus far, but inside the edges remained steak-raw and even at her most optimistic she knew they must for the foreseeable future. Being talked about on the public airwaves would be an unpleasant experience.

But she thought she ought to listen. Inevitably the talk of the town tomorrow, she needed to know exactly what had been said and how much of the gossip was innocent exaggeration and how much malicious embroidery. She decided to grit her teeth and tune in. In a way, it was easier having the house to herself. She'd have hated someone listening along with her, sympathizing.

In the event the decision was taken out of her hands. As she was fiddling with the radio the phone rang; clicking her tongue impatiently she lifted it and said, 'Can you make this quick?' – and then her insides curled up with the fear that it might be Brian.

It was Shapiro. He sounded taken aback. 'Sorry?'

Liz sighed. 'Sorry, Frank, I was expecting – some-one else. What is it, your ram-raiders struck again?'

'No, but they have been sighted. The car Keith Baker saw? – it's heading north on the motorway with Scobie maintaining a discreet surveillance. I thought you'd like to help me pull it in.'

Fleetingly she considered telling him about the broadcast; but it was too much like fate stepping in. She'd tell him later, when it was too late for either of them to listen. 'I'll pick you up at the office.'

By the time she'd collected Shapiro and the area car for back-up, Scobie was reporting developments. The vehicle he was following had pulled into a service area and the two occupants, a large man and a young girl, had gone into the café. Scobie had used his initia-tive, and the hoof-pick attachment on his Swiss Army knife, to immobilize their car before following.

When he saw a knot of people, half of them in uniform, coming purposefully across the concourse, Charlie knew the game was up. He finished his tea then spread his hands on the Formica table-top. 'Remember,' he said dully, 'you say nothing.'

But Patsy wasn't a career criminal, couldn't accept the risk of imprisonment with the same glum fatalism. She leapt up from the table, spilling her drink, and took off through the concourse like a hot prospect for The Oaks.

Liz could hardly have hoped for a better antidote to her own problems. Slapping her handbag against Shapiro's chest she said firmly, 'Mine,' and set off in pursuit.

A rack of paperbacks and a cardboard cut-out chef went flying as they scattered startled travellers. An amiable drunk was still trying to decide if he'd really been pushed aside by a snip of a girl moving like an express train when he was definitely pushed aside by a woman moving if anything faster.

They swept through the sweets and tobacco, through the souvenirs and novelties, on past the washrooms, between the slot-machines and children's rides. Beyond the rocking-horses and space-ships beckoned the black glass square of the back door. Once through it Patsy had the whole of the lorry park in which to lose herself. Insofar as she had a natural habitat, motorway lorry parks were it.

Not for the first time in racing history the prize was won in the last furlong by the best farrier. Patsy was wearing boots. Liz had on her lace-ups, and they felt like part of her. As Patsy snatched for the back door Liz grabbed a handful of frizzy fair hair and swung her in a crisp arc against the wall. With what breath she had left she gasped, 'You, my girl, are nicked.'

The expression Honour Among Thieves had never made much impression on Patsy. Her only motive was self-interest, and she was still just young enough to blame that on other people. Perhaps a decent up-bringing wouldn't have turned her into the Singing Nun, but now there was no way of knowing. Now she was the Planet Patsy surrounded only by hostile space, and she put herself first, last and everywhere in between because no one else gave her any priority at all.

She'd been there, just outside the door, when the policeman begged for Charlie's help. She'd said nothing because, then, she quite literally didn't care whether Donovan lived or died. The situation was different now. She needed something to bargain with. 'I can help you! You know a guy called Donovan? Tudor's going to kill him. You can stop it, but you'll never find them in time without me.'

Liz's racing breath caught in her throat. Scenarios flashed across her eyes. She loosed the girl's hair, fastened both hands in her lapels and lifted her until they were nose to nose. With infinite menace she growled, 'I've had a difficult week and I'm not in the mood for this. Why don't you tell me everything you know before I accidentally drop you head first into the Magic Roundabout?'

The time for discretion was over. The little convoy raced for the cottage with every light flashing, every siren wailing, every corner taken at speed and preferably on two wheels. Scobie adored it: *this* was what he joined the police for!

Even in the dark Patsy took them straight there, pointing out the byre as Liz stopped the car. The swinging headlights picked up the big dark 4×4 and, behind it, Donovan's van.

'Well, it's the right place,' said Liz. 'And they haven't left yet. Everybody watch out for those dogs: if they're on the loose we may have to wait for Armed Response to deal with them.' She'd let PC Stark drive, spent the short rough trip on the radio getting help. Gates and the boy she'd have tackled, but not the dogs. Patsy had left the cottage too soon to know how Gates intended to use them, but the mere fact of their presence here demanded caution despite the urgent need to find Donovan.

'Remember who brought you here,' whined the girl.

Liz turned on her an unforgiving stare. 'Don't worry, Patsy, nobody's going to forget your part in this.'

The prisoners were driven away then. Liz shouted after Scobie, 'I want Armed Response back here fastest. If they haven't left when you reach Queen's Street, put a bomb under them.'

Shapiro glowered. 'I should have thought of that sooner. I *knew* Gates had fighting dogs, I should have realized we'd need some way to neutralize them. Well, we'll just have to manage till the firearms get here. The uniforms have truncheons: you and I had better find something to carry.' He raised his voice. 'And if one of those things comes at you, beat its brains out first and we'll agree a story for the RSPCA later.'

There were five of them, the two detectives and three uniforms. It had been a matter of grabbing whoever they could without turning Queen's Street into the *Mary Celeste*.

Armed with a torch and a stout stick from the woodpile, Liz moved towards the byre. She knew the risks, but if she didn't go first then either a man nearing retirement or a junior officer would. And in an odd way recent events had not so much cowed her as made her reckless. She was just about ready to face another assailant: with her wits about her and a length of kindling she could begin getting her own back.

The door of the shed was ajar, hemmed with light. She listened a moment but heard nothing. She glanced back: the men with her were ready. 'If they're in here, try not to let them by. If they get as far as the wood we'll never find them.'

Someone ventured, 'Shouldn't we wait for the guns?'

'With DS Donovan in there?'

The hand on her arm was Shapiro's. He said quietly, 'Liz, if he is—'

She knew what he was saying, rounded on him furiously. 'I know. But certifying death is a doctor's job, and even they reckon on being in the same building when they do it! Now, *if* everyone's ready—?' She flung the door open.

No maelstrom of thick bodies, thick legs and snapping jaws hurled at her. The single dusty bulb hanging from the low roof, reinforced by the torches crowding the door, revealed no movement of any kind. But a sickly-sweet pungency hit her in the nostrils and there was something lying on the floor.

Prepared as she was, it took her a moment to be sure it was a man. The clothes were torn to rags, dark and heavy with blood. Through the rents gaped ragged flesh. He lay on his back, face destroyed, arms flung wide. Even through the shock that struck her as odd until she realized they'd done it – the dogs – grabbed at his flailing hands and tugged him between them like children fighting over a toy.

'Oh, dear God,' whispered Shapiro. Liz felt him sway against her.

'It isn't him,' she said hoarsely. 'Frank, look. Look at the head. Under the henna rinse that isn't black hair, it's blond. It isn't Donovan.'

When he made himself look closer Shapiro saw she was right. Donovan was six foot, this boy inches shorter. And he was only a boy, Shapiro thought; and now there was no chance of him ever being anything more.

'Then where is he?'

It was Liz. Shapiro looked at her blankly for a

moment, his mental processes numbed by what they had found. 'Hm?'

She shook his arm fiercely. 'Donovan. Where is he? What happened here? There were three of them, and three dogs. This must be – what did Patsy call him? – Andy. So where's Donovan, where's Gates, and where are those bloody dogs?'

Andy's mistake was in kicking not one of his own dogs, that associated him with nice things like food and walks, but Brian Boru, who didn't. It was an easy mistake to make – in a mill of agitated dogs one over-muscled backside looks much like another – but that moment's carelessness cost him his life. Brian had run the gauntlet of men's boots since he was a pup, didn't know there was such a thing as a friendly kick. Goaded to attack, he chose his own target.

Any one dog would probably have sunk its teeth somewhere soft, registered the resultant yell with a smirk and left it at that. But there were three of them, and three dogs is a pack. A pack doesn't behave in the same way as a single dog. It has no inhibitions, lacks that judicious combination of foresight and self-interest that serves dogs, and many people, as a conscience. It has no sense of fear.

A single dog will rarely bite because it feels about people the way most people feel about the police: they're strong, they have long memories and they never forgive. But the same dog in a pack situation is like a man on speed. Nothing scares him. He can't see that he's making trouble for himself: all he cares about is being in the thick of things, showing what he's made of. Mutual reinforcement escalates the situation until the pack has a nature and purpose of its own and all the well-trained, nice-mannered, thoroughly reliable dogs within it have shrugged off the trappings of civilization. By then it's out of control.

Brian's attack pressed the pack buttons in Gates's dogs. Swept away on a surge of adrenalin they forgot that the boy filling the air with screams and the scent of blood was their friend. As pack members their only allegiance was to each other. In the excitement of the moment instinct and training meshed so that they reacted as they always did to something struggling and shrieking and bleeding: they dragged him down and went for his throat.

Donovan cringed against the back wall, his eyes saucering, his forearms over his ears to muffle the sound. He made no attempt to intervene; nor would he have done had his hands been free; nor, he truly believed, had the victim been not a boy who'd tried to kill him but a casual bystander, even a friend. Afraid to his heart's core, he didn't think he could have waded into that frenzy to save his very soul.

He thought when they finished with Andy they'd turn on him, that his only hope was to get past while they were still fully occupied and before Gates shut the door. He dragged his eyes away from the mêlée and saw Gates watching too, gape-mouthed, through a six-inch gap, like a child watching something scary on TV from behind the couch.

There was a chance if Donovan moved now: if he left this corner running and hit the door before Gates could shoot the bolt.

The boy was quiet, dead or dying; though his body

still jerked under the dusty bulb, that was the dogs worrying at him. If they lost interest in him and looked round . . . But waiting could only make things worse. Donovan tore himself out of his corner and made a determined assault on the world sprint record.

Gates saw him a moment too late. He should have bolted the door as soon as Andy was beyond help. But the dog hadn't come near him, and by the time he realized the danger was not the animals, Donovan was two strides away. With a wordless howl he dropped his pitchfork and slammed the door.

But Donovan's shoulder hit it as it closed and he was travelling fast enough to burst it wide, flinging the smaller man half-way across the yard before he too stumbled and crashed in the dirt.

The vehicles. Inside one he'd be safe. The van was nearest: Donovan lurched to his feet and yanked at the door. But he'd locked it: he hadn't thought there was anything inside that could give him away but he didn't want anyone poking through it just in case. The 4x4 then.

He peered towards the shed. The weak light inside was enough to show him the broad-shouldered bulk of a dog standing in the doorway. He caught his breath and shrank back. But the frenzy was over, at least for now. It swaggered out like a boxer, unhurried, the big head swinging from side to side, scenting for him. The dark was no shield – it knew he was there, it would smell him out.

He didn't know where the other dogs were. But the longer he stayed here wondering, the more likely one of them was to find him. It didn't matter if they saw him as long as he reached the 4x4 first. He filled his lungs, cursed Gates's belt that he hadn't time to worry loose from his wrists, and ran.

Silhouetted against the light the dog's head came up as it saw him. Then it headed for him – not at speed, in a steady powerful lope. It could have caught him if it had tried but he reached the car with metres to spare and was already venting a relieved sigh as he reached for the nearside door.

It didn't move. He tried the handle again, anxiously – none of the dogs was more than a few seconds away – but still the door resisted him.

He scrambled round to the back – he hadn't realized how *long* the damn thing was! – and grabbed for the tailgate. The handle moved just enough for him to think he was safe, then stopped. Too scared now even to curse he kept going, down the long side to the driver's door.

A dog's head, raised in interest, appeared round the back of the vehicle.

Inside the light came on. For a fragment of a second Donovan thought it was because the door was opening. But someone inside had turned it on.

Gates had had the same idea; better luck or a sharper memory had brought him to the 4x4 first, and once inside he'd locked the doors. His elfin face was in profile; Donovan rattled the handle urgently but he didn't look round. He'd turned the light on only so Donovan could see that it was not luck that had defeated him. Then he turned it off again.

Donovan tugged at the door hard enough to rock the car, but he knew he was wasting time. A second dog joined the first at the rear of the vehicle, watching him. Breathing lightly, keeping his eye on them, he backed away round the bonnet. He threw a hunted glance towards the kitchen door, caught the hint of a stealthy movement. God, they had all his bolt-holes covered! Was it just luck or were they stalking him?

If he could reach the road, sooner or later a car would come. Sooner or later was too late. His eyes returned to the van. He must have had the keys: what happened to them? He patted his pockets, without success.

Still slowly backing he came against the broken fence and almost fell. One of the dogs bounded forward at that, just a single bounce that ended as Donovan righted himself. That would be the end. If he went down they'd have him.

He didn't want to go into the wood. Against other men he'd have held his own in there; against dogs he had no chance. But they were driving him that way. He didn't dare advance on them, they were bound to take that as a challenge. He picked his way carefully over the fence, still with his face to the dogs, and after a moment the green hem of the wood lifted for him.

He thought, I can climb – even with my hands tied I can climb six feet up a tree. They can't. If I can get higher than they can jump I'm safe, I can sit them out – for frigging days, if need be!

The last thing he meant to do was run. The dogs were curious about him, were trailing him at a distance – he could see the glint of eyes in the darkness – but there was no overt aggression about their movements yet. If he did nothing to make himself a target, like running, they might decide he was no fun and curl up for a snooze instead.

He backed steadily, and before the branches closed

round him he could see the distance between them stretching. The dogs were staying with the familiar smells of the cottage yard. The broken fence, that they could have sailed in an instant, seemed to mark the limit of their territory.

Another moment and he'd have been out of sight. But then one of the dogs seemed to realize he was escaping. It let out a sharp bark, hurdled the remains of the fence and bounded through the tangle of briars and long grass towards him, the others on its tail.

Donovan turned and fled. There was no sense in it – he didn't think he could outrun them, not in the open and not among the trees. But nor could he stand and wait for them. He ran as fast as he could, with the branches whipping his face and the black trunks looming out of the darkness almost, and sometimes entirely, too late for him to avoid them. Twice he fell, rolled and was on his feet and running again before the impetus of his flight was lost. He could hear the dogs crashing through the undergrowth, couldn't judge how close they were.

The third time he fell he knew it was over before he hit the ground. More than the pain, he heard his ankle break. He couldn't run any further, or climb, or defend himself. Andy's death had bought him a little time, nothing more. Instinct made him grope, on his hands and knees in the leaf-mould, for a tree to put at his back; when he found one he turned towards the sounds crashing towards him, just in time to catch the gleam of errant filtered moonlight off a sleak-coated, surging body sweeping down on him out of the blackness. He threw up his arms, and yelled once, and then it was on him.

Chapter Twenty-two

'Sir.' PC Stark was standing beside the 4×4, shining his torch inside. 'There's someone in here.'

Though he knew Donovan wouldn't be lurking in a darkened car, Shapiro found himself hurrying. There was no need: the man inside wasn't going anywhere. With the doors locked and the windows up, what he was sitting in wasn't so much a get-away car as a bunker. Despite the torches playing on his face he stared ahead almost without blinking, and Shapiro thought that if they hadn't come he'd probably have sat there until he starved.

'Shock?' asked Liz.

Shapiro nodded towards the shed. 'If I'd seen that happen I'd be pretty shocked, too.'

'Is it Gates?'

'I think so. He fits the description, plus he's the only one unaccounted for.' He tapped on the window. 'Mr Gates, you can come out now. It's quite safe.'

Gates looked at him then, his head turning slowly, mechanically. His eyes were glassy and he seemed quite disconnected from reality. He neither spoke nor reached for the door. After a few seconds his eyes slid forward again.

Stark said, 'Shall I open it, sir?'

Shapiro nodded. 'He can't stay in there forever.'

'Ask him about Donovan,' Liz said edgily, playing her torch round the yard while they waited. 'Better still, let me ask him.'

Shapiro's glance was faintly amused. 'You've been watching *Dirty Harry* films again. Calm down a minute. Let me talk to him. A minute won't make any difference at this stage.'

'No?' she shot back. 'Well, Donovan's missing and so are those dogs. If they're together, a minute could make all the difference in the world.'

Stark had the door open. Shapiro leaned his hand on the wheel. 'You're Tudor Gates, aren't you? Sergeant Donovan told me. And the boy inside is your friend Andy.'

At that, something flickered in the vacant eyes.

'There's an ambulance on its way,' Shapiro said gently, 'but I think he's dead. The dogs killed him, did they?'

That, finally, got a response. Puppet-like, Gates nodded. 'The dogs.' His voice was a broken whisper.

'Where are the dogs? Andy's in the shed but the dogs aren't there now. Where did they go?'

'Ask about *Donovan*,' hissed Liz.

Shapiro hissed back, 'I *am*!'

Gates whispered pathetically, 'My poor boy,' and a tear slid down beside his nose.

'They turned on him, didn't they?' Shapiro said softly. 'Then what? They took off? We have to find them before they attack someone else. Did Sergeant Donovan go after them?'

Gates blinked his eyes clear, intelligence creeping back; his head came up and the gaze that met the policeman's was haughty. 'No, Superintendent Shapiro, he did not.'

'Then where is he?'

Gates indicated the wood.

'And the dogs?'

'The same.'

Shapiro frowned. 'You said—'

Gates spat his hatred like venom. 'You think I'm lying? Why on earth would I bother lying to you? I said your spy didn't chase my dogs into the wood. You're the detective: you work it out.'

Liz already had. 'He wasn't chasing them,' she said briefly, already heading for the fence, 'they were chasing him.'

Shapiro wanted to lead the search. But someone had to stay with Gates, and pragmatically it had to be him. 'If things get hairy in there, seniority won't hold a candle to the ability to shin up a tree,' said Liz.

That earned a grim chuckle. 'I'll stay till the firearms get here and I can pass this' – he couldn't find a suitable word, shook a finger at Gates instead – 'on to someone else. Be careful, Liz. Stay close together. Don't even try to catch the dogs, just find Donovan. If he's hurt, stay with him and wait for us. We won't be far behind.'

Powerful torches turned the black wood into architecture, ranks of trunks receding into the shadows like columns, arching branches forming a vault like the undercroft of a great cathedral.

They spread out across a front thirty metres wide, close enough to bunch up if danger threatened, far enough apart to search a useful swathe of woodland. They weren't looking for a carelessly discarded cigarette butt, they were looking for a man, possibly injured, possibly worse. Speed was more important than precision. They moved at a pace between a strong walk and a jog, and they called and every thirty seconds they stopped and listened.

They'd been searching for a few minutes when Stark heard something. He didn't know what – a hoarse cry, the bark of a dog or fox, the grunt of a badger, maybe only an old tree groaning as the night grew cold. No one else heard it at all. But they wheeled in the direction he indicated. In the benighted wood one way was as good as another, and there was at least a chance that what Stark had heard was the missing man.

A minute later a shout came from that end of the line, and when she looked Liz saw that the beam of light from the furthest torch had stopped panning through the colonnade of trees to rest at the base of one of them. 'I think it's him, ma'am!'

Not until she was beside him could she see what Stark had seen. Grey on grey in the flat light of the torch, a shapeless heap among the roots of the tree, it didn't look much like a man. Her heart stumbled and she hurried down the track of Stark's torch.

'Ma'am!' The sharp note of warning brought her up short. From behind the bole of the tree another grey form was emerging. It moved deliberately, its massive head low. The light gleamed greenish off its baleful eyes. Less interested in her than in the man on the ground, it was already within one good bound of him. There was nothing they could do as quickly as the dog could reach Donovan.

Liz was breathing through parted lips. 'Everyone stay still, we don't want to alarm it.' Alarm it? Three divisions of Panzers wouldn't alarm that dog! 'Unless it goes for him, in which case we'll have to rush it.' Tightening her grip on the stave she edged forward. 'Come here, boy, come and talk to me. There's a good dog. Leave the nice man alone and come and talk to me.'

The average Labrador would have been putty in her hands, but this was no household pet. It made more sense to think of it as not a dog at all but a wild beast, savage and unpredictable. It responded to her blandishments by fluttering the lips over its scimitar teeth and emitted a growl like the starter-motor on a power-shovel.

She advanced a step at a time, her voice rhythmic, talking by turns to the dog and the men behind her. 'Good boy, take it easy. He doesn't like me this close. There's nothing to get excited about, old fellow, only me and this fence-post I'm going to beat your head in with. If he comes at me, somebody get to Donovan. Come on, there's a good boy, you don't want to take chunks out of the nasty policeman – he'll taste of engine-oil and antifouling.'

Finally, the heap under the tree stirred. A pale hand sketched a weary salute, and a voice thick with accent and frail with pain said, 'Boss – that's my dog.'

Liz sent two of the uniforms to find the paramedics; Stark stayed with her and Donovan. She sat by the tree and leaned the injured man against her, cushioning him. She took off her jacket and spread it over him. Stark took off his and put it round her shoulders.

She was content to wait for help, but Donovan couldn't rest. Wasted by pain and shock, awareness waxing and waning as if with fever, he couldn't let go of the horror, returning to it as if haunted. 'Did you see – in the byre?'

She nodded. But he couldn't see her face so she said aloud, 'Yes.'

'That should have been me.' With an effort he lifted his hands from his lap. Stark had untied him but they were swollen, clumsy and too painful with returning circulation to do whatever he had intended. He lowered them again, defeated. Under Liz's tweed jacket his thin body shivered.

She held him against her, sharing her warmth. 'Don't think about it. It's over.' By his side Brian Boru sat like a dog carved in jet.

'I can't stop seeing it,' said Donovan, his voice husky. 'Hearing him. They meant for that to be me. I was doing my job, and they wanted to see me torn apart for it.'

Anger stirred in Liz's breast – for him, for all of them. 'They're sick,' she gritted. 'They're sick, and they're vicious, and now one of them's dead and the others are going to prison. And you're going to be fine. Come on, Donovan, you've been hurt worse than this. Little old ladies of ninety-three get over broken ankles.'

That coaxed a fractional grin from him but it didn't last. 'Jesus, boss, I don't know. I think maybe this is the end. I don't think I can do it any more.'

Liz settled her arms about him firmly, holding him not like a lover, perhaps like a friend. 'What're you talking about? You'll be in plaster a couple of months, after that you'll just need to build up the strength. Footballers who break their legs are playing again before the end of the season.'

He shook his head weakly, insistently. His voice

238

was breathy as if his senses were slipping again, the words slurring. 'That's not what I mean. The leg'll mend. It's the rest of it. I don't think I can face – this – again.'

'This?' Her voice soared incredulously. 'You'll never have to face this again. This was one for the record books.'

'You're not *listening*,' Donovan whined fractiously, twisting against her, the pain of his broken ankle a hiss in his teeth. 'I'm scared, God damn it! I was never so scared in all my life. I was so bloody scared I didn't know what to do. I lost it. And I don't know how to get it back. I don't even know if I *want* it back.'

The breath caught in Liz's throat. Shocked as he was, clinging to reality by his fingernails, she knew what it cost him to say that. He was absolutely serious: for the first time in the two years she'd known him he seemed beaten. The ordeal of the last hours had been too much, psychologically and emotionally, and it had broken him.

Instinct warned that what she said now mattered.

By the time the professionals got hold of him the die would be cast: if he believed he couldn't function as a police officer any more they'd never convince him differently. But in the next few minutes, before the cavalry arrived with a stretcher and a bottle of nitrous oxide, she could do something for him. Not make things as they were: that was beyond her. And maybe not get him back to work. If he'd really had enough, she wouldn't even try.

What she could do was stop him sliding into a bad decision through being too exhausted to make a good one. She could get him back on the horse that threw him. After that, if he wanted to shoot the damn thing, stuff it and put it on castors, that was his choice. He had a right not to be a detective any more. But there were people who cared about him enough to want what was right for him, and it was his good fortune that one of them was here.

She said fervently, 'Donovan, of *course* you were scared! Do you think you shouldn't have been? Of course you freaked out! Do you think I'd have done any better? That the chief would? You can't win a situation like that, all you can do is get through somehow. It doesn't matter how. All that matters is surviving.

'And now you feel – flayed. Vivisected. It's not just the hurt, it's the helplessness. Something was done to you, something demeaning, that you were powerless to stop, and the humiliation is eating like acid into the bones of what you thought you were. A week ago you were a man with an important job, a good income, the respect of colleagues, the love of friends. Now that seems a world away. You're in a kind of limbo – alone and palely loitering in a place where no birds sing. Because something evil can crawl out of a nightmare and sink its claws in you, and use you in ways that make ashes of everything you've built.

'You know what that is, Donovan? That's rape; in every way that matters. It's not the physical assault that hurts, it's the loss of free will. We're not used to that, we thought we left it behind with childhood. Oh, we do lots of things we'd sooner not, but for adults there's always a choice. You can quit the job, end the relationship, whatever. Only the very young, maybe the very old and people in prison have no freedom and even they have rights. We assume that, between the extremes of dependency and providing we stay out of jail, we're in charge of our own lives.

'That's what the rapist destroys: the sense of autonomy. If anyone who's strong enough can dump all that about intrinsic human value and inalienable rights and use you any way he wants, the fabric between the nightmare and the real world has stretched so thin it seems it'll split wide any second and let the chaos in.'

He'd gone very still in the compass of her arms but Liz knew he was listening. Stark had gracefully withdrawn a little way, but she thought he was listening too. Only the dog, motionless at Donovan's side, holding her in its basilisk stare, was obviously listening and it couldn't understand a word.

She wanted to finish before they were interrupted. Her voice took it up again, soft but threaded through with a certainty that surprised even her. Crystallizing her thoughts for Donovan's benefit was sharpening her own understanding. 'What happened to us – both of us – was outside our control. We're not responsible, any more than if we'd been hit by a runaway truck. There was nothing to do except what we did: we endured.

'But now we have a choice. We can't pretend it never happened but we don't have to carry it through life like some great emotional burden. It happened, it's over; you got your ankle bust, I got away pretty lightly too. The scars will heal in time. It's what scars do – all they can do.' She took a deep breath that came out as a sigh. There was a kind of release in putting it into words. Her only regret was that she could talk like this to Donovan but hadn't managed to explain it to her husband.

'What I'm trying to say is that I'm not cut out to be a victim and I don't think you are either. After an air disaster, the victims are the ones who go to the funeral in boxes. The ones there on sticks are survivors.'

She was done. There was nothing she could usefully add; perhaps she'd said too much already. Among the dark trees wove the fireflies of distant torches.

Even though he'd been told the dog was Donovan's, the sight of it crouched over him made Shapiro's heart lurch. Constable Sutton edged towards it with a catching pole from the kennels. Brian Boru sat impassively to be lassoed, making them all feel rather foolish.

When it was done Shapiro hurried forward, anxiously taking in the white, strained face and shut eyes of the man on the ground. 'How is he?'

Liz looked up with a tired smile, made no effort to rise. 'He'll be all right. His ankle's broken, he's a bit battered – nothing more.'

'Does he know about—?' He gestured back towards the cottage.

Donovan raised one eyelid and squinted at him. 'Oh yeah.'

'You saw it happen?'

'I was a captive audience.' He flinched as the paramedics examined his leg.

'We've got all the people involved,' said Shapiro. 'How many of these killer dogs are we still looking for?'

Donovan had watched those dogs in action. He knew Andy would be alive now but for Brian's attack. But he'd be dead, and when he'd been defenceless with his back against this tree it had been Brian again who stood between him and carnage, snapping and snarling until Gates's dogs lost interest and moved off.

For a moment he appeared to consider Shapiro's question. Then he said, very firmly, 'Both of them.'

Chapter Twenty-three

It was the middle of the night before they finished. Though she had a backlog of work waiting, Liz thought she'd earned a lie-in: with no one but herself to consider – that's a joke, she thought bitterly, who else do I ever consider? – she threw Polly an extra slice of hay and set the alarm for an hour later than usual.

In the event she slept for perhaps an extra thirty minutes before wakening to the smell of coffee.

Before she was aware of knowing what it meant she was flying downstairs, dressed only in an over-sized t-shirt bearing the legend 'Teachers do it AGAIN and AGAIN until they GET IT RIGHT!' and with her tangled hair streaming in a sunshine train behind her. Brian Graham just had time to put the tray down before she flung herself on him.

'You *bastard*!' she sobbed, clinging to him like a vine. 'How could you *do* that to me?'

'I'm sorry,' he murmured, holding her, feeling the rich warmth of her body through the thin cotton, breathing in the fresh-from-sleep smell. 'I – thought it was what you wanted.'

'Jesus, Brian,' she hissed down the neck of his shirt, 'How could I want that? I love you: don't you *know* that? I love you and I need you. There's other stuff that

I want, but the only thing I *need* is you. How could you think I wanted you to go?'

'Just because you said so,' said Brian mildly, shaking his head. 'Silly me.'

She pulled back and looked at him suspiciously; and yes, she was right, he was laughing at her. Or at them. And why not? They'd behaved like idiots, got hung up on words at a time when anyone could have told them the only reliable guide was instinct. 'Oh – come upstairs.'

'Shall I bring the tray?'

She stared at him. 'Are you mad?'

Afterwards he said pensively, 'We should have done that before.'

'I wanted to.'

'I wish you'd said. I thought it was the last thing you'd want. I thought maybe you'd never want it ever again.'

She put her head on one side. 'It?'

'It. This.' Brian gave a rueful grin. 'All right, sex. You know I had a sheltered upbringing: I was fifteen before I stopped saying "toilet" '.

Laced by his arms she giggled. Then her brow knit in the search for words that said exactly what she meant. 'The point is, Brian, this wasn't sex, this was making love. And what happened out there' – she nodded towards the yard – 'wasn't even sex. Not to me, probably not even to him. It was a mugging. Love is in the commitment and sex is in the joy; without either it's just a violation. They stick something up you when you go for a smear test, too, but nobody thinks of it as sex. It was a violent assault, neither more nor less. A forcible intrusion. Breaking and entering.'

Brian shook his head disbelievingly. 'Can it really mean so little to you? But what does that say—?' He heard himself reopening the argument, stopped abruptly. Nothing mattered to him as much as having her here.

But Liz wanted all the doubts resolved. 'About what?' Her eyes saucered with understanding. 'My God, Brian – what does it say about *us*? About us in bed? You think that because I'm not prepared to fall apart over this it means I put no value on what *we* do? That's it, isn't it? – that's what you think!'

Her astonished stare made him uncomfortable. He could have denied it, but they'd come close to the abyss by failing to make their feelings clear, lying was no way back. 'I suppose. Yes, that's what I was afraid of. Does that sound stupid?'

She rolled eel-like in his arms, came to rest on top of him, staring into his eyes from a range of inches. They were the blue of well-washed denim, and the hearts of them were warm but tucked in the corners she saw worry and fear. She'd done this to him. Not the man who raped her – Liz herself. He'd worried himself sick about a phantasm, something with no reality, a bad dream with no power to hurt them, and she hadn't seen it happening and stopped it. Perhaps he had been stupid, but she'd been cruel.

'Yes,' she said honestly, 'to me it does. But then, I know it isn't true. I can shrug this off – maybe not as easily as I make out, but I can put it out with the trash – because I know how pathetically ersatz a thing it was. And I know *that* because I have the real thing to compare it with. It doesn't touch us, Brian – it doesn't come anywhere *near* us.

'It's – like getting home and finding you've had burglars. It's a horrible feeling: somebody's been in your home, helping himself to things that belong to you, trespassing in a place where you'd always felt safe. Ask anyone who's been burgled: it's not what you lose that matters, it's the invasion. People spend weeks spring-cleaning to get rid of the feeling that the place where they live has been sullied.

'They say being burgled is a bit like being raped. It's not trivializing what happened to me to say that's how it felt. Vicious, dirty and offensive, and not like sex because sex is better than that. I'm hurt and angry, and when I'm angry I don't always hit the right targets – I don't know if you've ever noticed that? – but I swear to you, Brian, nothing that can be done in five minutes to a woman who had to be knocked out first can possibly affect a relationship she'd die for.'

When they'd had breakfast Brian said, 'Are you going into work now?' Liz nodded. 'Me too. Leave your car at home today.'

She frowned, puzzled. 'Why?'

He smiled. 'Because I want to drive my wife to work.'

So he was there to witness perhaps the strangest sight ever seen at Queen's Street, not excluding a Jewish Santa Claus at the Christmas party. Later Liz quizzed him closely, sure he must have known, but he hadn't. He'd just wanted people to see them together.

The police station was full of flowers. Bouquets wrapped in cellophane, bunches tied with wool, hyacinths in pots, a dozen long-stemmed red roses in a crystal vase, a clump of what looked like ragwort – it couldn't have been, it was too early in the year, perhaps it was a rare Japanese dahlia – and two boxed orchids. Additionally there were great mismatched armfuls of flowers that had arrived one at a time and been hurriedly introduced by a desk sergeant who was more concerned with clearing a corner of his work-space than running a match-making service for horticultural lonely hearts.

Liz stared at them open-mouthed from the back door. 'Somebody's birthday?'

WPC Wilson appeared from behind a small camellia. 'They're for you, ma'am.'

'*Me*?' Liz was genuinely staggered. 'Why should anyone send me flowers? Let alone' – she indicated the riot of colour with a stunned wave – 'Kew Gardens.'

'I take it you didn't hear the radio last night,' said Wilson diplomatically.

'Radio? Oh – that thing of Gail Fisher's? No, I was busy.' Her eyebrows, which had reached her hairline, fell suspiciously. 'Whatever did she say?'

Wilson shook her head blithely. 'Nothing special. Only what everyone here's been thinking for four days: that this town's lucky to have you, and instead of making cheap jokes it should send you flowers and then give you all the help and support it can. I think people took the flowers part more literally than she expected.'

'But—' Liz couldn't get her mind round it. She'd seen nothing similar in twenty years on the force. 'Who are they all *from*?'

'Some have cards attached, some haven't. A lot of

the single flowers were kids dropping them in on their way to school. Mostly the others were women.'

They'd hurried in red-faced, embarrassed by what they were doing, anxious to deliver their gift and get away; but aware at the same time of being part of something important, standing up to be counted on an issue that mattered. As the flowers mounted Wilson loved watching the women's faces change as they came in from the street, from the troubled certainty that they were making fools of themselves to delight at joining a groundswell of female solidarity, a regiment levied by a ten-minute radio slot rushing to the barricades armed with flowers.

Wilson indicated a bunch of parrot tulips. 'Those are from us. From Queen's Street.'

Sergeant Tulliver cleared his throat. 'There's a couple of empty cells, we could put them in there.'

Liz shook herself, got her brain back in gear. 'No, find me a van. Some I want to keep, and I think we should leave some on view here, and I'll take the others to the hospital. There's enough here to decorate the whole damn place.' She shook her head in wonder. The threat of tears pricked behind her eyes. 'Is Mr Shapiro in?'

Sergeant Tulliver nodded. 'Went up a few minutes ago.'

'At least, it was probably Mr Shapiro,' added Wilson with a grin. 'It could have been some carnations wearing his hat.'

He'd brought in a couple of vases as well. She found him in her office arranging the flowers with deep concentration and no skill. 'Did everybody hear this broadcast except me?'

His eyes avoided her. 'Somebody made a tape, I

248

listened to it after you'd gone home. I thought—' He made a shy gesture towards the carnations. 'I didn't expect everyone in town to have the same idea.' He drew her attention to a pot on the windowsill. 'Donovan sent that.'

She was past wondering how *he'd* heard the broadcast or managed to send her a plant from his hospital bed. She peered at it. 'What *is* it?'

'It's a Mother-in-law's Tongue,' said Shapiro. 'I told him it was a funny choice but he insisted.'

Liz thought it was funny too. After what had passed between them last night it was so funny they could hear her laughing all over the building.

When the phone rang it took her a moment to find it. It was Gail Fisher.

Liz said severely. 'I suppose I've you to thank for the fact that this police station looks like the Chelsea Flower Show.'

She could hear Fisher's delight. 'Really? I hoped somebody might take it up, but – well, I sent some narcissi just in case. They're not alone then?'

'Not exactly. If you can spare ten minutes, have a look before I take some of them to the hospital. It's enough to renew your faith in your fellow man. Or fellow woman, mostly.'

'Funny you should mention that,' said Fisher, her tone changing. 'I do want to see you, though not about the flowers. And not at Queen's Street. I have a friend who wants to talk to you. Could you meet me at her house?'

Liz sat up sharply, the flowers receding into a soft multi-coloured haze. 'Is this the same friend we were talking about before?'

'Yes. She – I think she feels she let the side down. She wants to help you find this man.'

The house was in Rosedale Avenue, a pleasant piece of stockbroker Tudor with a long front lawn running down to a stone bird-bath. You could tell you were in the nice part of town. In less salubrious areas people put their bird-baths in the back gardens; and there were places where they took them in at night, like washing.

Liz wasn't aware of having met Amanda Urquhart before but she seemed familiar: after a moment, queasily, she realized it was because they were as much alike as sisters. She was aged about forty, fair, well-built, tall, and a professional woman – an architect.

Liz said, 'I don't need to tell you that I understand how you feel. I'm glad you agreed to see me. Any way you want to handle this, that's what we do.'

Mrs Urquhart twitched a smile. 'However it'll do most good. I'm only sorry I couldn't get up the nerve to do it sooner. If it turns out the attack on you, or anyone else, could have been prevented—'

Liz interrupted. 'Don't even wonder, there's no way we'll ever know. If you help us find him now, that's the most we can ask for. Even if you can't help it's still the best you can do.'

Mrs Urquhart was a partner in the firm responsible for the Mere Basin redevelopment which had recycled the old warehouses as apartments, offices and cafés. Donovan called it 'yuppification' and threatened to cut his boat's warps if it got as far as Broad Wharf. But any such project would have been doomed to failure: with

The Jubilee only a spit away across Brick Lane the bulldozers would have been stolen. They didn't have bird-baths at all in The Jubilee, and at night they took the washing-*lines* inside.

She was attacked in the hallway as she left work late one evening. The firm had its offices in The Barbican. Like the other converted warehouses it was shops at ground level, offices on the first and second storeys and flats above that. Electronic access kept kids and drunks from wandering in but it wouldn't have stopped a professional burglar and anyone with business elsewhere in the building could have found his way to that corridor.

Mrs Urquhart finished about midnight, locked up and headed for the lift. Aware that she'd be late she'd deliberately parked her car beside the lifts in the basement garage.

She never reached the lift. A gloved hand reached over her shoulder and closed on her mouth, swinging her like a pendulum into the wall. 'I don't know now where he came from.' A slight tremor disturbed the even rhythm of her voice from time to time, and the toe of one court-shoe was tapping a beat of which she seemed unaware, but that was all. It was as if she was explaining why a flat roof she'd designed kept leaking rather than how her life flew apart one night. 'I must have walked right past him, but the first thing I knew was his hand over my face.'

'Could he have come from one of the offices?' asked Liz.

'I don't see how. There are two doors on my way to the lift, one on each side. But I know one of them was locked – it's the door to our back office but it isn't used, everyone goes through reception. The other office has never been let so it's locked, too. He must have squeezed into the doorway, but with the corridor light on I don't know how I missed him.'

'Could he have broken into the empty office?'

'I asked afterwards.' She gave a self-deprecating smile. 'Carefully, I'd already decided I wasn't going to report this, but I was confused and scared. I didn't know how it happened so I didn't know if it could happen again. I wanted to know how he'd surprised me like that. But there were no signs of a break-in.'

'Then he must have had a key.'

'Apparently not. I told the caretaker I'd heard someone in there late at night, and he checked and said there was no sign of a forced entry and, apart from the one at the estate agents, he had the only key. He obviously thought I'd imagined it. You know: hysterical middle-aged woman alone in the office late at night, frightening herself over nothing. I couldn't put him straight without saying more than I wanted to.'

'Could it have been the caretaker?' Liz asked.

Mrs Urquhart was sure. 'No. He's a tall man, particularly tall. The man who attacked me wasn't.'

'You got a good look at him?'

'Good enough, through the shooting stars. Not his face: he had a scarf over it. Absurd as it sounds, I think it was a white silk evening scarf. And soft leather gloves. A grey track-suit, the sort with a hood which he had pulled down. He was about my height, average build.'

'A young man, would you say?'

'He was fit enough: he went at it like going for a record. But—' She hesitated, thinking. 'Not very young. I don't know how I know that. My impression was of someone about my own age. Perhaps it was his voice.'

Liz's pulse skipped a beat. 'He *spoke* to you?'

'Yes; just a few words. But it wasn't a youngster's voice. He was an educated man, too.'

'What makes you say that?'

Amanda Urquhart's brow crinkled. 'It was something he said. What was it? You'd think it'd be branded in my memory, wouldn't you, but it was something – silly. It made no sense. And I was dizzy.'

'It could be important,' said Liz. She didn't want to put it any stronger than that for fear of scaring the memory away. 'Try and remember.'

Mrs Urquhart squeezed her eyes shut, trying to get it back. 'He bounced me off the wall, I banged my head; I staggered and he kicked the feet from under me. I went down on my hip. He grabbed my hands, pulled me on to my back and – did it. He didn't hurt me. If I'd been any more dazed I mightn't have noticed. I mean, we're not talking Guy the Gorilla here, all right?'

Liz grinned. 'Bit like a Chinese meal? – half an hour later you're ready for another?' They chuckled together, a conspiracy of women not diminishing the wrong done them so much as absorbing it, grinding the edges off in some emotional gizzard. The things that made them vulnerable also made them strong, and they felt that strength stir in their veins like the first twitch of a waking volcano.

Mrs Urquhart went back to what she was struggling with. 'I think he knew me. Well, he was waiting outside my office door, it was no great feat to read what was written on it; but it was more than that. Because he said—' Her eyes came up, startled, as the key finally found the right lock. 'He said, "*That's* what *I* call Decon-struction." Like that: as if it were the last word in an argument we'd had.'

Liz ran the words round her head but they didn't connect with anything. 'Do you know what he meant?'

'I know what Deconstruction is. I've no idea what he meant by it.'

'Um – what *is* Deconstruction?'

'Syncopated architecture,' said Mrs Urquhart with a terse grin. 'Deconstructionists like to pull the bits of a building apart and make them do something differ-ent. They think it's challenging. It never occurs to them that buildings evolved the way they did because that's what the people using them find most con-venient.'

'You're not a Deconstructionist yourself, then.'

The architect shook her head. 'I'm a sort of Ante-Post-Modernist – I bet on certainties.'

'Then what was he saying?'

'I can't imagine. It's pretty esoteric stuff, and while people do get hot under the collar about modern archi-tecture it's a hell of a distance from there to rape.'

'Perhaps it wasn't architecture he was talking about,' hazarded Liz. A ghost of a possibility hovered at the edge of her vision. 'He's an educated man, he knows what it means, he knows that as an architect it means something specific to you. What? – paradox? Turning things on their heads? Was he saying that when you met before you had the upper hand and this time it was different?'

Mrs Urquhart shrugged helplessly. 'It's possible.'

They were coming to the end of what the interview could usefully yield. Liz nodded slowly. 'All right. You know, you've told me quite a lot about this man that we didn't know before. That *I* didn't know. He's educated, he's probably quite well-off – the silk scarf, the leather gloves – and he's someone you've met and maybe slighted. Think about that. Try to picture a man of that type that you got the better of in some way. A competitor? That'd explain him knowing about Deconstruction. A dissatisfied client? If you start getting any feelings about who it could be, call me. It doesn't matter if you're wrong: we can check him out so discreetly he'll never know. If someone comes to mind, let me look into it.'

Liz rose to leave, and was about to do her usual parting speech about the courage of rape victims putting other women's interests first when the sheer fatuity of it hit her. She must have made it a dozen times and it had never struck her how bloody impertinent it was. Mumbling, she went to make her escape.

But something else occurred to Amanda Urquhart. 'I don't know if this'll be any help, but there was something odd about how he used his voice. He'd just committed rape in a building where people lived and worked: he should have been whispering – better still, he shouldn't have said anything at all. But he was so anxious for me to know how clever he was, how much cleverer than me, that he didn't just say it, he *declaimed* it. Do you know what I mean? He wasn't shouting, more – projecting. Like an actor. I even thought at the time: "This man's putting on a show." I half expected him to take a bow as the lift doors closed.'

'But he didn't?'

'No. He looked back up the corridor, and his eyes went through me as if I wasn't there.'

Chapter Twenty-four

'An actor?' exclaimed Shapiro. 'We're looking for a stage-struck rapist?' He'd been persuaded to adopt a couple of hyacinths for his desk. He peered between them like a startled badger.

It didn't sound too likely. Maybe in London or Cambridge, but Castlemere didn't have a great theatre tradition; hence the paucity of travellers on the Luvvies Train.

'Perhaps not an actor as such,' allowed Liz. 'How about an amateur? There's the Castlemere Players and the Gilbert & Sullivan Society; and some of the churches have drama groups.' Brian had helped out with the scenery.

Shapiro remained scathing. 'A church-going amateur Thespian rapist, then? Oh, yes, that's a question I can just see myself asking. "Tell me, vicar, that Wise Man in the Nativity Play – show any tendency to jump the angels, did he?" ' Then he remembered who he was talking to and his broad face softened with regret. 'I'm sorry, Liz. I keep forgetting—'

'Good,' she said briskly. 'Once we have the sod we can all forget.' Thinking about Brian set her on another track. 'He might not be an actor at all. What about a teacher or lecturer – someone who's used to addressing large groups of people? Or—' Running out of suggestions she sighed dispiritedly. 'We're really not making much progress, are we?'

Immediately Shapiro was contrite. He hadn't much to offer her, he could at least avoid undermining her hope. 'Yes we are: we know a lot about him that we didn't four days ago. Perhaps the most important thing is that he knew Amanda Urquhart before he attacked her. That makes it likely that he knew the other victims, too. Well enough to know where you lived and that you'd be out alone first thing in the morning. Well enough to know Mrs Andrews would be walking home late at night past Castle Mount.'

Liz hadn't thought of that. She hadn't thought that her attacker could be more than just a pervert with patience and an eye for detail: could be a man she knew, perhaps knew well. Before she could stop it the camera in her head began to reel fast-forward all the men she could think of – friends and colleagues and friends of colleagues and colleagues of friends and men who served in the greengrocer's and the butcher's – who fitted even part of the description. When she found herself contemplating Dick Morgan, who though he was not big as policemen go was still bigger than the man who raped her, she yanked herself up short with an audible gasp.

'What?' asked Shapiro, concerned.

'Nothing,' she said quickly. Then, slower, 'I hadn't thought that I might know this man. It's a bit of a shock, that's all. But it could help. If the three of us get together and discuss acquaintances we have in common—'

'It'll amount to most of the male population of

Castlemere,' said Shapiro wearily. 'You'll use the same shops, tradesmen, restaurants, pubs and sports clubs – there are only so many to go round, you're bound to use the same ones some of the time. Even your social circles will overlap. Damn it, he chose the three of you *because* you were of a type.'

Liz moved the hyacinths to one side of his desk to give her somewhere to rest her elbow. Her chin cupped in her hand, she thought.

Watching her, Shapiro saw the moment that the seed of an idea germinated and took root. Her eyes sharpened and narrowed as she scrutinized it, not in every detail but enough to decide that it was worth planting. When her gaze snapped up to meet his, he saw the old battle-light, that compound of determination, intelligence and hope, that put him in mind of a she-panther shaking out her serviette.

'What?'

'If Mrs Urquhart's right and she's not only met this man but argued with him on a professional matter, there should be some record of it. Maybe it goes back years, maybe he's nursed the grudge and it's only now he's turned to sexual violence that he saw the chance to avenge himself. But somewhere in a filing cabinet at Brewster & Urquhart there's an exchange of letters referring to Deconstruction. I'm going to call Mrs Urquhart and agree some cover-story so I can look through those files.'

Shapiro swivelled his chair to and fro, his gaze travelling between Liz and the view of the canal from his window. He pursed his lips. 'Aren't you forgetting something? This isn't your case. For very good reasons, this is definitely not your case.'

'I know that, Frank. But for the same very good reasons it had to be me who saw Mrs Urquhart and it has to be me who follows this up. I can't ask her to start dealing with someone else now.' She gave an apologetic shrug. 'You could tackle the caretaker at The Barbican. The attacker must have come from that empty office, and if there was no break-in he had a key.'

'All right,' agreed Shapiro, standing up, 'I'll go and see him. And you can start your paper-chase. But if it looks like leading anywhere, Liz, call me. I don't want you dealing with this man. For your sake – I know, you're fine, you don't need molly-coddling, but still – and also for the sake of the case. I don't want this man getting off on a technicality.'

'Like, being unable to plead on account of having had his head kicked in by a Detective Inspector?' She grinned tightly, though it may not have been a joke. 'Don't worry, Frank, I'll keep the secateurs out of sight.'

Shapiro went to Mere Basin. He'd been here often enough before, couldn't think why he suddenly felt so ill at ease. Then he understood. This was Donovan's backyard, he knew every cobble and stanchion on the waterfront. Shapiro couldn't remember the last time he was here without him.

Though in fact the bistros, boutiques, offices and apartments of the redevelopment were not his sergeant's natural habitat in the way the derelict wharves and crumbling warehouses further down the tow-path were. When Donovan died he'd come back as an alleycat. Unless he'd been the cat first.

The caretaker was as Mrs Urquhart described him –
tall and unhelpful. He gave his name as Bibby: Shapiro
assumed it was a surname and his first name was even
sillier. He showed the way to the vacant office on the
first floor, pointedly marking time while Shapiro
looked round. He was a man of about thirty with the
manners of an adolescent.

Shapiro fixed him with a cold eye. 'You said nobody
was in here.'

'When?'

'A fortnight ago, when Mrs Urquhart told you she
heard someone in this office late at night.' Bibby didn't
ask why a detective superintendent was asking about
so trivial a matter and Shapiro didn't offer a reason.
He was ready to lie to protect the victim's privacy but
for the moment it wasn't necessary. Bibby showed no
curiosity about his presence, only a continuing resentment and the desire to see the back of him. 'You said
she couldn't have, that no one had been in here.'

Bibby shrugged, unconcerned. 'That's right. I
checked the door: there wasn't a mark on it.'

'Then you must have let him in.'

The caretaker regarded him with vulpine eyes. 'Get
real, squire! I'm here to keep the burglars out, not to
let them into the offices of their choice.'

'But you do have a key. You let people in here from
time to time.'

'Sure I've let people in. The place is to rent, people
come to see it, sometimes the estate agents show them
round and sometimes I do. Then I show them out and
lock up behind me.'

'When was the last time?'

Bibby had to think. 'A month maybe? There hasn't

been much interest – it's too small for most people who want to spend serious rent on an office.'

'And when did you last clean the place? I suppose you are meant to clean it occasionally?'

He was; but it wasn't a part of his job that he gave high priority to. He shrugged again. 'Probably about then.'

Shapiro crooked a forefinger and beckoned him. 'Then who's been perching his backside on this windowsill in the meantime?'

It wasn't a recent mark, fresh dust had fallen on the sill since it was made, but there was a definite bottom-sized depression where the older layers had been disturbed.

'I wouldn't claim to be a dust expert,' said Shapiro, 'but I don't think that's a month old. I'd guess it was made about the time Mrs Urquhart heard someone in here. He wasn't viewing the place, not that late at night. If you didn't let him in and he didn't break in then he had a key.'

Bibby shook his head. 'Not mine. These keys go nowhere without me.'

'You're sure of that?'

'Damn sure.'

'You never lend them to anyone?'

'More than my job's worth, squire.'

Reluctantly Shapiro accepted his word. He didn't like the man but he doubted Bibby was hiding anything. Too casual for a bad liar, not quite casual enough for a good one.

'The agents have their own keys?' Bibby nodded. 'Could they have shown someone round recently enough to make that mark?'

'Not that I know of.'

'Do they ever show people round without you knowing?'

Bibby scowled with justifiable irritation. 'You'd need to ask them, squire, wouldn't you?'

'I will,' promised Shapiro. 'I'll be sure to mention what an asset you are to them, too.'

They don't have irony where Bibby came from. For the first time his eyes warmed. 'Thanks, squire. 'Preciate it.'

Liz agreed with Amanda Urquhart an explanation of why the police needed access to the firm's correspondence files. They would say she'd received a threatening letter from someone who may have been a client at some time. But when she went to the office Mrs Urquhart said quietly, 'Never mind the cover story. I've told them.'

Liz tried not to let her eyes widen too noticeably. 'Everything?'

The other woman shrugged, only a little edgily. 'Yes. I'm damned if I'll let him make me a liar as well.'

'How were they – your colleagues?'

'Shocked. And angry, and kind. Like friends. I don't know what else I expected.'

'A bit of advice,' said Liz. 'Stock up on vases.'

They went through the correspondence disks on the firm's computer, working back from the date of the attack. Then they hunted through the filing-cabinet for anything relevant. They weren't sure what they were looking for. Ideally, a letter of complaint containing a veiled threat and the word Deconstruction. In reality, any communication from a man short of his dotage indicating real and sustained dissatisfaction. It was the nature of the business that there were more than a few of them.

There were several threats of legal action, a few of them aggressive on a personal level. But they all read as if they'd been written in anger and shouldn't be taken at face value. People who threaten to go to law rarely turn to violence as an alternative. And in all the letters they read, the only reference to Deconstruction was by a man who thought it was the same as demolition and was worried about an extension he'd built without planning permission.

There was one more possibility. Liz went through the more-than-slightly-dissatisfied list again, looking for a name she recognized. There were a few – as Shapiro had said, there were bound to be. None of them, so far as she could remember, were rather small men of about her own age with whom she'd crossed swords.

After two hours she sat back on her heels – running out of desk space they'd moved on to the carpet – and scowled. 'Damn. I thought we'd find something.'

Mrs Urquhart was frowning too. She looked as if she was trying to remember something. 'The man who thought Deconstruction was something you did with a bulldozer.'

Liz glanced around the confetti of papers. 'We didn't keep him. If you remember, you sorted him out and he was eternally grateful.'

'Yes,' said the architect pensively. 'But somebody else did that once – made that mistake, thought he was being clever by using technical jargon. Whoever was it? And why, and where?'

Mrs Urquhart's secretary was on the computer. 'The court case. That business of the swimming-pool roof that fell in. They tried to claim it was faulty design but it turned out the contractor had been using substandard materials.'

The architect's face cleared. 'That's what it was. About three, four years ago. We actually had to go to court over it. We won, but it was nasty enough for a while. I'd never been in court before.'

'Who brought the action?'

The secretary was busy with her disks again. 'Jason Fielder, 212 Cambridge Road.'

Mrs Urquhart nodded slowly, remembering. 'Yes. That was a very angry man – with every reason, if the roof had come down an hour earlier it would have killed his son.'

Liz felt the hairs standing up on her neck, like a terrier swelling at the sight of a rabbit. She didn't recognize the name but that might not mean they'd never met. 'What sort of a man is he – what does he do?'

'Something in the motor trade. He owns that big garage on the ring road.'

'A business which attracts its fair share of cowboys,' Liz observed pensively. 'What does he look like? How old is he?'

Mrs Urquhart shook her head decisively. 'He can't be our man. Yes, he's about the right age and build, and yes, he'd some reason to be bitter. But Inspector, it can't be him!'

'Why not?'

The architect didn't know whether to laugh or cry.

'Look, I know I didn't give you much of a description. His face was covered, his hands were covered, I only saw his eyes *and* I was stunned. I imagine it was the same with you?'

'So?'

'In spite of that,' said Amanda Urquhart, 'one of us would have noticed if he'd been black.'

Chapter Twenty-five

Four years on, Jason Fielder was still angry enough for his voice to quake when he described what happened. 'An hour earlier my son was in the pool. That Sunday all three of us spent half the morning in it. I could have lost my whole family, Inspector Graham – you wonder I wanted someone to pay for that?'

As Amanda Urquhart had said, he was not a big man. But what he lacked in stature he made up in sheer dynamism. He was never still: pacing the room he took Liz to, fiddling with the ornaments on the mantelpiece, opening and shutting the bureau. Liz thought at first that he was nervous, that she was finally on the right trail, that somehow she and the others had failed to notice that the man who attacked them was black.

But watching him prowl she realized he wasn't nervous at all: he just wasn't used to being awake and doing nothing. It was easy to see how a man with that sort of compulsive, unquenchable energy could come from a back-to-back in The Jubilee, skip school to work in a car-breaker's from the age of fifteen, and end up with a valuable business and a house in the best part of Cambridge Road.

'The court said you were blaming the wrong

people,' Liz reminded him. 'That the contractor cut corners, and Mrs Urquhart didn't know and wasn't in a position to know.'

'Oh, sure,' said Fielder savagely. 'Only the contractor had moved on without leaving a forwarding address by the time the pool roof damn near fell on my boy's head! All I know, Inspector, is that I paid a reputable firm for a swimming-pool extension and the first winter it fell down. If clever Mrs Urquhart didn't know what the contractor was doing she damn well should have done.'

'You're still angry with her.'

'Damn sure I'm angry! Wouldn't you be?'

'Probably,' admitted Liz. 'But I think I'd let it drop after a court told me I was being unreasonable.'

Fielder frowned, brows gathered over the fierce eyes. 'So did I. Is somebody saying different? The Urquhart woman – what's she saying about me?'

'Nothing,' Liz said honestly. 'She's – had a bit of trouble, but she isn't accusing you. Only something was said that reminded her of the court case. Does the word Deconstruction mean anything to you?'

He laughed aloud, a deep and still bitter laugh. 'What it doesn't mean,' he said, heavily ironic, 'is the roof falling into your swimming-pool. That was made quite clear to me.'

Liz allowed herself a wry smile. 'Extracting the Michael, was she?'

'That the same as taking the piss? Yeah, she did that all right. Left me feeling about so high.' The blunt fingers weren't even at full stretch. 'That was cheap. I wasn't trying to make a fool of her, only to make her take responsibility for her mistake – whether that was the design or the people she gave the contract to.'

'Have you seen her since?'

Fielder nodded. 'It's a small town, sooner or later you meet everyone.'

'What did you say to her?'

'Nothing. I crossed the street.'

There was nothing else to ask. Amanda Urquhart hadn't believed Jason Fielder raped her; Liz didn't believe it either. Using his hard-earned wealth to bring a legal action, that was his way. In certain circumstances she could imagine him shouting, waving his arms about, even slapping the woman he blamed for the near-tragedy. But stalking her, lying in wait and raping her to vent his fury? He'd have considered it beneath his dignity. It took him twenty years to make himself a man to be reckoned with. Liz couldn't see him resorting to a form of revenge that had been available to him when he was poor.

As he walked Liz to her car Jason Fielder gave a sudden deep chuckle. 'She didn't have it all her own way, though. The clever Mrs Urquhart. She might have made me feel like something she'd found in a bad bit of wood but my brief gave as good as he got. She didn't get any of those long words past him! Born with a silver dictionary in his mouth, that one.'

Liz smiled. 'Let me guess. Dan Fenton?'

Untroubled by false modesty, Fielder beamed. 'If you can afford the best, why settle for less?' Then he shook his head regretfully. 'We should have won. The work he put into it, we deserved to win. He said afterwards we would have done if it had been her partner's project. No offence, Inspector Graham, but he reckoned the jury would have expected a man to know

268

whether or not the contractor was skimping on the materials. He reckoned they accepted a lower standard of competence because she was a woman.'

When Shapiro went to the building society which acted as agents for The Barbican he was astonished to find Helen Andrews behind the manager's desk.

A cocktail of hope and dread quickened her voice as she recognized him in return. 'Mr Shapiro! Is there some news?' She meant, had he found the man who raped her.

Recovering his composure he intoned reassuringly, 'We're making progress. Forgive me, I wasn't expecting to see you here. I came to ask about a vacant office at the Basin. You told me where you worked but I'd forgotten.'

She ushered him in, left word at the front desk that they shouldn't be disturbed. She wielded her seniority with grace: she knew she'd earned it and so did everyone round her. Like Liz Graham; like Amanda Urquhart. 'Then how can I help you?'

Shapiro had intended to fib, as Liz had to Jason Fielder, about the reason for his questions. Now there was no need. 'The man who attacked you also attacked a woman working late in The Barbican. She was his first victim, so far as we know, and he seems to have come out of an empty office that you have keys for. I need to know who has access to those keys.'

Mrs Andrews called up the information on her screen. 'That's the office on the first floor, opposite the architects.' A tremor shook her and she stared at him wide-eyed. 'It was Amanda Urquhart? Oh no. I know her, we were at school together. We were always called The Book-ends – we're the same age, height, build, colouring.' She blanched. 'Dear God, did he make a *mistake*? Was he looking for me that time, too?'

'No,' said Shapiro quickly, 'we've no reason to think that. My inspector fits the same description and he knew exactly who she was – he went to her home to rape her.'

'I heard what she did,' said Mrs Andrews softly. 'That took courage.'

'Yes,' agreed Shapiro. 'We're very proud of her.'

The woman gave a slow smile. 'Today's my first day back at work. I kept putting it off till I heard that thing on the radio. Then I thought, why am *I* hiding? I've done nothing wrong! I thought, as long as the victims hide their faces the perpetrators don't have to. So here I am.'

He wanted to say something encouraging, was afraid of offending her. Because he was a man and the victims were women the opportunities were legion, or felt to be if they were not. He settled for returning her smile. 'Good. So, the keys. They're kept here, are they?'

'In the safe. They're signed out if someone wants to view and in again afterwards. According to this' – she tapped the screen – 'they're there now, but I'll check.' She did, and they were.

'Who's had them out in the last six weeks?'

That information was there too. 'I have, four times. No one else.'

'To show people round? Who?'

'Different people. One was an accountant, one a barrister. Neither was interested after they'd seen the place: they liked the situation but both needed more room. Then there was a financial adviser – not a very good one, I don't think, he liked it but couldn't afford the rent – and a woman who runs a domestic service agency. She was the most recent, she's still thinking about it.'

'Apart from that your keys would have been here?'

'Yes.'

'Could members of your staff take them out without it appearing on the record?'

Mrs Andrews was taken aback but took time to consider it. 'I suppose so, but I can't imagine why they would. There's no one here I don't have total confidence in. Dealing with other people's properties you have to be sure of your staff.'

'Fair enough.' Shapiro was disappointed but not surprised. It would have been nice to get a positive response, something like: 'We've always wondered about Mr Wiggins, something about the way he dribbles around the female clients,' but that wasn't usually how it happened. Sometimes, if you were lucky, you got a snippet of information that looked like nothing until you put it together with snippets of information obtained elsewhere. Dutifully he jotted down the names and addresses of the people who'd viewed the office.

He arrived back at Queen's Street as Liz was parking her car; she waited and they went up together.

'Any luck?'

'Not that you'd notice. You?'

'A curiosity, but I don't think I'll call a Press conference yet.'

They went to Shapiro's office and he made some coffee. Living alone made him handy like that. This was the first posting Liz had had where it wasn't automatically assumed – until she put the record straight – that she'd do the catering for any group of officers which didn't include a WPC.

'The curiosity,' said Shapiro, hanging up his coat, 'is that the keys for the empty office are held by Helen Andrews.'

Liz stared at him. 'That *has* to mean something. So he could have met both of them there – Mrs Andrews was showing him round as Mrs Urquhart came out of her office.'

'I got the names of the people Mrs Andrews has taken there in the last six weeks. One's a woman, we can rule her out. The others are professional men, two financial wizards and a lawyer.'

'A lawyer.'

Shapiro thought she hadn't heard clearly so repeated it. 'Yes, a lawyer. A barrister.'

For several seconds, which is a long time for a pregnant silence, Liz said nothing. Her eyes were narrowed, calculating, and when she spoke again her tone carried an edge. 'We're looking for an educated man trained to use his voice, yes? That's a pretty good description of a barrister. Half his job is addressing large gatherings. And I know a lot of lawyers, so one viewing an office in The Barbican could easily have met all three of us. Who was it, Frank? Not Beanpole Barraclough, I hope, or Tubby Taylor?'

'No, it was Fairly Ordinary Fenton,' said Shapiro; and wondered why to all intents and purposes the world stopped turning. It was a modest enough joke by any standard. Usually he found he had to draw attention to his jokes; he couldn't remember the last time one had stopped a conversation dead. 'Liz, what is it?'

Her heart was thumping and she was fighting to keep her respiration under control. If he'd hit her with a wet sock wrapped round a gold brick she couldn't have looked more dumbfounded. 'Frank—'

'*What?*'

'I don't want to say it.'

'Say it anyway.'

She took a deep breath. 'About three years ago Dan Fenton and Amanda Urquhart crossed swords in court over the use of the word Deconstruction.'

Over the coffee they took a sober look at what they had. A man of the age and build described by the victims. A man who would own a silk evening scarf and soft leather gloves. A man for whom an unusual technical term had a peculiar significance. A man all three women had had dealings with.

'But – this is an important man we're talking about!' Liz said, doubt already creeping in. 'A respectable man. Would he really risk everything for the sake of a quick thrill in the hayshed?'

Shapiro shrugged ponderously. 'Perhaps he doesn't see it as a risk. It's the nature of his job to have more than a lay knowledge of rape: perhaps he thinks he can fox us. Perhaps that's what he's really after: not sex, he wasn't long enough to enjoy it, but the pleasure of seeing us every day and knowing we'd give our eye-teeth to collar him if we could only work it out.' His jaw tightened. 'That performance in court. That wasn't a wretched coincidence. You were in his way, he wanted to shut you up and he thought that would do it.'

'Amanda Urquhart got in his way when she got the judgement against his client,' Liz proposed slowly. 'Frank, is that who he targets – women who stand up to him, who cut him down to size? Call Helen Andrews, ask if she ever got the better of him.'

Mrs Andrews had no trouble remembering the man she showed round the office a fortnight before – just two days before the attack in the corridor. 'We'd met before. I was at another branch a couple of years ago and there was a misunderstanding. I showed someone a house, and while they were thinking about it I showed it to the Fentons. He made an offer, but the first couple came back and bettered it. I asked Mr Fenton if he wanted to reconsider. He obviously thought I was inventing the other buyer because he said that was his final offer and if it wasn't accepted promptly he'd withdraw it. So the sale went ahead.

'When he realized he'd lost it he got very shirty, threatened me with all sorts of legal action, but I'd done nothing improper and we both knew it. I stood my ground and there was nothing he could do. I was surprised when he phoned about the office in The Barbican, but not as surprised as him when I arrived to open up. We weren't five minutes before he said he wasn't interested. I don't know why he thought he might be – it's a fraction the size of the place they have now.'

'He never intended renting it,' Shapiro told Liz grimly. 'All he wanted was to get inside, so he could lay an ambush for Amanda Urquhart. She was top of his list: he'd watched her, he knew she worked late, he knew if he waited in the empty office two or three nights running she'd be alone when the rest of the floor was empty. He needed access to the office to fix the door so he could get back whenever he needed.'

'That's a lot of time to invest in a two-minute rape,' Liz objected; not because she thought he was wrong, more wanting to hear his argument.

'Yes. But these aren't casual attacks, they're planned like a military campaign. Like a legal battle. We know he's a perfectionist, he takes it personally if things go wrong: well, he commits rape the same way. He picks his target – a woman who's trodden on his toes anything up to four years previously – follows her round to learn her routine, when she'll be vulnerable; then he waits for the perfect moment when he can strike with minimal risk to himself.'

'That's what he did with me.' It was half a question, half a statement.

'Yes. He identified the half hour in the day when you always do the same thing, and you do it alone. You work some evenings and not others, you get around during the day, you go home different routes at different times. But almost always you get up at seven o'clock to feed the horse. Your fence runs alongside Belvedere Park – all he had to do was climb it and hide in the hayshed for ten minutes. It was the only time in your whole day he could be sure of getting you alone. Yes, to know that he must have watched you.'

'Then in God's name, Frank, why didn't I spot him? Why didn't I know I was being watched? I was *trying* to draw him out – if I knew I'd succeeded I could have stopped him there and then! He must have been laughing his leg off, watching me ponce up and down the waterfront with Miss Tunstall's powder-puff, knowing he was going to jump me when I was least expecting it. But I *should* have expected it! Damn it, it's my *job*!'

'Liz, stop this,' Shapiro said sharply, capturing between his own the hand she was tapping fiercely on his desk. 'Don't start looking for ways this could have been your fault. You didn't see him because he didn't want you to. This is a town of eighty thousand people and you have a job that takes you out among them: you're always in the public eye. You think being a police officer makes you psychic? It doesn't. You have the same faculties as everyone else. No blue lamp flashes in your head when you look at someone who's planning a crime. Damn it, I've had this conversation with Donovan before now but I never expected to have it with you!'

She gave a ragged sigh. 'I know that, Frank. Honestly, I'm not blaming myself. It's just, I can't help wondering if I'd done something different whether the result would have been the same. If I'd seen him watching me, could we have had him behind bars by now?'

Shapiro shook his head wearily. 'You'd just have thought, "Nosy sod" and got on with what you were doing. Same as I would, same as anyone. It doesn't work that way. We solve crimes; we don't often manage to prevent them.'

'All right,' said Liz, swallowing the sudden bile. 'Well, we knew he didn't pick his victims out of the phone-book. But there's more to it than just raping women who've annoyed him, isn't there? There has to be. Why do we all look alike? It can't be that every woman who ever crossed him looked the same. And why, in heaven's name, did he wait years to attack the first woman who offended him and then rape three in quick succession?'

'You've met his wife. What's she like?'

'Nice enough woman; bit on the quiet side, at least compared with him. She's—' She broke off. 'Ah.'

'About your age?' hazarded Shapiro. 'Fair, tall, well-built?'

'Four of a kind. What's going on, Frank? What does he think he's doing?'

Shapiro considered. 'Something's happened, in the last month or so, and I bet it involves her. Somehow she's both earned his fury and put herself out of reach. She's – I don't know, left him, got another man? Anyway, made him feel small. He hates that above all else. The most bitter moments of his life have been when strong women made him feel small. For what-ever reason he can't do much about his wife, but he can start paying back some of the others. Beginning with those who remind him of her.'

There was a long pause before Liz spoke again. Then: 'Are we serious about this, Frank? It's not just an idea we're kicking round any more – we genuinely think Dan Fenton raped me and two other women? We don't have any proof. We have some circumstantial evidence but nothing' – she flashed a quick, tight grin – 'that a good lawyer couldn't kick out of court.'

'Forensics got a reasonable DNA sample. If it matches Fenton's, even he might have trouble explain-ing it away.'

'All right,' she conceded, 'it would convince you and it would convince me. But even DNA isn't the complete answer we used to be told it was. You can't

use it *instead* of a case, you need a case as well. If we
take liberties with Dan Fenton he'll tear us to shreds.
This is a clever, clever man, remember, and this is his
field as much as it is ours. He won't even run. He'll
call in some favours, fix up some alibis, buy an expert
witness to question the procedure for taking and analysing the samples, generally fog the issues so much
no jury will convict him. We need something specific
connecting him to one of the attacks.'

'A fingerprint would be nice,' Shapiro said wistfully.
'But you can't take them off rhododendrons and you
can't take them off hay. The office is about the last
chance. I'll have SOCO go over it with a magnifying
glass.'

Even after a fortnight the Scenes Of Crime Officer
found traces of adhesive clinging to the lock plate.
'Easiest trick in the book, that,' he said disgustedly.
'Only takes a few seconds; you could do it with someone a few feet away and they'd never know. You push
the tongue back into the lock-case and hold it there
with sticky tape – the clear sort, nobody'd notice unless
they had their nose up against it. Then you shut the
door and rattle it to show that it's locked. Only it isn't,
it's just held by the latch. When you come back and
turn the knob the door opens, you do what you've
come for, you strip off the tape and leave, and this
time the door locks behind you.'

He sniffed critically, a man in the pay of the law
with the instincts of a criminal. 'In a perfect world
you'd have a meths-impregnated tissue to wipe the
lock-case afterwards; then if you smeared a bit of dust

over it no one'd ever know. But that's maybe asking a lot of an amateur.'

'What makes you say he's an amateur?' asked Liz.

SOCO plainly thought she was being dim. 'He left something for us to find. When he didn't have to. And he left his bum-print on the windowsill while he was waiting. A professional would have dusted that off before he left. A *real* professional would have sat on the floor.'

Another phone-call to Helen Andrews pushed the case over the threshold of reasonable suspicion. 'Who left the office first? Well, he held the door for me if that's what you mean, then he shut it behind us. About the first piece of gentlemanly behaviour I ever had from him.' She wasn't a stupid woman, she knew this amount of interest in one of the four parties she'd shown round that office meant something. Her voice dropped and hardened. 'And, I take it, the last.'

Shapiro put the phone down, carefully, as if afraid it might break. 'I think,' he said, weighing his words, 'we have all we need to ask Mr Daniel Fenton for a blood sample. See if the DNA matches.'

'And if it doesn't?' asked Liz.

The superintendent looked thoughtfully at the ceiling, then at the backs of his hands. Then he scratched his chin and sniffed. Finally he said, 'Everybody has to retire sometime.'

Chapter Twenty-six

It was the habit of the Crown Court to rise as soon after four in the afternoon as was convenient. That is to say, a witness who was on the point of confessing to the crime himself would not be interrupted and told to come back in the morning, but no new witnesses would be sworn.

At a few minutes to four, therefore, Shapiro had the choice of intercepting Fenton as he left the court or meeting him as he returned to his office. The discreet thing would have been to go to his office. The slightly less discreet thing would have been to wait in the broad hall which served the four court-rooms as a mustering place, somewhere to give last-minute instructions, an arcade for the disbelieved to express their outrage to the agents of their disappointment.

Shapiro went into the court to wait. He found a seat at the front of the public gallery.

They knew one another, of course. Shapiro didn't give evidence as often now as he had a rank or two back, but police officers and lawyers in the same town inevitably know one another. That was almost the hardest thing for Shapiro to deal with: that this man knew Liz Graham, had traded pleasantries with her – outside in the hall, if they met in the street, at the

Civic Ball for pity's sake! – and after that he knocked her down and raped her. It was worse, much worse, than attacking a stranger.

So was what he did after that. In open court, knowing the answer, knowing the state her emotions must have been in even if she was making a supreme effort to hide it, he'd dared her to confess her own experience of sexual violence. A man swept away by a madness over which he had no control? No doubt that would be his defence; it might even be believed. But to Shapiro, sitting in the gallery watching the busy, self-important man dominate the front of the court even when the prosecuting counsel was on his feet, it looked more calculated than that. They were three uppity women that he wanted to take down a peg or two, and he did it that way because he wanted to and because he thought he could get away with it. Shapiro continued watching him with a dull deep anger, not savage but unforgiving, a sober and abiding enmity.

At first, Fenton barely registered his presence. From the corner of his eye he saw the slight disturbance as Shapiro took his seat – a bulky man, getting no more agile with the passage of time, he had never been able to slip through a crowd unnoticed; now he left a wake. Knowing the superintendent was not involved in the present case Fenton wondered briefly what his interest was, particularly at this point in the day, before returning his full attention to events outside The Fen Tiger on a Saturday evening last summer.

It was a critical moment for the defence. If the jury believed the two student nurses who were passing when someone got his face slashed with a broken bottle, Fenton's client had a new career opening up in the mail-bag industry. So it was vital to find the weakness in their story. Rising to cross-examine the second girl he fed the little inner flame that helped him to think of people who stood in his way as hostiles, wondering how he could trap her into undermining her own credibility.

So his mind was full of important thoughts, more than enough to eclipse a passing curiosity about a surplus detective superintendent. He had a difficult task, one which would have defeated many of his colleagues. Cometh the hour, he often thought with a certain inner smugness, cometh the Dan. He turned to the girl in the witness box with a smile as sincere as a crocodile's.

She was, he had to admit, a good witness, sure but not cocky, not deferential but polite. A lesser man might have despaired of shaking her. Fenton never despaired. But just when he needed his concentration most he began to feel Shapiro's eyes.

He tried to ignore them. The policeman had no business with him, was probably just filling time till the court rose. Even if he had something to say it couldn't be anything important; even if it were it would have to wait till this day's work was finished. There was no higher duty than that of a barrister to a client facing prison. He tried to put the sense of being watched – no, not that, he was constantly being watched, of being *scrutinized* – out of his mind while he got on with what he was being paid to do.

But Shapiro's gaze was steady – on his cheek as he faced the witness, on the back of his neck as he turned to the judge – its weight unvarying, its significance unavoidable, and Fenton found himself stumbling in his argument and omitting words from his sword-thrust submissions, like a comedian dying on his feet in a working-men's club.

He felt his cheek go ashy. He felt his command of the jury – of his audience, that he'd always played like a maestro – crumbling. He felt the judge watching him with puzzlement, then with concern, and the witness waiting tensely for the onslaught she'd been warned about and which had yet to materialize.

He didn't shake her story. He got through the cross-examination somehow but without making any dents in the nurse's account. A dew of sweat beaded his smooth face as he resumed his seat. Everyone had been expecting a rigorous review of the girl's testimony lasting an hour or more; now suddenly it was over and they could go home. The sense of anticlimax was palpable.

With a minuscule shrug, Judge Carnahan drew a line under his notes. 'Make a prompt start tomorrow, gentlemen, shall we? Ten-thirty suit?'

Fenton was looking at Shapiro, and Shapiro at Fenton. With difficulty the defending counsel dragged his eyes back to the bench. He rose slowly, as if smitten by a sudden palsy. He cleared his throat. Even then his voice was barely his own. 'I think it may be necessary, Your Honour, for the defence to seek an adjournment.'

'*Why?*' asked Shapiro.

It was no longer a question of If; even the blood sample taken by Dr Greaves was no more now than gilt on the gingerbread. Faced with a direct accusation,

Fenton had disdained to lie, had admitted – with hardly a flicker of guilt – the rape of Amanda Urquhart, Helen Andrews and Elizabeth Graham in Castlemere on sundry dates in March and April.

He sat in the interview room, the recording equipment on the table in front of him, a stony-faced constable by the door, Shapiro watching him as he might have watched Dr Jekyll turn into Mr Hyde, and marvelled that he wasn't afraid. He had no illusions about what this meant. It was the end of everything he'd worked for and enjoyed.

He felt it odd to be so little moved by the prospect. He'd known it could come to this but never expected it would, so it wasn't that he was prepared. Rather, he was detached from it – all of it, from what he'd done and from what would happen now. He shrugged negligently. 'Because I wanted to. Because it made me feel good.'

'Raping women made you *feel* good? Why?'

'Raping those women did. I don't really now why.'

'But—' Shapiro was unsettled by the surrealism of the situation. Not arresting a man he'd respected: he'd done that before, it wasn't a pleasant duty but he'd learned to step back and let professionalism take over. What he was finding hard to deal with was the lack of any emotional feedback from Dan Fenton.

It would have been easier if the man had denied it, so that the interview took a shape from the necessary direction of the questioning. But Fenton just sat there, meeting his gaze, answering his questions, making no attempt even to put a gloss on what he'd done; offering nothing that advanced in the least degree an understanding of what had happened.

Shapiro tried again. 'What you had, what you were in this town, that was all your own making. For damn near twenty years you put everything you had into building your career: time, energy, skill, commitment. And then – this. *Why*? Why does a man who's been a model citizen for twenty years suddenly rape three women? And not just any women: career women, women who've climbed the same greasy pole. Not for sex – you can buy that on the corner of Brick Lane any night of the week for less than what you'd charge to enter a plea for a careless driver.'

Fenton shook his head, once, precisely, the thinning fair hair stroking his brow. 'No, not sex.'

'Revenge, then. You were punishing them. Why that way, and why them?'

'Because—' He had to think about it, came up with an answer of a kind. 'Because they offended me. Because I found them offensive.'

'*Offended* you?' exclaimed Shapiro. 'What – laughed at your wig, made jokes about the Lord Chief Justice – what do you *mean*, they offended you?'

For almost the first time Fenton looked straight at him, eyes widening indignantly. 'Oh, come on, Superintendent, save the political correctness for someone who'll be impressed by it. It may be politic to pretend otherwise, and maybe you can't condone what I did, but don't tell me you like the way the girlies are muscling in any more than I do.'

'Muscling in?' Shapiro echoed faintly.

'Business, the professions – dear God, they're everywhere. The upper echelons of your world and mine are about the last remaining bastions: judges' chambers and the Association of Chief Constables are about the only places you can still walk without too much danger of tripping over a hat-box.'

'And that – bothers you?'

Fenton regarded him speculatively. Having nothing to hide and nothing to gain freed him to indulge the policeman's curiosity for just as long as it pleased him. For the moment he was willing to co-operate; when he got bored he would summon his own solicitor. He hadn't done so yet partly because he wasn't looking forward to meeting a colleague in these circumstances, and partly because he knew there was a limit to how much help a legal advisor could be. Also, he really didn't mind talking to Shapiro, as long as they kept it civilized. Shapiro was a civilized man. Shapiro remembered how things used to be.

'Don't misunderstand me,' Fenton said quickly, 'I like women. I enjoy their company, I like having them around. But I don't consider them my equal intellectually, and I resent being obliged to treat them as if they were. Positive discrimination: having to make room for them. If they were as good as they're supposed to be they'd make their own room.'

Shapiro scratched his nose pensively. 'It's a point of view. A lot of men share it; but most of them don't resort to rape. Why did you?'

Fenton smiled. 'I thought I could get away with it. Women who'd complain instantly of a smack in the eye hesitate to report rape. I thought Amanda Urquhart would prefer to lick her wounds in private. To start with, it was going to be just her. I owed her – you know that, do you? She treated my client with contempt because he misunderstood a piece of technical jargon. A man wouldn't have done that. The matter was of no consequence, she didn't have to make him feel he'd just stepped off a banana boat – whatever the pros and cons of the case, he was the victim, he was entitled to respect. A male defendant taking that attitude to a plaintiff would have been advised to mind his manners; and his pathetic little excuses for cocking up wouldn't have been accepted as an answer to the action. Against a man I'd have won that case.'

'So you waited four years and then raped her?'

His face closed, like a blind falling behind a window. He said stiffly, 'It wasn't – convenient – before.'

Shapiro made a mental note to pursue that later. 'But Mrs Urquhart did report it. It was her information that led us to you. You were so careful about everything else – why on earth did you speak to her? And something that specific: you might have known that could be traced back to you.'

Irritation flickered in Fenton's eyes. 'It's easy to be wise after the event, Mr Shapiro. Of course I should have kept quiet. But this was my first time, I was hyped up – somehow I wanted to put my signature on it. Anyone could have raped her: I think I wanted to mark it as my own work even though I hoped no one would ever unravel the cypher. I didn't think she'd remember, after four years. I didn't think she'd tell anyone even if she did.'

'You underestimated her. All of them. They were tougher than you thought, and they nailed you.'

'That's your interpretation,' Fenton said loftily. 'They were less modest than I expected, and that enabled you to nail me.'

Shapiro wanted nothing of his compliments. 'Why Helen Andrews?'

Fenton shrugged. 'I'd forgotten about her till she arrived to show me the office at The Barbican. After I'd finished with Urquhart I kept thinking about her. An absurd little co-incidence made it inevitable. A solicitor friend of mine was getting married and I was going to his stag night. It turned out the bride worked for the Andrews woman and *she* was going to be at the hen night. I knew where they'd end up and when – the happy couple agreed a two o'clock curfew to make sure we all got to the church sober. I made my excuses ten minutes early, drove to Castle Mount, changed my clothes – I had my tracksuit in the car – and waited for her. It was a clear night, she lives half a mile from the bride's home, she wasn't likely to drive home after a booze-up – yes, Superintendent, I did but then I knew I'd need to and rationed my drinking accordingly. I thought she'd be along within a few minutes and she was.'

'What if she'd had company? If she'd taken a taxi, or they'd organized lifts home?'

'Then I'd have haunted the rhododendrons till I got bored and went home. There's always another chance.' He gave a wry little smile. 'Until now, that is.'

Shapiro didn't return the smile. 'And Inspector Graham?'

The muscles either side of Fenton's mouth tightened, pursing his lips. 'She kept doing it, too. Making a fool of me. In court, in my own place. That's the trouble with women in the professions: you let them in and pretty soon they're trying to run things. I've worked hard for what I have: I don't expect to be pushed around by someone who's been fast-tracked to please the Equal Opportunities Commission. She pushed me, I pushed back.'

'You raped her! In her own back garden.'

'Well, I wasn't going to do it at the Basin with half CID looking on!'

Shapiro felt revulsion crawling up his skin. With difficulty he kept his voice even, measured. 'Were there any more, that we don't know about?'

'No.' The lawyer met the policeman's gaze with cool defiance. 'But there would have been.'

Shapiro considered that expressionlessly. It was one of the advantages, he'd found, of carrying some extra weight. A broad face could mask mental and emotional activity in a way a thin one never could. It was a real handicap to Donovan, for instance, that everything he felt showed in his face. He could never have sat here hating this man, wanting to tear him apart, concealing the fact right up to the moment that he could use it to best advantage.

Which, on mature reflection, he considered to be now. 'And what does Mrs Fenton think of the fact that you're going round raping clever women who look like her?'

That got a reaction, though it wasn't what Shapiro was expecting. Fenton said nothing and for long, long seconds did nothing either. Then he began to cry.

'Well, we were nearly right,' Shapiro told Liz afterwards. She'd waited in his office for him to complete the interview, containing her restlessness just barely. She didn't know what she was waiting for, what she hoped or expected to hear that would make her feel better. But she needed to know what there was to know about what happened, where the madness came from. 'We thought maybe she'd left him and so she did. She died, eight weeks ago. Cancer.'

It didn't make it any better. It didn't make it any more explicable. Perhaps it shaved a few grains off the knot of hatred gathered under her heart. 'How—? Why—?' She tried again. 'Why didn't we know? There must have been a funeral.'

'She was buried from her mother's house in Guildford. She died there – apparently Fenton couldn't cope with nursing her. He couldn't cope with her death, either. Nobody knew, not even the people he worked with – not even her friends in Castlemere.'

'Then – *is* he crazy? Diminished responsibility? Post-traumatic stress disorder?'

Shapiro couldn't tell from her tone how much of this was irony. He settled for answering as honestly as he could. 'No, I don't think so. It'll earn him some Brownie points with the judge but I don't think it'll be accepted as something beyond his control. Losing his wife was a catalyst, not a cause. He knew what he was doing. He isn't crazy, he's angry. She left him. She crossed him. He couldn't punish her so he took it out on you.'

'Because we crossed him too?'

'You were too good at your jobs. You each got the better of him in situations where his professional credibility was an issue. And you were still around after his wife was gone. Before it merely irritated him; after his wife died he couldn't bear to see you carrying on – wearing her face, as it were, and getting in his.'

'That *is* crazy,' swore Liz. She saw the prospect of a trial diminish, wasn't sure whether that would be easier or harder to deal with.

'Abnormal,' agreed Shapiro, 'not crazy. He could have stopped himself. He meant to stop after Mrs Urquhart. But by then he'd met Mrs Andrews again; and by the time he'd punished her you were getting up his nose. He knew about the decoy operation. We can guess how: somebody here let something slip, in all innocence, to one of the legal eagles and suddenly it's common knowledge in the robing room.' He squinted apologetically at her. 'If he'd any doubts about his next move, that decided him. I'm sorry, Liz. If I'd said no—'

She couldn't afford to think like that. She shook her head firmly. 'It might have taken him longer but he'd have got to me eventually. We'd locked horns too often, once he'd started down this road he'd have come to me sooner or later. And if it had taken longer he might have done more damage before we caught him.'

There was a lengthy silence, not because they were unsure what to say to each other but because there was nothing left to say. Finally Liz reached for her bag. 'Enough already.' She was hopeless at accents, even music-hall ones like Donovan's brogue and Shapiro's North London Jewish. Shapiro didn't in fact recognize the attempt. 'I've things to do. Believe it or not, I have to see a man about a dog.'

Chapter Twenty-seven

Liz drove. She got the van as close to the front of the clinic as she could, ignoring the No Parking signs, and Donovan manoeuvred himself out and on to his crutches. His plaster encased his leg from his toes to his knee and he hadn't got the knack of steering it yet. Liz watched him labour up the few shallow steps to the vet's front door.

There was no surgery: Keith Baker was doing his VAT. Donovan wasted no time on small talk. 'I want a certificate.'

Baker looked him up and down. 'You've got the wrong number of legs. You'll need one from a doctor.'

Donovan was not amused. 'Not for me. For Brian Boru.'

'Who—?'

'Doesn't matter what he is,' said Donovan firmly. 'What matters is that he's *not* a pit-bull terrier.'

The vet began to understand. 'And is he?'

'Oh, yes,' agreed Donovan readily. 'But I want a certificate saying he's something else.'

'You want me to lie.'

The policeman frowned. 'Is there not some dis-agreement as to what does and doesn't constitute a pit-bull?'

'Yes,' said Baker cautiously.

'And it comes down to someone's opinion, and if that person thinks he's a pit-bull he's put down and if they think he's a mongrel he isn't?'

'That's about the size of it,' admitted the vet.

'Well, this particular dog saved my neck. Not once but twice. He stopped a man who wanted to kill me and then he saw off some dogs that did. So I'm damned if I'm returning him to the kennels to be destroyed. I can keep him, and I can keep him out of trouble, if I can get him certified as something other than a pit-bull. There'll be no come-back. Everyone at Queen's Street knows what happened, nobody's gunning for him. If I get my piece of paper there'll be more blind eyes turned than at a convention of Nelson look-alikes.'

Baker considered. 'Can I see this dog?'

'He's in the van outside.'

The presence of Detective Inspector Graham at the wheel was not lost on Baker. Donovan was apparently telling the truth: there was a conspiracy to protect the dog from the consequences of its ancestry. He peered in at the back of the van. Brian Boru, one lip raised, stared back.

Baker sucked his teeth. 'I can see how people might think he was a pit-bull.'

Donovan gave a disdainful sniff. 'People *think* all sorts. I'm not interested in what people think, only in what can be proved. Can you make a definitive test that proves that dog there is a pit-bull terrier?'

'Well, no,' said Baker honestly.

'Right. Good. So what else could he be? Isn't he taller than your average pit-bull?'

There's no such thing as an average pit-bull, but

Baker knew what was expected of him. 'He could be, yes. I suppose he could be something like a bullmastiff.'

'Could he? Could he!' said Donovan with sharpened enthusiasm. 'And they're not dangerous, are they?'

'No, I believe the breed standard refers to high spirits and reliability. But he isn't pure-bred. He's too dark, for one thing, and his head isn't square enough.'

'OK. So if his daddy's a bullmastiff, what might his mammy be?'

'Dobermann pinscher?'

It was a shot from the hip. Donovan moved the target to make sure it struck gold. 'Dobermann pinscher, for sure! They're not dangerous either, are they?'

'They've been known to bite,' said Baker. 'Most breeds have. No, they're not required to be registered as a dangerous dog.'

'That's it then – he's a bullmastiff-Dobermann cross. For pity's sake, you only have to look at him! You'll put it on paper, will you?'

Baker considered, chewing his lip. 'What I will put on paper,' he said carefully, 'is that the owner understands the dog to be a bullmastiff-Dobermann cross and I see no reason to doubt it. That do?'

Donovan nodded slowly. Slowly a dark smile broke. 'Oh, yeah.'

Liz drove him home. So he wouldn't have far to hobble she drove down to Cornmarket and back up the tow-path. At one point she thought there was something wrong with the van, but it was Donovan whistling.

She parked beside *Tara*, accepted his invitation aboard for coffee. Then she glanced uneasily at Brian Boru. 'Um – is he going to want my biscuit?'

Donovan chuckled. 'I'll put him in the cable locker. He's used to being banished when I have callers.'

'You don't have any problem with him on your own?'

'No. He's not the sort of dog you get fond of, you know, but we've reached an understanding. He doesn't growl at me and I don't break his head with a tyre-iron.'

Of all those who were at the cottage, Brian Boru, armed with his certificate, was the only winner. Two of the original crew were dead, four were in custody, Gates was in a secure psychiatric unit and Donovan was in plaster. Gates's dogs were shot after one night's liberty by a farmer who found them couched on the carcase of a ewe. Even Chang was dead. Only Brian Boru, who had been marked for death and now had a chance for life, came out of the affair better than he went into it.

'What about your certificate?' asked Liz. 'When will you be back at work?'

'Next week, I hope. I can run a desk till this thing comes off.' He rapped the plaster.

She nodded slowly, relieved to hear him say it. She hadn't realized how much she relied on him until there was the chance he mightn't be there any more. There were other detective sergeants to be had, most of them easier on the nerves, but she felt about Donovan much as he felt about the dog: that they'd reached an understanding. Mutual respect was worth more to her than the uncritical fawning of a poodle. 'I wasn't sure you'd want to come back.'

He looked quickly up and down again, his narrow

face embarrassed. 'I – said some pretty stupid things. In the wood. It was a trying sort of a day.'

Liz laughed out loud. 'Yes, that's fair comment. But they weren't stupid things you said. Nobody could blame you if you decided not to get involved in anything like that again.'

He looked at her over his mug. 'Lots of people thought you'd have had enough after . . .' He left the sentence unfinished.

'After I was raped, Donovan,' she said shortly. 'You're a big boy now, you're allowed to use words like that. And yes, I dare say they did. Since it's what lots of people have been praying for since I got here, I expect they *did* hope this would be enough to see me off. Well, tough. It's a sod, but it's not enough of a sod to change my mind about what I want to do with the rest of my life. If I can deal with it, and Brian can – my Brian, not yours – then everyone else can too.'

Donovan was chewing his lip. There was something he wanted to say and he wasn't sure if he should. Liz rolled her eyes. 'Spit it out.'

After a moment, awkwardly, he did. 'I didn't know how to deal with it either. I didn't know – I still don't – how you're meant to face your boss when you know she's been raped. How you talk to her, what you say – if you say anything. It's too much. It goes beyond what we have the words for.

'If you'd been hit by a bus, now,' he hurried on, stammering in his discomfort, 'or shot even, however bad the damage, I'd have been there. I'd have *wanted* to be there, to see you, see how you were doing. Even if the news was all bad, I'd have wanted to be there. But you weren't shot, you were raped. I told the chief you wouldn't want to see me. What I meant was, I didn't want to see you. I couldn't face you. Jesus,' he swore disgustedly, 'this is pathetic!'

'Yes, it is,' she said frankly. 'But also pretty human. It's the same as avoiding someone who's been bereaved: you don't know what to say so you don't say anything. But anyone who's been there will tell you that *anything* you say, however clumsy, is better than nothing.'

He nodded slowly, the black hair lank in his face. He looked up from the coffee to meet her eyes; she saw him actually flinch. But he pressed on manfully. 'Then, I'm sorry. I'm sorry about what happened to you. I'm sorry if I made it worse. I wish I could've given you the sort of help you gave me. I owe you.'

There was something touching about such painful honesty from such a man. Liz smiled and shook her head. 'Donovan, you don't owe me a thing. You're good at your job. You only think you should be better because you're good enough to recognize what's possible and brave enough to measure yourself against it. But perfection isn't an option. Don't flay yourself because you make mistakes sometimes. Superman would make a terrible copper: humanity is an essential part of the job.'

He thought about that. 'If humanity means cocking up at regular intervals I could still make Chief Constable.'

'I'm talking about coppers,' Liz said reproachfully. 'Superman'd make a *wonderful* Chief Constable.'

That earned a black chuckle. But the eyes that met hers were finally clear, all the ghosts gone. 'What you said, about victims and survivors: I liked that. That's worth remembering.'

She elevated an eyebrow at him, disquietingly. Then abruptly she laughed. 'Tell me something. That stunt you pulled on the train, with the wedding-ring. You didn't learn that in Glencurran?'

'I did so,' he said, straight-faced. 'From my grand-mother.'

'Your *grandmother*?' Liz's voice soared in wonder.

'My grandmother,' Donovan said solemnly, 'said I'd go straight to hell if I ever made love to a woman wearing a wedding-ring. And the little buggers can be the devil to shift.'

Soon after that Liz became aware that he was listening to something. He put his mug down and let his head tilt to one side.

'What is it?'

He shook his head, listened some more. Then he hauled himself to his feet, hopped to the window and pushed it wide. 'Come here. Do you hear it?'

She did. A slow smile spread across her face. She looked at him and nodded.

All along the canal, between the water and the tumbleweed wasteland of Cornmarket, the birds were singing.